THE BLACK HILLS

M.J. Trow

CRÈME de la CRIME

This first world edition published 2019
in Great Britain and 2020 in the USA by
Crème de la Crime an imprint of
SEVERN HOUSE PUBLISHERS LTD of
Eardley House, 4 Uxbridge Street, London W8 7SY.
Trade paperback edition first published
in Great Britain and the USA 2020 by
SEVERN HOUSE PUBLISHERS LTD.

British Library Cataloguing in Publication Data
A CIP catalogue record for this title is available from the British Library.

ISBN-13: 978-1-78029-121-5 (cased)
ISBN-13: 978-1-78029-651-7 (trade paper)
ISBN-13: 978-1-4483-0350-2 (e-book)

All Severn House titles are printed on acid-free paper.

Severn House Publishers support the Forest Stewardship Council™ [FSC™],
the leading international forest certification organisation.
All our titles that are printed on FSC certified paper carry the FSC logo.

Typeset by Palimpsest Book Production Ltd.,
Falkirk, Stirlingshire, Scotland.
Printed and bound in Great Britain by
TJ International, Padstow, Cornwall.

*This book is dedicated to F Troop, for the laughter
and Companies C, L, I, F and E of the Seventh Cavalry,
for the tears.*

*And also to Doris Day, late and lamented; the best
Calamity Jane there ever was!*

ONE

George Armstrong Custer looked at himself in the mirror. He turned his head to the right, then to the left. Not bad. Not bad. Prince of the Plains, certainly. Major General already. Congressman? The White House? Why not? Why ever not?

John Burkman was fussing around him with razor and scissors, snipping here, trimming there. There had been a time when Libbie had demanded all those golden curls, to be worn in a topknot wig for gala balls. But the wig had gone up in smoke a year ago, along with half of Officers' Row – one of the perils of frontier life – and no one spoke of the glittering hairpiece again. Burkman stepped back, admiring his handiwork, angling the hand-mirror for Custer's approval. The General nodded but held up his hand as the orderly reached for a bottle. 'Easy on the pomade, John,' he smiled. 'I wouldn't want to upset Captain Keogh's chances with the ladies.'

Both men laughed, but the hilarity was brief. There was a knock on the barber shop door and Isaac Dobbs, bugler of Keogh's I Company stood there, back ramrod straight, arm at the salute.

'Beggin' your pardon, General,' he said. 'Lieutenant Cooke's compliments and would you join him on the southwest ramparts, sir. There's something you should see.'

Custer whipped the cloth from his shoulders and retied the red scarf around his neck. He held out his arms and Burkman slipped on the buckskin jacket, the one with the fringes and the porcupine quill beadwork. Dobbs stepped aside, straightening his braces in the hope that the General hadn't seen the slip, and he followed the man across the parade ground. Briefly, Custer stopped to watch D Troop going through its paces. Foot sabre drill. The General shook his head. In all his time in command of the Wolverines, all his time in the Wilderness, all his time chasing Black Kettle along the Washita, he had never been called upon to order his men to fight on foot with their swords. But it was in the Drill Manual, so foot sabre drill it had to be.

A knot of brawny sergeants were barking themselves hoarse, screaming at their men to tighten their line, swing harder. When they saw the General, they carried on shouting, but it was noticeable that all profanity had stopped.

At the foot of the stairway, two staghounds loped over to Custer, licking his hands and wagging their tails. 'Come on, Bleuch,' he shook the ears of one. 'Here, Tuck,' and he bent briefly to kiss the other on the forehead. Two officers stood on the ramparts, one resting his elbow on the timbers of the parapet steadying a telescope, the other peering into the mist. It was still early morning – the General had heard Reveille while Burkman was shaving him and cutting his hair – and the hollows outside Fort Abraham Lincoln were wreathed in grey. It would be an hour or so before the sun climbed over the Black Hills and burned the final wisps away in a wave of gold – it would be a perfect day for Libbie's picnic on the plains.

Both men straightened at Custer's arrival.

'Dubbya Dubbya,' the General returned the salute. 'What have we got?'

W.W. Cooke was Custer's adjutant, a lean Canadian with the longest flowing dundrearies west of the Missouri. He passed his telescope to the General.

'What am I looking at?' Custer had to adjust the barrel. He was the best shot in the Seventh but the thick glass of government-regulation telescopes combined with the haze over the plains could confuse the sharpest of sharpshooters.

'The bluffs above the hog ranches,' Cooke explained.

Custer swivelled the telescope. He took in the scrawny dogs, the squaws sitting cross-legged and blanketed in the hollows. He saw Murphy's Emporium and the bat-wing doors of the Dew Drop Inn. He noted, as his wife and her ladies did most days with tuts of disgust, the harlots already lounging outside the shanty that was My Lady's Bower. He let the lens trail to the west, to the point where the ground rose up and levelled, topped by a knot of pines. A lone Indian sat his pony custom-made octagonal shotgun in record time. 'But Charley Reynolds knows him. There's talk he killed Bloody Knife's son and anybody who has a beef with a scout of mine, has a beef with me. The Black Hills are a powder keg as it is. I don't want to provide any sparks.'

She passed him the cookies that Aunt Mary, her cook, had lovingly baked that morning. 'George Armstrong Custer,' she tutted, smiling. 'Providing sparks? Never!'

'You're a wicked woman, Libbie Custer,' he scolded her with a laugh. 'Ladies of a cavalry fort should know better. Anyway, we've got other problems.'

'Oh?' Libbie Custer didn't hear that sort of line often from her husband. He was the son of a blacksmith who had courted her, the daughter of a circuit judge. He was a West Pointer who had always ridden towards the sound of the guns; always charged even when there was strictly no need. He had whipped the bejasus out of Jeb Stuart, the best cavalryman in the world, according to many. And he had defeated Black Kettle's murdering Cheyennes along the Washita. Oh, and he'd also, because she'd asked him to, given up the booze and the bad language and the gambling. She didn't care that he had no chin to speak of and a nose four sizes too big for his face. If he cared, he didn't show it, being possibly the vainest man in the whole country. But men like George Custer didn't have problems; they had solutions.

'I got a letter from Washington this morning,' he told her, waving the piece of paper the galloper had brought. 'There's talk of a court martial if I don't comply.'

She paused with her coffee cup close to her lips. 'Belknap,' she said, putting it down.

'The Secretary of State for War himself,' Custer said. 'I guess if you tread on a rattler, he's going to try to bite you. I've been called to the capital.'

She looked at him, trying to read what lay behind those ice-blue eyes, the solemn face. 'Then I'm going with you,' she said.

'Now, Libbie . . .' he held up his hand.

'Or,' she cut him off at the pass, 'you can leave me in the hands of Chief Gall and Myles Keogh.'

Custer laughed. 'All right,' he said. 'You win. Pack a few things. We'll leave tomorrow. You'd be all right with Gall, I'm sure. It's Keogh I worry about.'

She looked at him, but her husband wasn't smiling.

'It will be all right, won't it?' she asked.

'Yes,' he said, after a pause. 'Yes, it will. But just in case, I'm going to send a letter to Matthew Grand.'

'Who?'

Mrs Rackstraw was quite tired of turning out breakfasts for two men who spent the whole time it was on the table hidden behind newspapers or letters. Kidneys, when all was said and done, did not griddle themselves. She could work her fingers to the bone, grilling sausages to golden, sizzling perfection, without so much as a grunt. She watched the toast like a hawk to snatch it from the fire just as the outermost crust reached its peak of slightly charred but still delicious crispness. She curled butter into iced water. She double-sieved the milk so that no cow hair or rat turd disturbed the perfection of her table. And yet, all of that being a given, still they shoved it into their mouths unheeding. Next time, she promised herself darkly, next time, she would give them lumpy porridge and burned bacon. See how they liked them apples. She glowered at them from the doorway and finally flounced back to the kitchen in disgust.

Without lifting his eyes, Matthew Grand muttered out of the corner of his mouth, 'Has she gone?'

James Batchelor didn't lower the *Telegraph* by so much as an inch. 'Yes,' he said. 'In high dudgeon, if I am any judge. We shouldn't really tease her like this, Matthew.'

'Perhaps not,' Grand said, slitting open the next letter with a butter knife wiped hastily on his napkin. 'But she'd only preen if we let her know how delicious her black pudding is. Oh.' He had unfolded the thin paper and was looking at it in amazement.

'A case?' Batchelor did lower the paper now. They were busy enough, he knew. They were even thinking of taking on a boy to watch the office while they were out. Possibly even a typewriter, for the letters, though he had heard that such women were often no better than they should be. But a case that made Matthew Grand say 'Oh' in quite that tone promised well.

'Hmm . . . not as such,' Grand said.

That let out anything family. He had been expecting to hear that his sister Martha was having another baby at any minute. She seemed the kind of woman who would be popping out children every year until her husband called time. Obviously, the letter was nothing to do with Grand's parents – they would warrant a little more than an 'Oh'. There was nothing left but to ask.

'Well . . . what is it, then?'

'It's a letter from an idiot I was at West Point with. Needs our help, he says, though it's hard to see what we can do.'

'Is he in England, then?' It seemed a little unlikely.

'No, that's the thing. He will be in Washington by now.' Grand turned the page back to check the date. 'Or back out West, even.' He carried on reading, to Batchelor's mounting frustration.

'Out West?' Batchelor was totally in thrall to stories of the West. 'You mean, the *Wild* West?'

Grand blinked. He had never really thought of it that way. Stories he had heard had made it sound hot, dry, unpleasant, yes. But wild? Who knew? 'I suppose so. He . . . that is, General Custer . . . has got himself into a bit of trouble. No surprises there. He's got to give evidence in a Congressional Hearing. Some fraud or another.'

Batchelor had seen the name of Custer in the Press so was surprised to hear that. 'He doesn't seem the kind of chap who would perpetrate fraud.'

'No, he's just a witness.' Grand frowned at the letter. 'At least, I think that's what this letter says. He isn't the brightest apple in the barrel. He was last in his class at West Point in '61. His spelling is appalling and his writing is worse. He is just asking me to go and be his . . . well, I don't know. His soldier's friend, I suppose.'

'Is he being court-martialled, then?' Batchelor was aghast.

'No.' Grand peered again. 'No, I don't think so. But anyway,' he folded the letter decisively and put it back in its envelope.

'He wants us to go to Washington and you know that isn't your kind of trip.'

Batchelor bridled. 'Why not?' he said, nettled. 'I am a perfectly good traveller.'

Grand snorted gently. 'I suppose you are, if you count lying on your bunk muttering "I want to die" for ten days straight being a good traveller. You had to be given brandy the other day when you went on that ferry for the Walberswick case.'

'It was rough.' Batchelor shook his paper out and retired behind it.

'It was flat calm. We're not going to Washington and that's final. I shall write to him later today. Or I might splash out on a cable. Although, God knows, I don't owe George Custer anything.'

Batchelor ignored him.

'Shall I? Splash out on a cable?'

Silence.

'James, don't sulk. The West isn't all it's cracked up to be. There's hardly anything there, just the odd cactus, I expect, and an Indian or two. And it's a long way. You Londoners have no idea of distances. You get a bit excitable over a trip to Brighton. In America, you're looking at thousands of miles, coast to coast.'

Batchelor put his paper down in annoyance. 'I do *know* that,' he said, in injured tones. 'I'm not stupid, just because I come from here. There are trains, aren't there? Coaches? What about the Wells Fargo Company? It isn't as if we would have to walk, exactly. You're so . . .' he searched for the right word, '. . . so *parochial*, Matthew.'

Grand raised his eyebrow. He supposed it took one to know one; Batchelor didn't even like going as far west as Wimbledon as a rule. 'I'm just thinking of you . . .' he began.

'I admit,' Batchelor said, as one condescending to a rather dim child, 'I admit that I was unwell on the crossing back from your sister's wedding. But I was not well before we set off, if you remember. I blame the cake, personally.'

Grand smiled bleakly. He was remembering the state of the stateroom when they encountered anything even approaching a moderate swell.

'And I am certain I am over it, anyway. That ferry nonsense the other day was just the stupid sailor – or whatever he was – overreacting.' He stared at Grand, who was on to his next letter and was jotting a note to himself across the top. 'Matthew. Matthew! I said . . .'

'I heard you,' Grand said. 'I think it's a waste of time, but Custer's ready to pay expenses and a fee, so if you're sure you won't be seasick, we'll go.'

Batchelor beamed and topped up his coffee.

'But, mark my words, you won't like it.'

TWO

Liza Grand loved both her children equally, she would tell anyone who asked her. But when it came to her son, there was perhaps just a little iota of extra doting that she had tucked away just under her heart. It swam in her eyes now as she plastered herself against his chest. Matthew Grand was used to it and, anyway, a little maternal affection was never unwelcome, especially when the mother in question lived far enough away to prevent it being a nuisance. He patted her back and let her lean against him, weeping happily.

Andrew Grand put out a manly hand for James Batchelor to shake. He loved his son too but left all the soft stuff to his wife. 'Morning, Mr Batchelor,' he said, formally. 'How was the trip?'

It didn't take an expert to see that James Batchelor had not had a happy crossing. The slight tinge of green still lingered on his skin and the six-hour train journey, stopping at various stations he didn't want to recall, especially the cheese and steak sandwich at the Philadelphia station, had not helped his constitution much. But he swallowed hard and told his host that he had had a marvellous voyage, thank you all the same.

Matthew Grand laughed and put his mother aside for later. 'Don't tell such lies, James,' he said. 'He hated every minute, Pa. He was sick the whole crossing and he's not that great on trains either. But we're here now and some good home cooking and a rest will see him right.'

The thought of food, home cooked or not, made Batchelor's stomach lurch and he hid his nausea behind a sickly grin.

Liza bustled over. 'Matthew, don't be cruel to poor James.' She smiled at Batchelor who felt a little better for it. 'Come with me, you dear soul. Annie will have something for you, I'm sure.'

Grand looked across at his mother. 'Is Annie here? I had it in my mind she would be with Martha these days.'

Liza Grand laughed. 'She would if she could, that's true. But, love her heart, she's a bit long in the tooth now for babies, though she sees them as often as she can. No, she is better here with us. Neither of us are getting any younger,' she looked fondly at her husband, who sucked in his stomach and threw out his chest, 'so some of Annie's notions and potions come in handy once in a while.' She took Batchelor's arm. 'Come on, James. Try some of Annie's jalap.'

Batchelor hoped it tasted better than it sounded. Sad experience had taught him to beware what he put in his mouth in this country. But he was too washed out to argue, so allowed himself to be towed out of the room.

Andrew and Matthew Grand stood looking at each other. There was a lot to say, but communication ran slow in the father's veins and the son had learned to wait.

'Here for any special reason, hmm?' It seemed to Andrew Grand that his son was somewhat of a stormy petrel, bringing chaos in his wake. He had been so since a child, he would tell anyone who asked him.

His son blew out a breath. 'To see you and Ma, of course,' he said. 'But also, Custer – you remember George?' Andrew did. A pesky loudmouth, as his memory served, over-promoted and over-dressed. 'Well, I had a letter from him. Some kind of fraud investigation?' He shrugged. 'His writing is terrible and his spelling is worse, so I don't know the details. But he is paying our fares and a fee, so it seemed like a good time to visit with you folks on someone else's dollar.'

Andrew Grand looked solemn. 'He's talking about the Belknap affair, I guess,' he said. 'It will have been in your papers.'

Matthew Grand thought for a moment and shook his head. 'No,' he said, finally. 'No, not in any paper we read and, believe me, we read them all. James is a print fiend; once a journalist, always a journalist, I suppose.'

'Not very good journalists in England if they missed this,' Andrew said. 'It's the scandal of the age. Or will be, once the trial begins.'

'There'll be a trial, then?'

Andrew Grand narrowed his eyes at his son. The boy was

no fool, but he'd been away far too long. There'd been a lot of water under Montgomery Meig's new bridge since Matthew had come home from the war and although the worst of it, foul with dead cats, lay buried under Constitution Avenue, there was still a stench of corruption in America's capital.

'You'll have seen new buildings on your way from the station.' The old man poured a bourbon for them both.

'A lot,' his son nodded. 'I barely recognized the place.'

'We've got "Boss" Shepherd to thank for that. He's paved a hundred fifty miles of road, built two hundred and eight miles of sidewalk. He's built over a thousand new houses and renovated many more. And don't get me started on the trees.'

'Trees?'

'Sixty thousand of them.' The elder Grand winced a little as the liquor hit his tonsils. He would have to speak to Liza – economies were one thing, but not when it came to his bourbon. 'It's gotten so a dog doesn't have a leg to stand on.'

'Sorry, Pa,' Matthew said. 'I don't see what rebuilding Washington has to do with George Custer.'

'It may have passed you by, boy,' the old man growled, 'living three thousand miles away and all, but we've got a madman in the White House.'

'Ulysses Grant? America seems to love him.'

'He's won two landslide elections, I'll grant you – no pun intended – but he's also the most corrupt president we've had since Martin van Buren. Never met a palm he couldn't grease. He and this fella Shepherd are bosom buddies, even though Shepherd voted against him back in '68. Rest assured, Matthew, we'll never see another Democrat in the White House. The man draws scandal like a fox to a henhouse. Belknap's part of that.'

'Our papers . . .' Matthew Grand stopped himself as his father raised a wry eyebrow. He already knew his views on the British Press.

'Our revered Secretary of State for War, it is rumoured, has been lining his own pocket for years. He and his former wife have been working hand-in-glove with the Indian agencies, providing cheap blankets and not-so-cheap whiskey to the

Indians and receiving pretty big backhanders from just about every sutler west of the Missouri.'

'And Custer?' Surely, the man would enter the tale sooner or later, but it did no harm to nudge every now and then.

Andrew Grand shrugged. 'I've never liked the cuss,' he said, 'but he's written some pretty hard-hitting articles recently about all this.' Matthew Grand could hardly suppress a snort. It would take a pretty talented copy-editor to make much of Custer's usual ill-spelled ramblings; he suspected that Libbie had had more than a small hand in it. 'He's been accusing Belknap up-front about substandard breech-loaders issued to his men while the Indians get brand-new Springfields.'

'Where's Custer based now? He may have said in his letter, but I could only make out one word in three.'

'Fort Abraham Lincoln in Dakota Territory. He's standing on the edge of an abyss, that man. They've just found gold in the Black Hills.'

'Gold?' Matthew sat up and took notice.

'It's not common knowledge yet,' his father told him, 'but I remember California in '49; you were only a child; do you remember it?'

His son half shook, half nodded his head. 'I remember it being mentioned, but no detail. Ma didn't like you talking about the news at the dinner table, do you remember?'

Andrew laughed. 'Lord, yes. No politics, no religion, no scandal, no violence – it was hard to know what we *could* talk about.'

'And yet look at the two of us. Martha with a baby three months after the wedding and me . . .' His face darkened, 'Well, me, I've seen more violence than most people have had hot dinners.'

Andrew Grand looked grave. 'Do you think anyone else noticed. About Martha, I mean?'

'Hard not to,' his son said, bluntly. 'But I doubt anyone cared. It is the Seventies, after all.'

'Tell your mother that – Washington etiquette says something rather different. I do worry about the life you live in London if that is really how you see things; do people *really* not mind . . . that kind of thing?' Andrew Grand had never been comfortable talking about personal feelings with his son, or indeed, anyone.

Matthew laughed. 'In London, they would be shocked and horrified by it, but they would love to talk about it, nonetheless. Martha's tea parties would be the best attended in the city, especially if they also knew about Hamilton's little financial peccadillos.'

Andrew shook his head. 'A mad world, my masters,' he sighed. His son looked askance. That sounded perilously like a literary quotation, something his father avoided like the plague as a rule. 'Yes, I know,' he said, seeing Matthew's expression. 'The theatre is also very influential here these days. I went to see the play, but you will be reassured to know that I slept right through it.'

'Anyway,' Matthew tried to get the conversation back on track. 'This Gold Rush news.'

'Yes. Back in the day, thousands of men swarmed west, without a brain in their heads or a bean in their pockets. Most of them came back the same way, having wasted their best years on a fool's errand.'

'You think the gold's an illusion?' Matthew asked.

'Oh, it's real enough. It was in California, after all. It just depends how you value the stuff. As someone who's pursued business all his life, I can see its advantages. But I can also see its cost. Rumour is the gold is on Lakota land – the Indian's sacred ground. If brainless prospectors turn up there in their thousands, their brains aren't all they're going to lose.'

Matthew let the logic of his father's statement go. 'So, Custer's career is on the line?'

Andrew nodded, refreshing the drinks of both of them. 'He's openly accused William Belknap of corruption. And Belknap is backed by the president. It's not going to go well. What I can't understand – and I mean no offence – is why he's asked for you. You were never close, were you? At West Point? In the war?'

'Let's just say we had the misfortune to be in each other's class on the Hudson and each other's unit along the Potomac.'

'Well, it's a different river he's riding along now. The Little Bighorn. I barely know where that is.'

'That makes two of us,' Matthew chuckled.

'Matthew,' the old man was suddenly solemn. 'We've had our differences, you and I, over the years.'

'What father and son have not?'

'Even so, this Custer thing. I want you, for your mother's sake, if not for mine, to be careful. *Very* careful.'

James Batchelor had not known quite what to expect. From the newspapers back home, including his own *Telegraph* when he had written for them, George Armstrong Custer was a hero of the civil war; old Iron Butt, his men called him for his determination and guts. But to men of discernment like Matthew Grand, he was Fanny and Ringlets, an altogether softer couple of nicknames. And bearing in mind Grand's memories of West Point and the outrageous non-regulation uniforms that Custer used to design for himself, Batchelor half-expected a curly-wigged clown to meet them in the foyer of the Baltimore Hotel that morning.

He was rather disappointed when Custer of the West turned out to be rather ordinary looking. He had longer hair, it was true, than most men Batchelor encountered along the Strand, but his auburn moustache, bleached blond by the prairie sun, could be seen in facsimile anywhere from the Coal Hole to the Garrick. His outfit owed less to the last frontier and more to Savile Row – a plain, dark grey frock coat and check kicksies. Only the ubiquitous scarlet cravat of the Cavalry of the Potomac set him slightly apart from other men. And Matthew Grand owned one of those too.

What caught Batchelor's eye a second after Custer was the dark-haired beauty on the man's arm. She wore the latest Parisian dress and her hair was curled just so with a lavish feathered hat set at a rakish angle.

Custer was extending a hand to Batchelor's partner in crime. 'Matthew Grand, as I live and breathe,' he smiled.

'General.' Grand's smile was a little more forced.

'General be . . .' Custer checked himself in his wife's presence. 'That's George to you, Matthew.'

'George,' Grand repeated, as though the name was trapped somehow in his throat. 'May I introduce my associate, James Batchelor?'

'Mr Batchelor.' Custer shook his hand too.

'General.' Batchelor found himself gushing in spite of himself. This was the man who had led the Sixth Michigan, his Wolverines, against impossible odds and had led them all out the other side. If miracles happened, they had happened courtesy of this man more often than Batchelor had had hot dinners. 'May I say what an honour . . .'

But Custer was holding up his hand. 'You may not,' he smiled. Then he winked. 'Not until you know me better. And by the way, it's Colonel these days. That major general nonsense was a brevet rank, held in the war between the states. It doesn't cut much mustard here in Washington. Every other cuss you meet was a general or an admiral. Gentlemen, allow me to introduce the little lady who really runs the Seventh Cavalry – my wife Elizabeth.'

The enquiry agents shook hands and half-bowed.

'Captain Grand,' Libbie said. 'George has told me *so* much about you.' For the sake of good etiquette, Elizabeth Bacon Custer could lie for America. 'Thank you for coming.'

'Amen to that,' Custer said.

'Mr Batchelor,' Libbie took his hand again. 'I understand that you and Captain Grand have premises along the Strand in London, England.'

'We do, madame,' he told her.

'Madame be . . .' she checked herself, looking up from under her lashes at Custer, who smiled indulgently. 'You must call me Libbie. May I call you James?'

'Of course . . . Libbie,' the Englishman smiled.

She linked arms with him. 'George will be chewing Captain Grand's ear from now to the trump of doom. Soldiers, eh?' James Batchelor always had to remind himself that Matthew Grand had been a soldier. He showed no signs of it these days. 'Come with me. There are some delightful tearooms right along the street and you must tell me all about London. For instance, do you know the Queen?'

'Er . . . not personally, Libbie, no . . .'

'But you've seen her, though?'

Batchelor smiled and nodded in such a way as to imply no, not really. But a little disappointment like that was not going to stop Libbie Custer and the pair swept from the hotel arm in arm and rabbiting away like old friends.

But there was another member of the Custer party, a tall, square-looking sergeant with yellow chevrons on both sleeves and yellow piping on collar and cuffs. He looked as if he hadn't smiled in years.

'Matthew, this is my striker, Sergeant Reilly. Reilly, say hello to Captain Grand of the Third Cavalry of the Potomac.'

Reilly stood even taller and saluted, but Grand held out his hand. 'That was a long time ago, Sergeant,' he said. 'It's just plain Mister these days.'

'Lose yourself, Reilly,' Custer said. 'Captain Grand and I have things to discuss.'

The tearoom right along the street could have been anywhere in one of London's better quarters. Lace at the windows and on the tables had attracted the ladies of Washington society and those who would like to join their number. To Batchelor's untutored eye, it was impossible to tell one from the other, but Libbie steered an unerring course between the tables, nodding and smiling here, averting her head there, until they reached a secluded booth at the back.

She tapped Batchelor on the shoulder as he stood aside while she settled herself. 'Land, Mr Batchelor,' she said, laughing. 'All the ladies of Washington will think I have a beau.'

There was something in her tone that made Batchelor's laugh a little tight and nervous. George Armstrong Custer might seem like a damned nice fellow, but that was before he heard the gossip about a Limey enquiry agent and his wife.

Libbie's laugh was genuine. 'Pay no mind to me, James,' she said, more quietly. 'If I had a silk chemise for every man I was supposed to have had an affaire with, I could open a lingerie shop. George pays no attention. And, for my part, neither do I.' She picked up the hand-written menu and looked it over. 'I like a hand-written list of comestibles, James, don't you? It shows everything is home-made and fresh.'

Batchelor had never given it much thought, but supposed it made a lot of sense. As he didn't recognize most of the cakes listed, it could have been in Greek for all he cared.

'What will you have, James?' Libbie asked, looking at him brightly. It suddenly came to Batchelor in a flash that she played the silly little wife so well that she clearly was anything but.

'I'll have what you're having,' he said, smiling. Glancing through the list, he had spotted some disturbing names; he had already experienced some American cooking so didn't fancy monkey bread somehow. Anywhere else, he would not suspect it of containing actual monkeys – here, he wasn't so sure.

'I was just going to have a piece of strawberry shortcake,' she said. 'It may be a bit early for fresh ones, but jam is just as good.'

'I'll have that, then.' Batchelor was relieved. He recognized both names as real food and when it came, he wasn't disappointed. Essentially, it was an English cream tea. But with coffee.

Libbie peeled off one of her fashionable mauve gloves and picked daintily at her cake. 'It is so good of you and Captain Grand to come and help George,' she said. 'He has been so worried, all this trouble. He hates dishonesty as he hates the devil, James. He just won't have it in his regiment and when he sees it in government . . . well, it breaks his heart, it really does.'

'I think it is going to be more a job for Matthew . . .' Batchelor began.

Libbie's eyes opened wide. 'No, no, James,' she assured him. 'I am sure you will be an enormous help to them both. Many heads make light work.' She nibbled a strawberry and smiled sweetly.

Batchelor was pretty sure that the phrase was many hands make light work, but it seemed rude to say so. Also, he couldn't help but remember the other phrase about cooks and broth. He wiped his lip carefully – it wasn't easy to look like a helpful addition with a lump of whipped cream under the nose.

But Libbie had changed tack again. 'So, James. Tell me about the London fashions. Are overskirts still in? I do like that look but George says it is impractical out West and I daresay he's right.' She sighed. 'But it is *so* galling to come back to

Washington and find that one is so behind the times.' She waited
and Batchelor filled the pause nicely.

'You look as pretty as a picture, Mrs Custer,' he said,
gallantly and with no more than the truth.

She smiled at him and lowered her lashes. 'Oh, London
manners. What a delightful man you are.' This was going to
be fun.

Grand and Custer discussed long and hard in the smoking
room of the Baltimore. Custer neither drank nor smoked, but
he downed coffee with a vengeance. He sat in the plush leather
of the armchair but hunched over and Grand knew why. Better
than Custer, he knew that every wall in Washington had ears.
Everybody was an enemy of somebody and real friends were
like hens' teeth. From their respective posts, nearly six thousand
miles apart, both men had stumbled into a hornets' nest.

'George,' Grand said eventually, 'can I ask you a personal
question?'

'Fire away.' Custer was pouring himself yet another cup of
coffee.

'Why me? You and I didn't exactly hit it off at West Point.
And I seem to remember we had our share of differences from
Gettysburg to Appomattox.'

'We did,' Custer smiled. 'In fact, I'd go further and say – now
that Libbie's not here to hear it – you were the Goddamnedest
most insubordinate son of a bitch I ever rode with.'

It was Grand's turn to smile. 'Well, let's not beat about the
bush, George,' he said. 'Tell it like it is.'

'I will,' Custer said. 'But you were also an upfront soldier.
If you thought I was wrong, you'd tell me. If you thought that
I was right, you'd follow me to the ends of the earth.'

'But you were usually wrong,' Grand felt obliged to point
out.

'It's whether I'm wrong now that counts,' Custer said
solemnly, looking his old comrade squarely in the face.
'Besides, you know Washington. You know Belknap. Hell, you
even know the President.'

Grand opened his mouth to say something, but Custer beat
him to it. 'And you're an outsider at the same time,' he said.

'You're not mired in scandal up to your neck like just about every other son of a bitch in this town.'

Grand nodded, leaning back, 'So . . .?'

'So,' Custer cut to the chase, 'all I'm asking is that you watch my back, just for a couple of days. After that, I'll go back to Fort Lincoln and round up a few hostiles. You and Batchelor can take in the sights and head home.'

'Fair enough,' Grand said and the men shook hands.

'By the way,' Custer was pouring another cup of coffee for Grand. 'I'm taking a look at some recruits tomorrow. Want to come along, for old times' sake?'

James Batchelor had seen cavalry recruits before. Every so often, a colour party with ribbons pinned to their tunics, drums beating and regimental guidons snapping, would wind its way along the less salubrious byways of London, looking for likely lads to take the Queen's shilling. The bringers were men like Sergeant Reilly, old soaks who had seen it all, been everywhere. They kept the pongolo coming, the cheap beer that glazed the eye and dulled the brain and had men reaching for their silver even before the tall tales of the regiment's valour were trotted out.

It was no different here. A ragbag of scruffy men were already wiping the froth from their mouths, trading insults with passers-by and scratching their clothing. As Custer and his friends approached, they tugged off their shapeless caps and tried to look indispensable to Uncle Sam.

'Here we go,' Custer murmured to Grand. 'Half of 'em'll be Irish. The rest a mixture of German and English. Mr Batchelor,' he half turned to the man. 'You speak the language. See if you can get any sense out of them.'

Sergeant Reilly slapped his boot with his riding crop, stood squarely in front of the gaggle and barked, 'Ten-shun!'

Three or four of them understood and stood taller, but it was a sorry spectacle. The rest barely moved.

'Silence for the General!' Reilly thundered, and a kind of stillness prevailed. What passed for a recruiting barracks was a dilapidated warehouse in Frogtown, one of the many antebellum buildings that Boss Shepherd's energetic refurbish campaign had not dealt with yet. Street gangs roamed here, indistinguishable from the lads now volunteering for the army and the gay ladies watched them from afar, knowing that none of them could afford the price of so much as a kiss.

'Gentlemen,' Custer stood centre stage on the muddy cobbles, his voice high and dramatic, ringing off the walls around the square. 'You are about to make the best decision of your lives. To join the finest army in the free world – that of the United States of America. More than that, you're going to enlist in the finest regiment of that finest army – the Seventh United States Cavalry. You'll get free board and lodge in the healthiest climate in the country. The beds at Fort Abraham Lincoln, let me tell you, are pure goose feather. Don't believe what the old sweats tell you about chewing leather and hard-tack. Look at Sergeant Reilly here – he was a puny hundred and ten pound weakling before he saw army food. You'll have furloughs aplenty, complete with wine, women and song. Talking of which,' Custer was into his stride now, 'the Seventh has its own band and Glee Club, so if any of you is of the musical persuasion . . .'

'That'll be me, sir,' an Irish voice piped up. 'I sing tenor. And I've never met a fiddle I didn't like.'

There was laughter but Custer ignored the man and carried on. 'All this,' he said, 'and thirteen dollars a month. There's no greater calling, gentlemen. You'll spend the first weeks in training at Jefferson Barracks on the Missouri, then it's out West by train.'

'Do we get to ride at all?' another Irish voice chirped.

'Sort them out, Sergeant,' Custer muttered. 'Dollars this way, boys!' he called and turned smartly away, Grand and Batchelor in his wake. Once they had gone, Reilly grabbed both outspoken Irishmen by the scruffs of their collars. 'You won't be singing tenor when I've finished with you. You're a long way from Killarney now, boyo. And you,' he prodded the other man in the ribs, 'want to ride a horse, do you? Believe me, bog-trotter, by the time I've finished with you, you'll never want to see a horse again.'

'That's not the way to win men's hearts, Sergeant,' yet another Irish voice rang out across the square.

Reilly turned to find the culprit and his eyes narrowed when he saw him. 'Well, well, what have we here?'

The man waited until the sergeant's face was close to his. 'Patrick O'Riordan,' he said. 'Late corporal, Sixth Iniskillen Dragoons.'

'You don't say,' Reilly nodded, smiling. 'Tell me, Corporal O'Riordan, if I was to rip your breeches off, would I find the letter "D" for deserter on your hip, burned there in all its shameful beauty?'

'We don't do that in the British army,' O'Riordan said, 'but I left the army with an honourable discharge.'

'Oh, you did?' Reilly beamed. 'Well, over here, mister, you'll start with the rank of private trooper and *I'll* decide how bloody honourable you are.'

The silence was palpable but Reilly had already turned away, pulling pen and paper from his wallet to sign up the latest batch of brave defenders of the frontier.

On the edge of the makeshift parade ground, Libbie was twirling her parasol and being delightful for James Batchelor's benefit. Custer looked at her fondly and ignored her after that. Grand looked at his colleague, not quite so fondly; he knew only too well how susceptible he was to a pretty face and hoped he knew where to draw the line. Custer might be an affable cuss when the mood was on him, but when it wasn't, he was a quick man to the draw and they weren't in London now, where a sharp comment was the way to deal with a man who dallied with one's wife. Here, even in what passed for polite society, it wasn't the comments that were sharp – it was the knife in the ribs and ask questions later. Grand promised himself that he would keep an eye on the couple before it went too far.

'Mr Batchelor . . . James, I mean. Don't you just *love* watching all these fine men parading? I look forward so much to meeting them all again at Fort Lincoln. I try to be a mother to the young ones; bless their hearts, just look at them. Some of them have hardly started shaving yet.'

Batchelor had seen something completely different. He had seen a body of men the bulk of whom were running from something, and if their destination had to be a fort somewhere out West, well, so be it. It beat prison, the shotgun wedding or the debt collector by a country mile. But he smiled down at Libby and agreed that yes, they were a fine body of men.

'Your husband was very impressive with them,' he added. 'And the full dress uniform was a good touch; gives the men something to aspire to.'

'Land, James,' Libbie slapped his shoulder and laughed. 'He doesn't do it to impress the men. He does it because he likes to dress up. You won't have to spend long in George's company to notice that. Any excuse. But yes,' she added, more seriously, 'he does care a lot for his men, wants them to be happy and to have the best he can squeeze out of the sutlers. That's why he got so angry over this Belknap affair. It was not right, cheating the men for his own enrichment.'

'But do they really have goose feather beds?' Batchelor had not known many soldiers, but those he did had always made a big thing about sleeping on rocks.

'No, bless you, of course they don't.' She chuckled. 'Oh, my, George will love to hear that. No, he just tells them that as his little joke, you know. And the food isn't that marvellous, though most of them will have known worse. The meals come three times a day, at least, and if there isn't much variety, it's good, hot and wholesome.'

Batchelor could see that she was as proud of the US army as any soldier could be and so forbore to say that if half the men now wheeling randomly to Reilly's orders on the parade ground made it to Fort Abraham Lincoln then he, James Batchelor, was a three-star general. Smiling, he turned to watch the men forming their ragged lines and tried not to worry about what would happen once they had weapons in their hands.

THREE

Colonel Custer was dressing up again the next morning as he made his way by carriage to the Capitol. He wore his full dress uniform complete with gold wire epaulettes and cap lines. His war medals flashed on his chest and his sabre clanked at his hip. His yellow-plumed helmet was bright with the bald eagle in brass and his hair, even without John Burkman's barbering skills, shone with pomade.

Batchelor had seen the Capitol before, but never from the inside. He tried not to look like a star-struck tourist but inevitably his neck craned upwards and his eyes bulged at the ceiling under the dome and the portraits of senators great and even greater who glowered down at him. Every one of them knew that Batchelor's ancestors had tried to burn down the White House down the road and that the Capitol building, unfinished at the time as it was, would have been next for Admiral Cochrane's torches.

But Batchelor didn't have long to dwell on the splendours of all-American architecture or the chequered relationship between his country and Grand's. There was an army of journalists on the marble steps where presidents past and present had taken their inaugural oath.

'Over here, General!' photographers were shouting, trying to balance their tripods and vanishing under black hoods.

'General Custer, is it true about Fort Sill?' at least a dozen of them wanted to know.

'Are you gonna tame the Indians any time soon?' was another question that Custer refused to answer.

As the little party reached the huge doors and flunkies held them open, the general who was only a colonel turned to the baying mob. 'Gentlemen,' he said, tucking his helmet under his right arm and holding Libbie's hand with his left, 'my wife and I have come to have a quiet chat with Mr Hiester

Clymer. Rest assured, your colleagues already inside the building will be making furious notes. And you gentlemen will be the last to hear about it.'

Batchelor was the only man to laugh. As a reporter who had faced such put-downs before, he thought that was rather a good one. Custer was pleased with it too, but Libbie hadn't even cracked a smile.

'Mr Batchelor,' the General murmured once they were inside the lobby, 'take Mrs Custer to the gallery, will you? If things get a little ugly in the next few minutes, I want to know she's safe.'

'Don't worry, General,' Batchelor said, 'I'll be there,' and he whisked the woman away.

'Anything I should know?' Grand asked as he and Custer faced the open doors of the Committee Room and the faces inside, craning to get a view of them.

'Just what I heard over breakfast this morning,' Custer said, 'William Belknap has resigned.'

'He has? Well, that's a victory in itself, George. You've got him.'

'Have I hell?' Custer sneered. 'The story goes he was on his knees to Grant, begging to be let go.'

'And?'

'And Grant did what he has always done, let his cronies have it all.'

'Like I said . . .' Grand began.

'Congress isn't having any of it. They're pushing ahead. Even if Hiester Clymer doesn't want the truth to get out, there are others who do. Crawling out of the john in the nick of time doesn't mean you're not covered in shit.'

Custer straightened and marched through the doors, Grand at his side. The noise was deafening. When the hubbub had died down, the tall bearded man in the centre of the podium banged his gavel like a high court judge and a kind of order prevailed. He was Hiester Clymer and this was his committee, one of several that had convened over the last few months into various aspects of President Grant's administration.

'Colonel Custer.' Clymer fixed the man with his steel-blue eyes.

The brevet-general stood there, back ramrod straight. 'Mr Clymer,' he nodded.

'Before we begin, Mr Custer,' Clymer said, 'may I enquire as to the name and purpose of the gentleman standing beside you?'

'This is Matthew Grand,' Custer told him, 'formerly captain of the Third Cavalry of the Potomac in the late war between the states.'

Grand stood up and nodded to Clymer.

'You don't need a soldier's friend, Colonel,' the chairman chuckled. 'This isn't a court martial.'

'Isn't it, sir?' Custer said. 'It sure feels like one to me.'

There was hubbub again and Clymer's gavel put another end to it.

'You have been invited here to tell us what, as the commander of Fort Abraham Lincoln, you have to say on recent Indian affairs. Your attendance is totally voluntary. You can leave when you like.'

'Not before I state certain facts,' Custer said as he and Grand sat down, 'relating to corruption and financial mismanagement by William Belknap, who I understand – as of an hour or so ago – has recently resigned.'

There were more rumblings. Grand noted that Belknap's resignation had come as a surprise to many in the Committee Room.

'Does that resignation mean that you withdraw your accusations, Colonel Custer?' Clymer asked.

'No, sir, it does not. Ex-Secretary for War Mr Belknap is up to his neck in fraud. He has been short-changing my troopers, not to mention the Indians, throughout his time in office. He has been lining his own pockets at the expense of the American taxpayer.'

This time, Clymer had to batter the desk before he could be heard. 'I assume, Colonel, that you have evidence of all this?'

'I have, sir.' Custer held up a leather-bound file. 'Chapter and verse.'

This time, the mutterings were more muted. Whatever Custer had in that file, it could smear more of them than just William Belknap.

'We will take that under advisement,' Clymer said as a clerk passed him the file. 'Was there anything else, Colonel?'

Custer's eyelids flickered. He glanced at Grand, up at Libbie in the gallery. 'Yes, sir, there is. And Captain Grand here is witness to my remarks – and to the reaction they are likely to cause.'

'Say on.'

'Mr Belknap is not the only culprit in this matter.'

Custer knew how to milk an audience. Had Libbie dropped a pin from her hair now, it would have set off echoes all the way to the Potomac.

'Indeed?' Clymer's eyebrow was raised. So was his gavel. Whatever Custer was about to say was likely to cause a storm.

'Someone else who had his snout in the pig trough, Mr Clymer, was Orvil Grant, brother of the President.'

The room erupted. Half the grey faces on the podium left, with snarls and expletives. Others waved papers at Custer, but old Iron Butt just sat his ground.

Clymer's 'Do you have evidence of that?' went unheard.

Grand was on his feet again. 'Time to go, I think, George,' and he pulled the man out of his chair.

Somehow, they struggled through what had once been a slightly bored audience that had now turned into an angry, shouting mob. Democrats in the hall slapped Custer on the back, laughing and clapping. Republicans glared at him, jostling and pushing.

'Custer!'

The General turned to face the speaker.

'From today, you're a dead man.'

Grand blocked the man's path. Custer needed no one to fight his battles for him, but Grand stood three inches taller and the red scarf of the Potomac he wore that day spoke volumes for his fighting credentials too.

'Libbie . . .' Custer craned his neck, trying to see his wife.

'She'll be safe with James,' Grand said. 'You and I have to talk, George.'

'So,' Batchelor was trying to make sense of the day. 'Does he actually have any evidence against the President's brother?'

'Always a little short on detail, was Fanny Custer,' Grand said, lighting a cigar.

'That's not going to go well.'

'Are you eating something?' Grand looked around to see where the snacks had disappeared to.

'In a way. It's this. Have you tried it?' Batchelor fished a small packet out of his pocket.

'What is it?'

Batchelor read the label. 'Adams New York Gum,' he said. 'Apparently, it snaps and stretches.'

'Tobacco?'

'No.'

'Paraffin wax?'

'No.'

'Not spruce resin?'

'Chicle.'

Grand was none the wiser. 'Really?'

'Want some?'

'What does it taste of?'

'Rubber – I should think; although I've never knowingly eaten rubber, so I couldn't actually be sure.'

'Thanks.' Grand waved his cigar in excuse. 'I'll pass.'

'Very wise,' said Batchelor, discreetly spitting the gum into his hand. 'It'll never catch on.' He looked down at the unlovely wad in his palm and searched around for somewhere to put it. In the end, he settled with pressing it firmly under the table. It shouldn't bother anyone there.

There was a knock on the door and Grand got to it first. A distraught Libbie Custer stood there, desperately trying to keep herself together. 'Captain Grand,' she flustered. Then she caught Batchelor's eye. 'James. Oh, please help. George has gone to the War Department.'

'He has?' Batchelor was on his feet, helping her to a chair. 'Why?'

'Read this.' She rummaged in her bag for a moment and finally brought out a letter, crumpled and half torn through. She tried to smooth it out but after a moment simply thrust it into Grand's hand. He read it quickly. War Department stationery. Scribbled, semi-literate scrawl. For Batchelor's benefit, he translated. 'George has been deprived of his command,' he said. 'He's lost the Seventh.'

'They didn't waste much time,' Batchelor observed drily.

'If you ask me,' Libbie said through tight lips, 'they wrote that *before* George gave his evidence. You recognize the signature, Captain Grand?'

'I do,' he nodded. 'Phil Sheridan.'

'Little Phil.' She raised a furious eyebrow. 'He's no taller than me, James, but he's George's commanding officer in terms of the Army of the Plains. I've never seen Georgie turn so pale. He stormed off as soon as he got that. Knocking Sheridan down is the least he'll do. He's right, but he's got himself into a position now. You were with him in the war, Captain Grand. What will he do?'

'He'll charge,' Grand knew, reaching for his hat, 'and he'll need some support. James, stay here with Libbie.' And he was gone.

The lights burned blue in the labyrinth that was the War Department that night. Soldiers in night capes saluted as people came and went and nobody challenged a man wearing the scarlet scarf of the Cavalry of the Potomac. It had been a long time since Grand had walked these particular corridors of power, and he took more than one wrong turning before he reached his destination.

Eventually, it was the noise of raised voices that drew him, like a good general to the sound of the guns, and he read Sheridan's name etched on the glass pane in the door.

'Who the hell are you?' the little man on the other side of the desk was already on his feet, his knuckles white, his face a livid scowl in the lamplight.

George Custer stood opposite him, the full-dress glamour gone now and replaced by a plain civilian coat. His ringlets had tumbled over his forehead in the absence of his hat and he did not look as if this interview was going well.

'Matthew Grand, General,' Grand said. 'I was a captain under your command back in the day.'

Little Phil Sheridan frowned and put on his glasses. 'Oh, yes,' he said. 'I remember. You were a tolerable soldier in the

Shenandoah Valley, Grand, but that doesn't give you the right to barge in here without so much as a kiss my ass.'

'Beautifully put, General,' Grand smiled, 'but I was hoping for a word with Colonel Custer.'

'Feel free,' Sheridan snapped. 'I've had all the words with him I intend to have.'

'For one last time, Sheridan,' Custer shouted. 'Will you reinstate me?'

Sheridan paused, breathing hard, trying his best not to bend a brass paperweight over Custer's head. He pointed to a large pile of War Department files on his desk. 'You see these?' he asked.

Custer nodded.

'That's a list of men available for duty in the West. George Crook, Nelson Miles, Alfred Terry – fine soldiers all, and all of them outranking you.'

'Those three gentlemen,' Custer growled, 'couldn't find their own asses with both hands and you and I both know that. You've taken the Seventh off me because of my comments about Orvil Grant and you know that too.'

'I don't play politics, Custer,' Sheridan insisted.

'The hell you don't,' Custer snapped back. 'Ulysses S. Grant says "Jump" and you say, "Certainly, Mr President, sir. How high?" So I guess I won't waste any more time on the monkey. I'm off to the organ grinder.'

He paused at the door. 'Don't get up, Phil,' he smiled. 'Oh, wait a minute, you already are.' And the door slammed behind him.

Sheridan threw an inkwell across the room. He had an orderly somewhere who would clean that up later. He looked at Grand. 'Are you still here?'

'They don't make men like George Custer every day, General,' he said, mildly. No point in riling the man even more by being aggressive, though if memory served, it didn't take much to rile Little Phil.

'And aren't we all glad of it,' Sheridan countered. He caught the expression on Grand's face. 'Look, Grand, you know George and I go back a long ways. Hell, he was the most loyal lieutenant I had in the Shenandoah. But he just can't go around bad-mouthing the President's family like that. There have to be consequences.' He motioned Grand to a chair.

'Adams Gum?' The General held out a packet that Grand had seen before.

'No, thanks.' The enquiry agent held up a hand. 'But I'd settle for a Bourbon.'

'Thank God,' Sheridan said, reaching for his decanter on the sideboard. 'That's another thing about Custer. Ever since he married Libbie Bacon, he's gone all blue light on us. Never trust a soldier who doesn't drink.' He poured the amber nectar for them both.

'Unlike the President,' Grand said, stony-faced.

'Now, Grand . . .' Sheridan wagged a finger at him. 'No, women'll do that to a man. They say he hasn't touched a drop nor thrown a dice since he tied the knot. Mind you, they say he hasn't dropped a profanity either and from what I've heard in the last few minutes, *that's* not true, I can tell you.'

Grand smiled. Little Phil was quick to anger but it never lasted long.

'As a matter of fact, I'm tying the knot myself in a couple of months.'

'Congratulations,' Grand said.

Sheridan passed a framed photograph and Grand was impressed. The future Mrs Sheridan was a stunner and could easily have been the general's daughter.

'I heard you'd emigrated to England.' Sheridan took back the photograph and smiled at his bride-to-be, polishing off an invisible piece of dust from her lovely nose. 'Slàinte.' He raised his glass to Grand.

'Slàinte,' Grand echoed. 'That's right.'

'Not still soldiering, I take it?'

'Enquiring,' Grand said. 'Of the private, criminal variety.'

'Ah. And that's what brings you back to DC? Not pursuing your enquiries, I hope.'

'No, no,' Grand half-lied. 'Just visiting the folks, you know. Not getting any younger, either of them, you know how it is. I ran into Custer by accident.'

'Didn't we all.' Sheridan drained his glass. 'Look, Grand. I've got no choice over this. A colonel in this man's army can't go around slandering the President's brother and be seen to get away with it. It'll blow over in a month or so and I'll get Custer a post somewhere. Jefferson Barracks, maybe, Inspector of Cavalry, something like that.'

'That would break his heart, General,' Grand said. 'You know George. It's a fighting command or nothing for him.'

Sheridan shrugged and sighed. 'Then, it's nothing,' he said.

For four days, Custer sat in the lobby of the White House. For four days, he was ignored, at least by the President. *Mrs* Grant swept past him once and smiled, not quite sure who he was. An Undersecretary of State cut him dead, and any number of aides, in crisp blue uniforms and white gloves, kept him supplied with coffee and cookies. But of General Ulysses S. Grant, there was no sign.

'He's using the back stairs,' was Matthew Grand's take on the situation. 'That's sort of like the back passage in England and with pretty much the same connotation.'

'So, that's it, then.' Batchelor put down the *Washington Post*. 'We're going home.'

'We are,' Grand said, 'but not just yet.'

Batchelor looked at him. 'Matthew,' he murmured, 'you've got that funny look in your eyes, the one that says, "I've just thought of a cunning plan that's probably illegal but we'll try it anyway".'

'I have,' Grand nodded, 'but there's no "we".'

'Come again?'

'If the President won't see Custer,' Grand said, 'he might see me.'

Batchelor guffawed. Then he realized he may have given offence and qualified it with, 'You'll forgive me for saying this, Matthew, but why would the President not see a decorated major general, albeit of the brevet type, and yet spare the time of day for a . . . and there's no kind way of saying this, a mere captain.'

'Oh, you'd be surprised,' Grand smiled.

'I'm sure I would,' Batchelor said, 'but tell me anyway.'

'I can't do that, James,' Grand said. 'It's too long a shot. Anyway, there's a snag.'

'There is?'

Grand nodded, looking at his partner in crime. 'How do you break in to the White House?'

Batchelor blinked. 'Well, we British did it a few years back,' he said. 'It can't be that difficult.'

'Ah,' Grand wagged a finger at him. 'That's as maybe, but you British aren't going to be involved this time. This one's on me.'

'What?'

'If I'm caught, they'll lock me up, quite possibly in a mental institution. If *you're* caught, there could be a war.'

Batchelor disagreed. 'After Lincoln,' he said, 'if you're caught, they'll hang you. And if I'm there, you won't get caught.'

Grand was shaking his head. 'Sorry, James,' he said. 'It's not going to happen.'

FOUR

'It's always best to reach some kind of compromise.' James Batchelor was feeling, if not smug, at least partially vindicated as he crept through the White House shrubbery in the dark of the night. Owls softly hooted from trees above his head, their gentle cries sounding something like agreement to the Englishman. He and Grand were dressed from head to toe in black, with streaks of lampblack on their faces, to break up the silhouette in any glancing moonbeam. Grand had been against the lampblack, but Batchelor's sense of the dramatic had won the day. It was easy to keep under the deep shadow now they had crossed the lawn, fifty seconds – according to the frenzied beating of Batchelor's heart – when a well-aimed bullet from a guard could have stopped the entire expedition in its tracks. They blessed the man who had decided to surround the building with gravel paths. Every minute, the measured tread of the sentry approached and then retreated and, in the spaces between, the two paced silently nearer and nearer to their goal.

Grand put his mouth against Batchelor's ear and breathed, 'We're near to the kitchen block. If a window is open anywhere, it will be here. The laundry room is our best chance; someone will have left a sash ajar to air the President's smalls, you mark my words.'

Batchelor nodded. Where Grand got his encyclopaedic knowledge of the ways of laundry maids he would prefer not to know, but sure enough, on a corner of the building and handily placed in the lee of a bush, a casement stood ajar and from within the room came a fresh smell of hot irons, starch and clean linen. Grand said nothing, simply smiling in the moonlight and putting an arm in to release the catch further. The window swung open with a deafening squeal of hinges subjected daily to steam and heat. Batchelor grabbed it as it swung and both men stood there frozen, waiting for the sound of running feet on gravel, but none came. Breathing again, Grand put a leg carefully over the sill, feeling gingerly to make sure he was stepping on to solid flags and not into a copper full of water. Everything seemed secure and he slid inside, swallowed up by the dark.

Batchelor followed him, pulling the window shut behind him.

'James!' Grand's hiss was harsh in the linen-muffled silence. 'I thought we agreed you would wait outside.'

Batchelor shrugged, though in the total blackness the gesture had limited value. 'I'm as much of a spy outside the White House standing by an open window at dead of night as I am inside, I would think,' he said. 'I'll be your backstop.'

'What? This isn't a game of cricket, you know,' Grand snapped.

'Cricket?' Batchelor was confused. 'Oh, I see. You're thinking of rounders.'

Grand snorted, but quietly. 'Let's not argue children's ball games now, James. The long and the short of it is, you are not coming with me. My business with the President is just between him and me.'

'I needn't come in,' Batchelor said, reasonably. 'I will watch outside the room, make sure you're not disturbed.'

'How . . .?'

'I'll think of something.' Batchelor had caught up with Grand in the dark by the simple expedient of cannoning into him and nearly sending him flying over a pile of ironing awaiting attention. 'Let's get on with it. The night isn't getting any longer, you know.'

Grand knew when he was beaten. Generally, Batchelor was an even-tempered, pleasant enough cuss, but when he put his foot down, he was as impossible to move as the White House itself. So he turned on his heel and led the way, tentatively and with several wrong turns, into lines of airing washing, out into the corridor, where at least a little light filtered in from the gaslit main areas beyond.

'Do you know where we are?' Batchelor asked, in the softest whisper he could manage.

Grand stopped himself just in time from saying 'In the

White House.' As they got nearer the hub of things, levity wasn't really appropriate. 'Not exactly,' he breathed. 'I know there are some back stairs along here, somewhere. But we will have to be careful. At least one flight goes all the way to the servants' rooms in the attics, with no stops at the intervening levels. So the President and his good lady don't accidentally meet a tweenie on the stairs.'

Batchelor was oddly annoyed on behalf of tweenies everywhere. What price democracy? 'How do you know all this?' he whispered.

Grand shrugged again and, this time, the movement was clear as his black outline showed against the relative glow from a window. 'We all know that kind of thing. Our fathers and grandfathers have been in and out of this building since they broke ground, or near enough.'

Batchelor felt suddenly very lonely. His partner was suddenly no longer Matthew Grand, Enquiry Agent, with offices in the Strand, London, but Mattie Grand, whose father was in and out of the White House. But there was no time for reflection. He was off like a rabbit along the corridor and then, suddenly, he was gone.

Batchelor froze. Had Grand been snatched by a prowling guard? Was he even now being pressed against a wall, a firearm's muzzle in his back? Batchelor crept along the corridor in the direction Grand had taken, placing each foot with care. Heel, toe. Heel, toe.

Grand's head appeared around the corner. 'Are you going to take all night?' he said, from the side passage he had slipped down. 'The stairs we need are just down here.'

Batchelor squared his shoulders and hurried along, his rubber-soled shoes making no sound on the flagged floor. Off to their right, a staircase rose into blackness, and Grand took it two steps at a time. On the first landing, lights burned at either end, green, flickering flames that made the whole length look strange, as though underwater. Grand gestured to Batchelor to come closer and breathed in his ear.

'These are the offices, on this level. Not the Oval Office, of course, that is down below and to the east. But the offices which count are up here. Back in the day, my father's office was just along there.' He pointed behind him. 'The stairs to the private quarters are along here. Follow me.'

Batchelor reached out to grab his arm, but the man had gone, loping down the corridor, carpeted now in hardwearing brown Turkey. Again, he disappeared, but now Batchelor was ready for it and he swung around the corner in his wake and up the stairs behind him like his shadow. Two steps from the top, Grand stopped and held out a warning hand.

'Guards patrol up here just like everywhere else,' he muttered. 'But I know Lincoln stopped them being any more frequent than every two hours, because there was a squeaky board outside Mary Todd's room and it woke her up. I should have thought mending the board would be easier, but . . . well, we all know how lax they were on security in those days.'

Batchelor grimaced. The whole world knew *that*.

'Don't worry about it, though. I happen to know that President and Mrs Grant have rooms adjoining along this corridor here.' He pointed. 'She prefers the morning sun to wake her up, so they moved to rooms facing east.' Grand looked carefully left and right and listened, his finger to his lips. 'I can't hear a guard, which is not to say they won't be here any minute. Look,' he turned to his left, 'there's a deep window embrasure there, with the curtains drawn back. Slip in there behind the curtain and you will be able to keep watch without being seen.'

'What shall I do if anyone comes?' It suddenly occurred to Batchelor that they had made no contingency plans regarding signs, warnings or any other sensible plans, come to that.

'You'll think of something.' Grand crept off along the corridor, listening at doors until he found what he wanted. Snoring like someone sawing wet timber with a dull saw came through the door in waves. That was simple enough, then. One door further on from this, Julia Grant's boudoir, had to be the President's. With infinite care and glacial slowness, Grand eased down the handle and pushed open the door. Batchelor, watching from the cover of the dusty brocade, saw him pause once more in the doorway, look both ways and disappear.

It wasn't as if it wasn't a sound that Ulysses S. Grant hadn't heard before – the cocking of a gun – it was just that he had never heard it in his bedroom at the White House. He sat up abruptly, his still-brown hair all over his forehead and the ties of his nightshirt caught up in his beard.

'If you're going to shoot me, you son of a bitch,' he growled, 'just get it over with.'

'I'm not going to shoot you, Mr President,' a voice in the darkness told him, 'unless I have to. No, I'm content to ruin you.'

Grant sat up still further, cracking his head a nasty one on some ornate carving on the bedhead. 'Who the hell are you?' He was still looking at the cold muzzle of the gun inches from his left eye, gleaming in the faint moonlight which crept in through the half-open curtains.

'Matthew Grand, late of the Cavalry of the Potomac.'

A silence.

'Grand.' The President was easing his hands out from under the bed covers. 'I remember you. You were with Custer in the Shenandoah.'

'Not to mention Gettysburg and Appomattox,' Grand added.

'Sure, sure.' The President's face broke out in a grin. He knew of many men whose nerves had cracked under the strain of war. Some of them turned their own guns on themselves, some on others. Nobody, since John Wilkes Booth, had turned a gun on the President. But the assassination of Lincoln, ten years ago and just down the street, was probably precedent enough.

'Let's talk about this.' Grant flashed his campaign-trail smile, the one that went with rosettes and bouquets of flowers and kissing ghastly children, noses always dribbling with snot.

'Yes, let's.' Grand stepped back a little, allowing his President some space. He sat in the chair in the corner, but he still held the revolver in his hand, the one he had promised James Batchelor he would not be bringing with him.

'What is it you want, Captain Grand?' Grant asked. He leaned over and scraped a match on a silver holder on the nightstand. The small flame of a candle flickered to life and grew, steadying until it lit the faces of both men and picked them out of the gloom. He hadn't expected Grand to be blacked up, but the after-effects of war took men in different ways.

'A favour,' Grand said.

'Oh?' Grant felt that he was making some sort of progress with this lunatic. 'What might that be?'

'I want you to reinstate Colonel Custer to his command of the Seventh Cavalry at Fort Lincoln.'

'Out of my hands, I'm afraid,' Grant said, with surprising smugness for a man staring death in the face. 'General Sheridan's in charge of the army out West. I hung up my sabre a long time ago.'

'Bullshit, Mr President,' Grand said, 'with all due respect, of course. Little Phil wouldn't so much as scratch his ass unless you told him he could. Reinstate Custer.'

'Or you'll shoot me?' A man didn't get to be a four-star general and President of the United States – twice – without being able to brazen things out.

'Or I'll expose your brother for the lying shit he is.'

Grant chuckled. 'We're used to besmirching here in Washington, Captain Grand. Why, it's almost a metropolitan pastime. Orvil and I can ride this out. There isn't an iota of truth in Custer's accusations.'

'I wouldn't know anything about that,' Grand said. 'It's other accusations I'm interested in.'

'Like what?' Grant was sitting up in bed now, like a recuperating patient enjoying the attention.

'Well, now.' Grand sat back too, the pocket Colt tilted back so that it no longer pointed at the leader of the free world. 'Let's not worry about Orvil. What about you? Where to start? To be fair to you, Sam – you don't mind if I call you Sam; I feel I've come to know you so well – you started out all right. There have been worse students at West Point – Custer, for one. And you did all right in the Mexican War. Then, old Mr Bourbon came calling, didn't he? I know,' Grand waved an understanding left hand, 'the Pacific coast's a bitch for a cuss with not enough to do. So you damned near drank yourself to death until they kicked you out of this man's army.'

'Technically,' said Grant, sitting up rather straighter and tugging his nightshirt straight across his chest, 'I was asked to resign.'

'Whatever,' Grand shrugged. 'Then what? Oh, yes, a seven-year apprenticeship drifting from one shitty job to another. The real high spot there was a clerk in your daddy's leather store in Galena, wasn't it?'

'All a matter of public record.' The President folded his arms. This lunatic was sadder than he had thought.

'Then, of course, came the war. What a Godsend, huh? The Union was desperate. Any man who could sit a horse could raise a regiment in those days. Still, Belmont was a fluke, wasn't it? Damnedest piece of military luck I ever heard.'

'That's your interpretation.' Grant was still smiling, as though his face had forgotten how to do any other expression.

'You made your name capturing Forts Henry and Donelson, even though that was at the expense of too many good men.'

'War is Hell, Grand, as General Sherman said to me only the other day.'

'It certainly is,' Grand agreed, 'witness the way in which General Johnston kicked your ass at Shiloh. And a lot more men died when you beat Beauregard. And don't get me started on Vicksburg and Chattanooga.'

'Where are you going with this, Grand?' The President wanted to know. 'Vicksburg was a long siege – men are going to die. As for Chattanooga, they made me a lieutenant general after that, conferred on me by the Senate itself. Nobody since George Washington has been accorded that. Or have you got something on him, too?'

Grand smiled. 'I've saved the best till last,' he said. 'Where were you on the night of April 14, 1865, Mr President?'

Grant bridled. 'I don't know, man, that was ten years ago.'

'It was,' Grand nodded. 'But that date is etched on your brain, sir, just as it is on mine. The night they killed Abe Lincoln.'

Grant said nothing.

'Well,' Grand said, 'since you seem so hazy on the matter, I'll remind you. You and your good lady wife were invited by President Lincoln to Ford's Theatre – the papers said so. I was there too, though not, thank God, in the Presidential box. You and your good lady wife cried off, anxious to visit your daughter at school in New Jersey.'

'That's right. I remember now. Poor Nellie; she was home-sick.' Grant looked smug.

'Except that wasn't the reason, was it, General Grant?'

A silence.

'No,' Grant said at last. 'It wasn't.'

'What was it?'

'If you must know, Julia and I couldn't stand Mary Todd Lincoln. Matter of fact, I don't know anybody who could. How Lincoln stood her I have no idea. I didn't want to put Julia through three hours of hell in that woman's company.'

'Aw, shucks.' Grand was pure South Carolina for a moment. 'Ain't you the perfect gentleman?'

Grant shrugged, smile back firmly on his face, lips clamped together in a mad rictus.

He watched as the intruder reached inside his coat and pulled out a letter. 'You know,' Grand said, 'I used to think we had the finest postal service in the world – Pony Express, that kind of thing. I guess, what with the war just coming to an end and all, things got a little confused. Anyway, long story cut short, I got this letter back in April '65. It was addressed to you, but delivered to me. Well, Grant, Grand, it's a mistake anybody can make.'

'What is that letter?' Grant wasn't smiling now. His lips were still pressed together but he looked about as affable as a rattler. He held out his hand.

'Uh-huh, Mr President. This is evidence. Or, perhaps I should say, a copy of the evidence. I have the original back in my premises in London. Just in case anything should happen to me tonight. It's a letter, written six days before Lincoln's death. From Mary Surratt.'

'Who?' Grant was fiddling with his bedcovers.

'Ah, how soon they forget,' Grand smiled. 'Mary Surratt, along with John Wilkes Booth, George Atzerodt, David Herold and Lewis Paine were all involved in one way or another with Lincoln's assassination. They all hanged on July 7, in the old prison right here in Washington. Truth is, Mr President, there should have been another man blowing in the wind with them. You.'

Grant was about to leap out of bed, but Grand's re-cocked pistol stopped him. 'That's a Goddamned lie,' he snarled.

'Is it, Mr President? That's not what Mrs Surratt says here.' He brandished the paper. 'Mrs Surratt says that you were in on the whole thing. You and Lincoln never saw eye to eye, did you? This was your way of getting revenge. And it worked, didn't it? Here you are, one of the most powerful men in the world, thanks to what happened at Ford's. Of course, you couldn't be there that night. Because with what you knew about the whole sordid operation, you had to be elsewhere; like visiting your daughter in New Jersey.'

Grant slumped back against the headboard. 'What do you want?' he asked quietly.

'I told you,' Grand said. 'Reinstate Custer.'

'And if I do?'

'Then this letter,' Grand tucked it away again, 'and the original will both be burned. You have my word as an officer of the Army of the Potomac.'

'Your word!' Grant almost spat the words.

'You've got pen and paper over here,' Grand lit the oil lamp on the table and the rest of the room, opulent, overblown and decadent, leapt into view. Grand looked around wryly, wondering what the vast proportion of the electorate who had thought they were putting a campaign-hardened soldier in the White House would think if they could see what he could see right now. 'Write to Sheridan telling him to send Custer back to the Seventh. *Two* copies, please, Mr President; one for Sheridan, the other for my records, shall we say? Otherwise, my next port of call will be the *Washington Post*. America can forgive a lot of things – financial misdealing, lies to Congress, bribery – but involvement in the murder of Abraham Lincoln? No, Mr President, America will not forgive that. Now, *sign!*'

Outside on the landing, Batchelor had had an eventful night. The guard had come round once, but scarcely looked about him and was certainly not listening very hard, singing softly under his breath as he was the judge's song from *Trial by Jury*. Batchelor was impressed. He had seen it twice and couldn't get his tongue around half the patter; it wasn't something you expected to hear in the dead of night on a landing in the White House. No sooner had the guard paced past than pattering feet ran down the corridor from the same direction. A maid, judging from the darns in her nightdress, sprang past Batchelor, running on tiptoe, her eyes alight with fun and her cheeks pink with the sport. Behind her came one of the boot boys, arms outstretched to catch her, as he did, just to Batchelor's right. He had to peer around the curtain to see what happened next and almost wished he hadn't. Obviously, spooning had come on in leaps and bounds in the White House of Ulysses S. Grant. After a brief scuffling, the pair legged it up a concealed staircase, no doubt in search of more privacy. No sooner had they gone than the door next to the President's and almost in front of Batchelor swung open and a matronly woman stood in the doorway, a candle in a brass holder in her hand. Batchelor shrank back behind the curtain and held his breath. As he always had when hiding as a child, he closed his eyes.

The moments ticked by like aeons and Batchelor risked another breath and opened one eye just a crack and almost swallowed his tongue. Standing not ten inches away was the matronly woman with the candle. Her madly crossed eyes sought for his in the gloom. He tried a smile, but she didn't move.

'You are?' she eventually barked.

'Ermm . . . I am with the . . . fabric committee,' Batchelor said, thinking relatively fast.

'Fabric? Do you mean the drapes?'

Batchelor blinked. He hadn't even thought of fabric having two meanings. 'No . . . madam.' He realized he had no idea how to address the First Lady of the United States, assuming this was she. 'I mean, the fabric of the building.'

She stepped back a pace. 'You *sound* like a lunatic,' she observed. 'What's that accent, for a start? You *German*?'

'No, no, ma'am . . . English.'

She was outraged. 'What's an Englishman doing looking at

the fabric of *my* White House? There must be Americans who can do the job.'

'Indeed there are,' Batchelor flustered. 'In fact, my boss is American. I am just a junior inspector of fabrics.'

She looked at him with one eye then the other. 'You're a bit long in the tooth to be a junior anything,' she said eventually. 'And why are you so . . .' she waved a hand vaguely in front of her face, 'dirty?'

'I've had other jobs,' he said, thinking on his feet. 'I've been a . . .' the truth was as good as anything else '. . . journalist . . .'

He got no further. She hauled off and fetched him a right hook on the jaw, all the more amazing in its accuracy as she clearly could hardly focus on him at all. 'I thought so,' he heard her hiss through the ringing in his ears. 'A *journalist*. You'd stop at nothing, wouldn't you, scum? Well, you'll get no stories out of *me*.' And so saying, she turned and went back into her bedroom, slamming the door behind her.

Batchelor sagged back against the window, nursing his jaw, and was still there, wondering what on earth had just happened, when Grand slipped silently out of the President's bedroom. He gave his friend an odd look. Surely, his face hadn't been swollen like that when they set out? However, no time for small talk; with a finger to his lips he led the way through the corridors of the White House and soon they were swinging along Arlington Avenue just like any other two gents on their way home after a spree.

Back in their hotel, Batchelor leaned into the lamplight on the side table to read President Grant's letter to Sheridan. 'How the hell did you get him to do it?' he asked. 'I thought he would never give Custer his job back.'

'Oh, he saw reason,' Grand shrugged. 'I knew he would.'

'You blackmailed him!' Batchelor clicked his fingers in realization.

'Me?' Grand was all wide-eyed innocence.

'You!' Batchelor laughed. 'But how?'

'With this.' Grand pulled the letter from his pocket, the one containing the most damnable of damning evidence.

'It's a hotel bill,' Batchelor said, unfolding it. 'From the Baltimore.'

'Yes,' Grand said. 'It came to me by mistake. See that George Custer gets it, will you, James? I'm going to get some shut-eye.' He stared at the man's face again. 'And I'd get some ice on that jaw, if I were you. How did you do it, again?'

There was no way on God's green earth that James Batchelor was going to admit that he had been socked in the jaw by a little cross-eyed woman who would never see fifty again, but on the other hand, Grand and Batchelor, Enquiry Agents of the Strand, didn't lie to each other, that was understood, so he compromised. 'I walked into a door,' he said, with a rueful smile. 'Clumsy.'

William Belknap may have been the ex-Secretary for War but he hadn't vacated his office yet and he still had odds and ends to tie up. The man's girth was becoming legendary in the corridors of power and the vast beard that threatened to reach it could not disguise its existence. It was late and the lamps in his office were dimmed. William Belknap was the sort of man who conducted much of his business after dark when few men were still awake to witness it.

One who was sat before him now, hat in hand, waiting for instructions.

'The President may have rolled over and reinstated Custer,' Belknap growled, tapping a cigar butt on his blotting paper, 'but I haven't. I sat in the White House with Grant and Phil Sheridan not two months ago and we agreed that all troops should be pulled out of the Black Hills. The place will be wide open to prospectors now that word's out about the gold strike and the United States will soon be one state larger. Or more.'

'And the Indians?' his visitor felt bound to ask.

'Savages, son,' Belknap thundered. 'Who the hell, in the scheme of things, gives a fiddler's bitch about them?' He leaned forward, the lamplight glowing on his thick lips and bushy eyebrows. 'But with Custer back with the Seventh, all that's blowing in the wind. I want that man stopped, closed down, finished. Nobody points a finger at me and

gets away with it. I can rely on you, can't I? To do whatever
it takes?'

Belknap's visitor nodded. He picked up a fat envelope from
the desk and stowed it away casually in his inside breast
pocket, almost as though it didn't contain an ordinary Joe's
annual pay. 'You most assuredly can.'

FIVE

The next day saw the Custers window shopping along Pennsylvania Avenue. Libbie was in agonies of indecision over a choice of hats, but all her angst was fabricated to deflect her real worries over George's future. Neither Grand nor Batchelor felt they could pass on the good news about the General's reinstatement until he heard it himself; and little Phil Sheridan seemed to be dragging his feet. They stayed with the Custers, but not with them, trailing a little behind and pretending to take an unhealthy interest in the latest Parisian fashions. Both of them stiffened a little as a soldier in white gloves came clattering along the sidewalk with an urgent message for the General.

'Well, well, well.' Custer's solemn face broadened to a grin as he read the contents. 'Thank the General for me,' he said to the messenger, a clean-cut young man with 'West Point' written all over him. 'Tell him I shall be in touch shortly, just before I take a train for the Dakota Territory.'

'Good news, General?' A dark-haired man with bushy sideburns had appeared from nowhere. There was nothing new in this. Ever since his performance at the Capitol, men had been approaching Custer, some to shake his hand, others to scowl at him or worse. Even so, Grand and Batchelor were uneasy. It would be a whole lot safer when the General was on that train.

'Do I know you, sir?' Custer narrowed his eyes at the man.

'Mark Kellogg, General.' He held out his hand.

The enquiry agents were impressed at Custer's perception when he said, 'I'm not giving interviews to the gentlemen of the Press today.'

'Ah, but I'm not your run-of-the-mill Pressman, General,' Kellogg persisted. 'I'm from back home.'

'Michigan?' Custer asked.

'No, sir. Dakota territory. I'm with the Bismarck *Tribune*.'

'Then you're as far from base as I am,' Custer smiled.

'I've been following you for days, General,' Kellogg said, which came as a surprise to Grand and Batchelor, who had never seen the man before. 'I'd be honoured if you could give me your story, sir; an exclusive, if you will, for the *Tribune*.'

'I've got a train to catch, Mr Kellogg,' Custer said, 'and a regiment to command. If you're intent on hearing my story, as you put it, you're going to have to come with me.'

'That'll be my pleasure, General,' Kellogg beamed.

'But first, Mrs Custer and I have some shopping to do.' He tipped his hat and Kellogg did the same. As the little Custer party went on their way, Kellogg stood on the sidewalk, watching them go, a hand raised in friendly greeting, a parting smile on his lips.

'I'm not sure I care for that,' Batchelor murmured to Grand. He knew all about pushy Pressmen; he used to be one himself. There was something oily about Mark Kellogg and it wasn't just his Macassar.

'Nor me,' Grand nodded, watching as the Custers disappeared inside South Market Hall, the great doors swinging closed behind them on a gust of perfume and exotic fruits with just a faint and unfortunate hint of fish. 'Watching Custer is like monitoring the intellectual development of a boll weevil.'

Batchelor had no idea what that was. But Grand was probably right.

The sun was setting over the Washington Memorial the next day and Custer had business at the War Department. His case against William Belknap and Orvil Grant was lodged in some bureaucratic limbo between the White House and the Capitol and he had more unfinished business in the Black Hills. This time, Libbie Custer stayed at the Baltimore, trying fruitlessly to fit her new purchases into the trunks she had arrived with; in the end, she knew, she would have to buy just one more trunk. Privately, the hotel maid helping her thought it would need to be two, but who was she to judge?

Grand and Batchelor walked with the General; it was Sergeant Reilly's turn to be a few paces behind. Pennsylvania Avenue was never quiet and, even as the gas lamps flickered into life, gigs and wagons rattled along, picking their way between the silver lines of the streetcars.

Everybody there had slightly different memories, later, of what happened next. Grand heard a scream, a woman panicking somewhere behind him. Batchelor heard that too, but he also heard the whinny of a horse and the rattle of a trap. Custer heard a whip, struck like thunder and echoing around the high, sunset-pink buildings. Reilly didn't hear anything at all before he was hit by the flying hoofs of a cab horse and he was thrown against a wall, the breath knocked out of him.

Grand and Batchelor were both turning when Batchelor realized that Custer was still in the path of the galloping animal. He launched himself, he who had never played rugby in his life, and drove his shoulder into Custer's chest, forcing him back on to the sidewalk to bounce off the Treasury Building wall. The next man in the gig's path wasn't so lucky. Grand barely had time to call out when the horse's shoulder hit a bystander in the small of the back, smashing the man's head against the brickwork so that blood and brains flew out in a grisly fountain. The right-hand wheel of the gig rolled over the dying man's legs, making him buck as though leaping back to his feet, though he would never move by his own volition again, except to draw one final, shuddering breath.

The cabbie somehow held on, his feet braced against the heel-board, his fist tight on the reins. Grand leapt upwards, trying to catch the door handle, but the cabbie lashed him with his whip and Grand fell back, his face bloody from a cut across his ear. The horse, maddened with fear and pain, losing its footing on the blood-slick cobbles, recovered by some miracle and kept going. Pedestrians, wise to it now, were jumping out of the way into doorways and alley mouths. In a clash of iron-shod wheels and the crack of the whip, the cab rocked from side to side, took a murderously tight right turn down Alexander Hamilton Place and was gone.

'I'm all right, James,' Grand said, as Batchelor reached him through the confusion. 'Custer?'

'Right as rain, Captain,' the General said, helping him up. 'Reilly?'

The sergeant limped over to them, his cap gone, his cheek

gouged by the brickwork. 'There's some pretty careless bastards driving cabs in this town,' he growled, pressing a handkerchief to his face.

'Careless be buggered,' Grand snarled, trying to staunch the blood running from his slashed earlobe. 'That was deliberate. Who's that?'

A knot of ghouls had collected around the body on the sidewalk and Grand and Batchelor parted them. Grand crouched down by the man's ruined head and felt for a pulse but it was a faint hope; the man was clearly dead.

'Dead as a nit,' a voice said callously from above. Grand didn't honour it with a reply but left it to the crowd.

'That's disgraceful!' a shrill female voice added her fifty cents. There was the sound of a furled parasol fetching someone a nasty one upside the head. 'That poor man . . . I saw it all. That cabbie drove straight at him.'

A Scottish burr droned into the conversation. 'No, ye're wrong, lady. It was nothing but an accident. The cabbie had lost control, that much was clear.'

Again there was the sound of a parasol meeting cranium and the woman returned to the fray. 'It was nothing of the kind,' she shrieked. 'I will never forget it, never. He had mad, crazed eyes. White they were, white, white I tell you!'

This time the sound was of Batchelor's palm striking maidenly cheek. 'Move along, ladies and gentlemen,' he said, as authoritatively as he could. There was something in his accent which unaccountably brought the crowd to order and soon nothing was to be heard except occasional shrieks of 'Never!' as the lady with the bent parasol was led away to a quiet place for a while and only the very firmest disaster-watchers remained, silently waiting for life to be finally pronounced extinct.

'No sign of Washington's finest,' Batchelor noted as he looked up and down the street.

'Did anyone get that cab's number?' Grand asked the residual ghouls. He might as well have been speaking in Lakota.

'These accidents happen all the time,' one said. 'What can you do about a spooked horse?'

Custer was the last of them to get up from viewing the dead man. 'You can make sure,' he said, slowly, 'that it doesn't run into the senator from Milwaukee.'

The senator from Milwaukee was lying in the front parlour of Hector Fonde, foreign bookseller, at his home along Boundary Street. There was a tradition of taking dead politicians to bizarre places in this city. The last one had been the President himself, Abraham Lincoln, who had been carried from Ford's Theatre, still alive, across the mud of Tenth Street to Petersen's boarding house.

News of the President's assassination had spread like wild-fire back in the day. That was because of who Lincoln was and what he stood for. Nobody felt that way about Hal Maitland, least of all the good voters of Milwaukee, who had begun to regret their actions as soon as the count was announced. Custer knew him by sight and vague reputation, but it took an old Washingtonian like Andrew Grand to cross the i's and dot the t's. He stood alongside his son in the candlelit room that had become a funeral parlour, gazing down at the corpulent figure on the undertaker's board.

Andrew Grand still didn't fully appreciate what his son did for a living, but it was slowly dawning on him, in those small hours before another dawn crept over the city – a dawn that Maitland would not see – that all this was in a day's work. A doctor had patched up Sergeant Reilly and put a makeshift dressing on Grand's ear, which was already coming loose and driving him mad with itching; it would be in the trash by morning, but it was a kindly thought. Grand was simply grateful that the whip had missed his eye and that he still had all his teeth. The undertakers had done a partial job on Maitland; embalming would come later. An urgent telegram had been sent from the government offices to Milwaukee, informing the electorate and the senator's family and friends of the dreadful accident that had befallen their man.

'Accident be damned.' Andrew Grand sounded so very like his son at times like these. 'The list of men who wanted Maitland dead would stretch to Arlington. You were there, Matthew; what do you think?'

Grand looked at the dead man. The dried blood had been wiped from his face, but it still clotted on the pillow and the blanket under his head. His own clothes were ripped and bloody, so the undertaker had dressed him in a sombre black suit two sizes too small. His greasy-looking stomach jutted out through the over-tight starched shirt. 'I think you're right, Pa,' he said. 'You wouldn't care to shorten that list to Arlington, would you? Suggest, for instance, who'd be at the top?'

Superintendent Alexander McGregor didn't like private detectives. Rumour was he had once run a Pinkerton man out of town with his pants around his ankles, but, to be fair, since said Pinkerton man was visiting a lady of the night in the Division at the time, they were probably already down in the first place.

Superintendent Alexander McGregor didn't like Englishmen either, being, as he was, of the Scottish persuasion. So, at one stroke, he loathed the very existence of the two men sitting in front of him in his offices at the headquarters of the Metropolitan Police. McGregor was a bear of a man, with a grizzly's beard and beady eyes and, like his animal counterpart in the wilds of the northwest and northeast, he didn't suffer fools at all.

'Aye,' he grated, 'I heard all about it. My boys were on the scene within three minutes.'

Batchelor looked at Grand. Despite the demise of the senator from Milwaukee in broad, if fading, daylight, outside the offices of several government departments in America's capital city, they had stayed there, supervising events, for half an hour, and within that time, not a single police officer had turned up.

'I have their reports here,' McGregor went on, although he appeared to be pointing to an ashtray. 'An accident. Clear as day.'

'An accident?' Batchelor repeated. 'So, what's being done about it? And have you questioned any of the bystanders? There was a woman with a parasol who saw everything.'

McGregor narrowed his eyes. 'Mr . . . er . . . Batchelor, is it?'

Batchelor nodded.

'I don't know how the police operate where you come from, laddie, but here, I can assure you, we leave no stone unturned. But finding a specific lady with a parasol in Washington in this weather would take rather more time than we have at our disposal.' The final word was thick with spit and sounded like the crack of a pistol.

Batchelor smiled. 'Reassuring, indeed,' he said. 'Where I come from, Superintendent – that's London, England, by the way – our police operate very like you. More so, in fact, because you pinched your entire organization, even the rank of superintendent, from us. If a cabbie had run down and killed, say, a member of the British Parliament, that man would, by now, be in custody facing charges of manslaughter at best; quite possibly murder.'

'We don't hang cusses for failing to control a horse, mister,' McGregor snapped back.

'Oh, I thought our man controlled his horse pretty well,' Grand chimed in, 'to the extent that he bowled over a sergeant of cavalry, caught me a nasty one with his whip and narrowly missed a brevet major general, *before* he got to Hal Maitland.'

McGregor sighed and lolled back in his chair. 'Like I said,' he murmured, 'no stone has been unturned.'

'Has been?' the journalist in James Batchelor caught the past tense at once. 'Do I gather, Superintendent, that your enquiries are at an end?'

'Afraid so,' McGregor shrugged. 'I have personally interviewed all the relevant witnesses to the aforesaid incident. I'm satisfied with their statements. Oh, we'll keep an eye out for likely cabbies, of course.'

Neither Grand nor Batchelor knew quite where to start. 'I have reason to believe,' it was Grand who broke the silence first; after all, it was his father who had provided the information, 'that the late Hal Maitland was under investigation by at least three government departments. There are also rumours about unhealthy activities with a child . . .'

McGregor slammed his fist down on his desk. 'I'm not here to indulge in fiddle-faddle about rumours and innuendo. Neither, as a good Presbyterian, will I continue speaking ill of the dead.' He looked defiantly at the two in front of him, his eyes wide and just a little spit gathered as foam at the corners of his mouth. He appeared to be holding his breath, rather like a thwarted toddler who had run out of options but still was determined to get his own way. Both Grand and Batchelor realized at once – and simultaneously – that perhaps Alexander McGregor was in the wrong job.

The superintendent finally took a deep breath and smoothed back his hair. 'I thank you for your time, gentlemen,' he said, on another inhalation, calmer now, his colour returning to somewhere approximating to normal. 'I'm sure you can see yourselves out.'

'So, that's it, then.' Batchelor shrugged over his steak at the Baltimore that night. 'End of the road, Maitland-wise.'

Grand nodded. 'As you hinted to the good superintendent,' he said, 'if this was London, it would all be different. And if it wasn't, you and I would get involved. As it is . . .'

'I know,' Batchelor sighed. 'Your family has social standing in this town and I'm a foreigner. So, I suppose . . .'

There was a frantic knocking at the door. Batchelor was up first, untucking the napkin from his collar and crossing the room, Grand-style, in three strides. A distraught-looking Libbie Custer stood there, a handkerchief in her hand and a worried look on her face. The enquiry agents had been here before.

'James,' she blurted out. 'Captain Grand. It's Georgie.'

'Where's he gone this time?' Grand asked. 'Not to the War Office again?'

'No, no,' the General's lady said, blowing her nose on her handkerchief in a way which owed more to Fort Abraham Lincoln than Washington society. 'Somewhere far worse. He's gone to Hooker's Division.'

'Fighting Joe' Hooker, the Civil War general, hadn't set up a ghetto for prostitution and every other type of vice; he just let his soldiers loose in the area to let off a little steam. Back in the day, Matthew Grand had once done just what Custer was doing now; getting his boys out of trouble. The nice church-goers of the Division complained long and loud to anybody who would listen – and to Superintendent McGregor, who wouldn't – but the ending of the war made little difference to the principal occupation of the area.

Grand and Batchelor were by no means the only well-dressed gentlemen strolling the litter-filled alleyways that night. Trees grew in Brooklyn; they grew here too and most of them had a flashily dressed girl flaunting her wares under the branches, advertising the more refined interiors of the Blue Oven, the Wolf's Den and the Devil's Own. Andrew Grand would have been appalled but his son felt quite at home here. James Batchelor had visited, too, some years before, and anyway, the gay ladies looked not unlike the promenaders along the Haymarket back home; he had seen it all – or at least, most of it – before.

'Black ass, sugar?' a beautiful coloured girl flashed an ankle at him.

'Thank you, no,' Batchelor smiled politely. 'I'm looking for a soldier.'

'Ain't we all, honey?' another tall, deep-voiced girl said from under the boughs of a neighbouring tree.

'I can kinda help you there.' A check-suited pimp was suddenly at Batchelor's elbow, his teeth flashing in the darkness, the smell of pomade enough to etch glass. He handed Batchelor a card. 'Brother Sebastian's,' he said, 'third on the left past Lafayette Square. Can't miss it.'

Despite Grand's attempts to drag Batchelor away, the Englishman persisted. 'A very specific soldier,' he said. 'Auburn ringlets.'

'Huh-huh,' the pimp nodded, pleased to be able to help. 'Brother Seb's got three or four of those.'

'No, no . . .' but Batchelor couldn't get any further before Grand dragged him away.

'What's Custer doing here, anyway?' Batchelor asked him. 'Surely, he's not . . . umm . . . well, with Libbie waiting in their room and everything . . .'

Grand raised an eyebrow. Batchelor hadn't spent much time with soldiers, that much was clear. However, he gave him a sensible reply. 'He's trying to keep his regiment out of yet more shit,' Grand explained. 'Sergeant Reilly is old enough and ugly enough to handle himself, but Custer's a marked man now. If he so much as sneezes in public, the Washington papers'll have a field day.'

'But how . . .?'

'There is a God,' Grand said, pointing to two men walking towards them, the one in blue staggering a little. The enquiry agents breathed a collective sigh of relief. Neither of them had much of a clue as to how to find Custer in this rabbit warren of iniquity, still less the relatively anonymous Reilly.

'What brings you gentlemen here,' Custer asked, adjusting Reilly's weight so he stood upright by himself, 'if that isn't a foolish question?'

'Mrs Custer was concerned about you, General,' Grand said.

'Mrs Custer's always concerned about me,' the General smiled. 'And I am grateful for your concern, also. But tomorrow I'm catching a train. And Sergeant Reilly here is coming with me, aren't you, Sergeant? Assuming you still have any stripes on your arm by then.'

'Wouldn't miss it for the world, General.' Reilly could salute for America whether he was three sheets in the wind or not. He did it now.

'Best get you back to the Baltimore,' Grand suggested, and the four of them marched on.

They had gone deeper into the Division than they had realized. To while away the time, Batchelor asked Reilly precisely where he'd been. Reilly didn't know the Division. He didn't know Washington, but the unerring nose of an old soldier had taken him with astonishing precision to the Haystack, the Ironclad and the Blue Grouse, entertainment establishments all. He had tried his luck at Madame Wilton's Private Residence for Ladies, but a *very* large man at the door had told him that only soldiers with bars on their shoulders were allowed in. When Reilly had asked if there was a back passage he got some very funny looks and a boot up his backside. Naturally, such reconnoitring in strange streets was thirsty work and Reilly had blown much of his striker's allowance at a whole variety of watering holes, nearly all of which had a barman called Sam.

'Eleven o'clock,' Batchelor muttered to Grand at the sight

of three men lounging on some steps ahead of them and to their left.

'Huh-huh,' Grand nodded. 'They'll be with the three behind, six o'clock.'

Batchelor ventured a half-turn. He could only see silhouettes because gas lamps were a rarity in the Division, but he knew the outline of a shillelagh when he saw one.

'Irish,' he murmured to Grand.

'So keep your mouth shut,' Grand advised. 'These cusses aren't particularly fond of Americans, but you guys . . . well, I don't have to paint you a Fenian picture.'

'No,' Batchelor said, 'you don't.'

'Top of the night to yer.' The three men on the step had stood up now and fanned out, blocking the sidewalk.

'Gentlemen,' Custer nodded, suddenly feeling quite naked without his brace of Webley Bulldogs.

'That's a nice shirt,' a second man said, looking the General up and down.

'Is that a bulging wallet in your inside pocket?' the third asked, 'or are you just pleased to see me?'

James Batchelor couldn't resist a comeback, ignoring Grand's very wise advice. 'Three clichés in as many minutes,' he said. 'You've outdone yourselves, boyos.'

Until now, there had been no sign of weapons ahead, but suddenly, two shillelaghs and a long-bladed knife filled the sidewalk. Grand sighed. He *had* warned Batchelor, but it was too late now.

'What are you Killarney bastards doing here?' Reilly wanted to know. 'On the run from the police for sheep-shagging, are yer?'

Marvellous, thought Grand; it just gets worse.

'Well, well,' the first man said. 'Paddy,' he was talking to one of the three behind Custer who were blocking any avenue of retreat, 'was that a County Tyrone accent I just heard? Or do I have shit in my ears?'

If Sergeant Reilly had been sober, he might not have done what he did. On the other hand, had he been sober, he might have done it better. He launched himself at the first thug, missed him completely and landed heavily on the sidewalk.

Paddy swung his club at Grand, but the American was faster, dodging aside and smashing the man's face with the butt of his pocket pistol.

Custer put up his fists in the manner of West Point but only succeeded in having his knuckles rapped by a heavy blow from a shillelagh. Cursing under his breath, despite his promises to Libbie, he lashed out with his right boot and caught one of the assailants a nasty one between the legs.

'Nice one, sor!' Reilly was on his feet again. 'The General's wallet yer after is it, Paddy me boy?' he growled. 'Take mine instead!' In an instant his belt was off and he was ramming the buckle into Paddy's eye, the civilian Irishman screaming as the blood began to run.

'You English bastard!' another thug yelled, crashing his club down on Batchelor's shoulder with a wild two-handed swing. The English bastard dropped to one knee, then drove his head into his attacker's groin and the two of them rolled in the mud.

In the Haymarket, whatever the altercation, it would not be long before a whistle would shatter the night air and the giant boots of C Division would come running. Everybody knew perfectly well that that wasn't going to happen here, so Grand decided to shorten the odds. Whirling his Colt in his hand, he cocked it and blew a hole in his attacker's shoulder. The man cursed and fell backwards. A second thug came into the fray, as tall as Grand but wider, and Grand levelled the gun again, cocking it and holding the muzzle against his forehead. 'I don't suppose you'll miss this lion of Celtic intellectualism,' he called to the others, 'but I'm going to kill him anyway.'

One by one, the attackers backed off, one nursing his shattered shoulder, another trying to see through the tears caused by Custer's kick to his unmentionables. The man with Grand's gun to his head didn't move at all, just in case his opponent's trigger finger had a nervous tic.

From somewhere, Reilly had got hold of a shillelagh and he swung it levelly now, crunching it into the man's head with a sickening thud. The man's eyes crossed and he went down with a groan.

'Sheep-shagger!' Reilly cursed and spat at the fallen body.

Grand looked around. The threat, four and a half men where once there were six, were running down the street for all they were worth. As for his own side, they seemed to be all right. Reilly was swaying a little, but he had been before it all started. Custer looked ready to go a few more rounds, were it not for his bruised knuckles.

Reilly looked from one to the other of the men beside him, closing one eye from time to time to do an accurate count. Then he smiled his long, slow, Irish smile. 'Are we going on somewhere?' he asked.

In the soft light of their rooms at the Baltimore, it was obvious that the evening's encounter had left more of a mark than either Grand or Batchelor realized. Custer was presumably wrapped in the relieved and loving arms of Libbie. Reilly was sleeping it off in his narrow little bed beyond the back yard. As for James Batchelor, he was looking into the mirror by the flickering lamplight, dabbing at the purple patch on his shoulder and hissing with pain every time he moved his arm. Alone of them all, Matthew Grand sat propped on his bed, watching the rings of his cigar smoke disappear into the wooden panels of the ceiling. The man was untouchable.

'You know what's occurred to me, James?' he asked.

'That you lead some kind of charmed life?' Batchelor said, reaching with difficulty for his nightshirt. 'Yes, I had noticed.'

'What have Grand and Batchelor, Enquiry Agents of the Strand, London, Sergeant Reilly of the Seventh Cavalry and Hal Maitland, Senator for Milwaukee, got in common?'

'Er . . .' It had been a while since Batchelor had been called upon for any actual sleuthing. He was rusting up.

'Precisely,' Grand nodded. 'Nothing. The common denominator is Brevet Major General George Armstrong Custer.'

'What?' Batchelor winced as he hauled the nightshirt over his head.

'Think about it.' Grand sat upright, flicking his ash into the nightstand. 'The senator for Milwaukee may have been a bent son of a bitch and had more enemies than the average street dog has fleas, but nobody's tried to kill him, or even punch him on the nose, before now.'

'Assuming the whole cab thing wasn't an accident.' Batchelor felt he still had to play McGregor's advocate.

'Yes, we've already assumed that, James,' Grand said. 'Do try and keep up.'

'Say on.' Batchelor was fighting to keep down a scream as he bent to remove his boots, so he didn't say much.

'We've both been to the Division before and seen our share of scraps – here and back in the Old Country . . .'

Batchelor hated it when Grand called his home that but said nothing.

'Yet six toughs from the bogs decided to have a go at us tonight.'

'Just after our money,' Batchelor shrugged. 'It's common enough.'

'I'll lay you odds it wouldn't have happened without Custer.'

'So,' Batchelor eased himself down on to his bed. 'Whoever drove that gig was out to get the General.'

Grand nodded. 'An unmarked vehicle,' he said. 'Van Niekerk, Austen, the Central – all those companies have their names painted on the side.'

'Private hire?' Batchelor offered the logical alternative explanation.

'Precisely again,' Grand said. 'Somebody was hired to kill Custer. Only, it backfired. Tricky weapon, a one-horse gig. Imprecise.'

'And the toughs?'

'A cover. They were hired to take out Custer. The rest of us were just unfortunate side effects of that; they would have killed us, yes, but there was no malice in it. Did you notice, at one point he had two of them on to him?'

''Fraid I was too busy staying alive,' Batchelor groaned, his shoulder reminding him how true that was.

'Take my word for it, then.'

Batchelor ruminated for a while. 'If you're right . . .' he said.

'. . . which I am.' Grand was sure.

'Who's your money on? Sheridan? Grant? You've already accused the man of being involved in the plot on Lincoln. Killing Custer wouldn't cost him much sleep.'

'Grant had no more to do with killing Lincoln than you did,' Grand said. 'And you were three thousand miles away at the time. No, Grant rolled over as quickly as he did over something else, and maybe we'll never find out what. I just got lucky.'

'We'd better move the Custers, then,' Batchelor said. 'Different hotel. Word'll have got around that he's staying here.'

'Ordinarily, I'd agree with you,' Grand nodded, 'but he's on the train tomorrow. We'll shadow him over breakfast, kiss him goodbye at the railroad station and then, he's somebody else's problem.'

'And then we go home?'

Grand didn't like unfinished business; neither did Batchelor. So Grand really spoke for neither of them when he said, 'Hell, yes.'

'Well, George,' Matthew Grand had momentarily lost James Batchelor but the man was a leech – he'd be around somewhere. 'I guess this is the parting of the ways.' His hand was already extended for the farewell.

'Not necessarily . . .' Custer murmured but before he could finish the sentence, Libbie turned up, three porters in her wake struggling with trunks and cases, and Batchelor on her arm.

'I've just persuaded James to come back to the Plains with us,' she trilled. 'He's delighted to accept. Aren't you, James?'

'Yes, ma'am.' Batchelor's attempt at North Carolingian needed work.

'You see,' Libbie was always generous, 'he even sounds like a cavalryman.'

Neither Custer nor Grand had caught that, but Mrs Iron Butt was not to be denied.

'So, it's settled, then.' She smiled at them all. 'James was telling me how he'd love to see the West, Indian Territory and all.'

'It's not the safest place in the world.' Grand was just getting started on his list of reasons why the mere suggestion was preposterous.

'It will be,' Custer said. 'Trust me.'

Grand was still not sure he could do that.

'I've had Reilly get your trunks from the hotel,' Libbie said, and they all looked at the scowling Irishman, as buried in luggage as the porters were.

'James . . .' Grand began.

'Now, Captain Grand.' Libbie was faster, with the old pioneer woman's skill at heading people off at the pass. 'None of your negativity. George and I are living with History at the moment. The Plains are changing, believe me. Oh, Washington is one thing. It'll never change. It'll always be dog-eat-dog here, everybody stabbing everybody else in the back. I predict that in a hundred years' time, there'll be more horses on the road, is all. Land, you won't be able to move for the droppings. But the West is vanishing. A whole way of life is disappearing. It's all rather sad, but you'll want to see it. And besides,' she linked arms with Batchelor again, 'it'll give you English some tips as to what to do about *your* buffalo problem!'

There was really no answer to that. Grand sighed and shrugged. He had never been west of Kentucky himself and the Great Plains and the Black Hills *did* have a romantic allure of their own, even if he wasn't especially enchanted by the notion of a little house on the prairie. 'Well, I guess . . .'

'Excellent!' Libbie reached up and kissed his cheek. Custer rolled his eyes. He never tired of indulging Libbie Bacon Custer. Hell, he'd been court-martialled for going absent without leave to visit her before now. Just as long as these greenhorns didn't get under his feet.

'General Custer!' There was a shout along the platform as the locomotive snorted and steamed.

'Mr . . . er . . . Kellogg, isn't it?' Custer shook the man's hand.

'I hope I haven't held you up,' Kellogg said, lugging his portmanteau. 'I thought for a minute there you might go without me.'

'Oh.' Custer's smile was icy. 'Fat chance of that,' he said.

SIX

They took on water at Indianapolis – or at least, that was the only place they took on water that Batchelor had ever heard of before. After Des Moines, the number of passengers dwindled considerably. The Custers were reading; this journey was old hat to them and they had no need to look out at the speeding countryside. The General had his nose in a book about Napoleon; Libbie was, rather belatedly perhaps, absorbing the etiquette advice of Mrs Bisbee Duffy on exactly what to do when and with whom when in Washington. She could try it out in the fort; she bit her lip as she tried to work out how to adapt the rather strict rules of Mrs D., but Libbie Custer was nothing if not adaptable. Sergeant Reilly, as ever, was relegated to the guard's van and Grand was asleep. That left Batchelor and Kellogg.

'So, Mr Kellogg; a newspaperman, eh?'

'Mark, please.'

'James.' The men shook hands anew. 'That used to be my calling before I saw the light.'

'Really? Who were you with?'

'The *Telegraph*, back in London. Tell me, did you ever come across George Sala? He covered your Civil War, back in the day.'

'Indeed he did.' Kellogg handed Batchelor a cigar. 'But I never had the pleasure, I'm afraid. He was legendary, of course.'

'It seems our lot in life to be associated with legends.' Batchelor nodded to the General, sitting several seats away.

'Yes, indeed. What exactly do you do now, James? Not still in the hack trade?'

Batchelor hid a minor bridle. Hack, indeed! 'No, Grand and I are writers. We were doing some research for a book, but we're done with that, now.'

'Really?' Kellogg paused in mid-puff. 'And what were you researching into?'

'Oh, nothing important,' Batchelor smiled. 'Grand has family in Washington and knew the General at West Point – and beyond. This is a sort of holiday . . . er . . . vacation, I suppose.'

'Do you know the Plains?'

'No. That's one reason I was delighted to accept Mrs Custer's invitation to come West.'

Kellogg smiled. 'She's a pistol, that woman, isn't she?'

It was not a metaphor that Batchelor would have used, but he found himself nodding. 'How long have you been with the . . . *Tribune*, is it?'

'The Bismarck *Tribune*, yes, sir,' Kellogg said. 'Ooh, it must be five years now. As soon as Clem Lounsbury – that's my editor – got wind of the General coming to DC, he said, "Kellogg, get your ass on a train east. This is a story the *Trib* just has to have."'

Batchelor felt sorry for the man. If Kellogg's impression was even close to reality, Clem Lounsbury had to have the worst-fitting dentures in the Black Hills.

'Actually, Clem wanted to cover the story himself, but his wife got sick, so here I am. You were with Custer, weren't you, in the Committee Room? Hiester Clymer?'

'Technically, I was with *Mrs* Custer. Grand was with the General.'

'I couldn't see a damned thing from the back. I'd give my eye teeth to see what Custer had in those files he handed in.'

'Ah,' Batchelor nodded. 'Wouldn't we all?'

'Look, James.' Kellogg became confidential. 'Can I be straight with you, newspaperman to newspaperman, so to speak?'

'Of course,' Batchelor said.

'You're going to hear some pretty strange rumours regarding the General over the coming weeks, depending on how long you stay.'

'I am?'

'Stories about a black cook,' Kellogg's voice had dropped to a whisper, so that, what with the racket of the Baldwin loco eating up the miles, Batchelor could barely make out what he was saying. 'Even about an Indian squaw.'

'Really?'

'Don't you believe a word of it,' Kellogg said, sitting up straight again and looking out of the window. 'There's something about a cavalry fort and Abraham Lincoln is no exception. Things fester, glances can be misinterpreted, tensions build. In particular,' he went on, 'don't pay any attention to anything said to you by Marcus Reno or Fred Benteen. Catch my drift?'

'Er . . . yes.' Batchelor had never heard those names before, but he played along anyway.

'By the way, do you have a family, James?' Batchelor knew the abrupt changing of a subject when he heard one. 'Wife? Kids?'

'Neither,' Batchelor said.

'That's a pity.' Kellogg hauled out his wallet and put on his glasses. 'My Martha went of the cholera a few years back, but here are my daughters. They're at college in Northfield, Minnesota.'

Batchelor looked at the pair in the photograph, pretty girls with bows in their hair. He glanced at Kellogg. 'Must look like their mother,' he said.

'I guess,' was Kellogg's only comment.

The end of the line was an inconspicuous hole called Billings. While Custer waxed lyrical about how one day there would be a railroad station here and billboards and the West would become civilized, James Batchelor looked with horror at the contraption which would take them on the final leg of their journey to the fort. It was an open-sided carriage with four wheels and it was harnessed to four of the smelliest mules Batchelor had ever encountered. The animals stamped in the Dakota sun, twitching their outsized ears and flicking at the flies with their tails. Their coats were thick, dull and dusty; Batchelor had seen some sights at London cab ranks, of poor spavined horses keeping upright by the willpower of the cabbie alone, but they looked like prime horseflesh compared with these beasts. That said, they rolled their eyes and lifted their lips in a sneer that said they had seen better than Batchelor, should anyone be asking. It was difficult to tell which sight alarmed them more – the hissing, snorting Baldwin, straining to be on its way, or a fully fledged Limey greenhorn out West and way out of his depth.

After several false starts, mainly due to Libbie Custer's luggage, which had seemed to grow in extent even since they had got on the train in Washington, they all managed to clamber on to the buckboard and the whip cracked away and they were off. This was the Deadwood coach that linked the lawless mining town with all points in Indian Territory. No one had told Batchelor about conveyances like this. An avid reader of the Wild West tales of Ned Buntline, he expected the stage to perhaps be a little rough and ready, no extra cushion for the back, for instance, or possibly fewer windows than he was used to at home. Both of these expectations the coach met with ease, but what Batchelor was not ready for was the nauseating motion. There was nothing resembling a road over the Great Plains, just tracks of flattened grass, and if Batchelor found Atlantic crossings bad – and he did – they had nothing on the roll of the Black Hills. To take his mind off things, he glanced back to where Sergeant Reilly rode his troop horse in the stage's dust, his yellow scarf across his face and his campaign hat pulled down. Not even Libbie Custer's incessant babble about the beauty of the prairie could take his mind off his stomach and the bob of Reilly's hat through the dust cloud helped not a jot. He groaned. He hoped it was silently but didn't really care a hoot if it wasn't.

'Ride up top, James,' Grand advised. So, the groan had been out loud, then. 'More air up there.'

When the mules halted for a rest and water and everybody stretched their legs, Batchelor took the advice, but he wasn't sure he was much better off. The smell on the roof where the lashed-down luggage rattled was worse than inside. At first, Batchelor silently blamed the mules, then he realized that his fellow passengers were to blame.

'Bill McCune.' The driver thrust out a gloved hand. He appeared to be a hundred years old but Batchelor reasoned that the weather on the Plains would do that to a man who spent most of his time perched on top of a stagecoach. 'This here's Calam,' he nodded his head to a second figure who had just jumped up alongside Batchelor, squeezing in between the men, bringing yet another fragrance to the heady mix already wrinkling the Englishman's nostrils. 'Calamity Jane Cannary.'

Batchelor felt so ill that his usual suavity and gentlemanly demeanour deserted him and he found himself staring at whatever it was sitting beside him. Jane, surely, was a woman's name, but McCune's shotgun today could easily have passed for a man. She had cold blue eyes in a hard, square face, her dark hair strained back under a shapeless hat. She wore greasy buckskins, fringed, Indian-style, at the shoulders and cuffs, and wore a pistol at her hip. A Sharps rifle lay cradled in her lap.

'Ain't ya seen an Injun scout before?' she growled, with a voice deeper than Batchelor's.

'Er . . . no,' he said. It was no more than the truth.

'You still ain't, mister.' McCune spat out his wad of tobacco. 'Jane here signed on all right, with General Crook, no less. But she made the mistake of going swimmin' with the fellers. Now, the army, it don't go swimmin' with wimmin, so old Crook, he ups and fires her right there, on the spot.'

'Man's an asshole.' Jane was chewing tobacco too, slurping it across from cheek to cheek. 'All right, so maybe I'm not a scout. But I'm a mule skinner and that's the next best thing.'

Bill McCune narrowed his eyes. He knew Jane Cannary of old – most men in the Dakota Territory did. She didn't just dress, swear and drink like a man, she fought like one, too. With Jane, you had to know when to give a little. 'There's no denying that,' he growled and whipped the mules into action.

'You stayin' at the fort, Mister?' she asked Batchelor.

'Yes.' He tried to smile, but with his eyes shut and his teeth clenched it was a poor effort. 'Yes, I am.'

'You'll be needing some laundry done. I'm neat with starch and don't cost the earth. Come see me in the Dew Drop.'

'Um . . . thank you,' Batchelor said, 'it'll be my pleasure.'

James Batchelor had no idea what to expect of Fort Abraham Lincoln, but when he saw it, it reminded him of photographs he had seen of the hill stations in India, where officers of the Raj cooled down after months of sweating it out in the hot season. Officers' Row in particular was a series of new villas, with dormer windows in the roofs and tall chimneys. Each house had a neat garden, bright with late spring flowers and a low, white-painted fence around it. Apart from the choice of flowers and the colours of the curtains swagged at the windows, each was identical with its neighbour. Batchelor almost expected every door to spring simultaneously open and women dressed in pastel shades and carrying matching parasols to sweep out of them. But the doors remained resolutely closed, the windows blank; not so much as a curtain twitched as they sped by.

The Deadwood stage rattled past a shantytown on the fort's outskirts and Calamity Jane got off, throwing her rifle to McCune and slapping Batchelor on the back.

'Listen to that, Libbie!' Custer's head popped out of the open window. 'It's good to be back.'

The music got louder as the stage clattered over the planking between the open gates. Flags flew everywhere and there was a brass band mounted on grey horses, the sunlight dazzling off trumpets and tubas, the plumes of the musicians' helmets swaying in the breeze.

'All the tunes of glory,' Kellogg muttered to Grand as they alighted. 'The Garryowen' was in full swing.

As Custer and his lady reached the ground, a voice roared over the parade ground, 'Draw . . . swords!' and there was a rush of steel as the blades flew clear. It had been a long time since Matthew Grand had seen a cavalry regiment drawn up in revue order and it gladdened his heart. He didn't miss the shattered soldier boys crying for their mothers in the carnage of Shiloh and Gettysburg. But somewhere deep within him, he missed the flutter of the guidons, the jingle of bits and the thunder of hoofs.

Batchelor stood there open-mouthed. The sickening roll of the coach and the smell of his travelling companions had gone as he looked at the lines of blue coats, their campaign hats white in the sun, their sabre blades at the slope on their shoulders. He half-expected Kellogg to be scribbling away in his notebook, but he was just watching Custer; no doubt he had seen it all before.

An officer with a buckskin jacket and huge flowing dundrearies walked his horse out of the line as an orderly brought up Custer's horse, the General's full dress shabraque over the saddle.

'Thank you, John.' Custer smiled at the striker who held the animal's bridle. 'I hope Vic's been behaving himself.'

'He has, General,' the man beamed.

Custer kissed the horse's nose with its white blaze and swung into the saddle. The officer with the dundrearies saluted him with his sword.

'Welcome back, General,' he said.

'Lieutenant Cooke,' Custer returned the formal greeting. 'It's good to be back.' He urged Vic forward so that the men were sitting almost side by side. Neither Grand nor Batchelor could hear what they were saying. Libbie Custer was surrounded by a bevy of ladies, fans fluttering like chickens in a henhouse, all of them desperate to hear tales of the capital. Batchelor nodded to himself, glad to note that he could do that now without wanting to vomit. So *that* was why no one had come out of the houses; they were already here.

'Anything untoward,' Custer asked his adjutant, 'while I've been gone?'

'Nothing in particular, sir,' Cooke said.

'Hostiles?'

'Gall came back a few times after you'd gone, but he caused no trouble. I can't say the same for Bloody Knife.'

Custer raised an eyebrow. 'Drinking again?'

'Had to drag him out of the Dew Drop. You know how he is.'

'I do,' Custer sighed. 'I'll have a word. He may be the best Indian scout west of the Missouri, but there are standards.' He scanned the lines of the Seventh, waiting patiently as they had been for over an hour. You *could* set your watch by the Deadwood stage, but if you did, you would rarely have the right time. He saw his officers – Tom, his brother; Autie Reed, his nephew; Myles Keogh at the head of I Company.

'No Major Reno today?' he asked. 'Captain Benteen?'

'Patrols, sir,' Cooke said. 'As soon as we got your telegram, they went out.'

'Well, well,' Custer murmured. 'There's a surprise. I've got a few guests with me, Dubya, as you see. One is an old comrade, Matthew Grand. Army of the Potomac. Tell him nothing. The other is a Limey, harmless but nosy. Ditto with him. The third is a newspaperman, Kellogg of the Bismarck *Tribune*. He is to know *absolutely* nothing. Understand?'

'Perfectly, sir,' Cooke nodded.

'Right, then.' Custer hauled back on Vic's reins. 'Let's see what you've done with my regiment.'

Libbie Custer had enjoyed her time in Washington – the shops, the crowds, the hotel with as much running hot water and maids as she could take – but she was glad to be home. Something in her liked being the Queen Bee and there was no way in which she could pretend to be that in Washington. Julia Grant may well be built like a wrestler and have eyes where one was looking at you, the other looking for you, but even so, she ruled the White House, the President and Washington – not necessarily in that order – with an iron fist. Just *how* iron, perhaps, alone of the people in Fort Abraham Lincoln, only James Batchelor really knew. So it was good to be home.

'Libbie,' Frabbie Benteen squeezed her arm gently, 'the ladies have got a little tea party planned for you. You were a bit late arriving . . .'

'Sorry about that,' Libbie smiled indulgently over to where Batchelor and Grand were watching the cavalry go through their paces. 'One of our guests was taken sick on the way. We had to keep stopping.'

Frabbie backed away a little. 'Sick? Nothing . . .'

Libbie tapped her with her fan. 'Nothing catching, Frabbie, of course not. Just a little motion-sickness.'

The woman was puzzled. 'On the Deadwood? Why?'

Libbie shrugged. 'I have no idea, Frabbie,' she said. 'It struck me as a very smooth ride but . . .' again the fond smile towards Batchelor's unheeding back '. . . he's English.' She mouthed the last word and all the women smiled understandingly. They had never actually met an Englishman before, but they had all heard stories.

Mary Reno stepped forward and took Libbie's other arm and the women, in an excited gaggle, led her off to her own house, where they had prepared the tea. The room looked lovely. Although nothing like even the most modest home in Washington, Libbie had made it nice with some touches that only a woman knows. Nosegays adorned the photograph of the General and potpourris hung from the moose horns over the fireplace. The ladies of the fort had made it even prettier with flowers from every garden and a 'Welcome Home' banner, made by the patchwork club who met every Thursday, come hell, high water or Indian attack.

Libbie clapped her hands when she saw her sitting room. 'Land!' she exclaimed. 'Girls, you have done me proud. Now, tell me everything that has been happening while I have been away.'

Myles Keogh was on the parade ground bright and early the next morning, the gold Medaglia given to him by the Pope flashing in the weak rays of the sun. Long before Grand or Batchelor were up, the captain was introducing the new recruits who had arrived the night before, after a nightmarish journey through the wasteland, to life in the Seventh US Cavalry.

They were drawn up in front of him now, twelve of them, the advance guard whom Reilly had enlisted in Washington. There was a reason they had been hurried West from the training depot at Jefferson Barracks and Keogh wanted to know what it was.

Sitting on his buckskin horse, he had one leg cocked nonchalantly across the pommel of his saddle and his nose buried in a book, the novel *Charles O'Malley, the Irish Dragoon*, which he dipped into most days. The men looked up at their new troop commander with a mixture of suspicion and disbelief. He was a ladies' man, that much was certain, with his neat goatee, dark eyes and dazzling smile. He was also the most casual officer any of them had ever seen, but they hadn't heard anything yet. He closed the book and popped it inside his bib-fronted blue shirt, easing the Medaglia aside, tilted the peaked forage cap at a jaunty angle and began to sing.

'Let Bacchus' sons be not dismayed
But join with me each jovial blade;
Come booze and sing and lend your aid
To help me with the chorus.'

The Irish lilt was taken up by someone in the ranks and Keogh stopped singing, letting the lone trooper go on alone.

'Instead of Spa we'll drink down ale,
And pay the reck'ning on the nail;
No man for debt shall go to jail
From Garry Owen in glory.'

Keogh laughed and clapped. 'I knew there'd have to be an Irishman among you,' he said, 'but there's more to it, I'll wager. What's your name, soldier?'

'O'Riordan, sir,' the man said, standing to attention. 'Late of Her Majesty's Iniskillen Dragoons.'

'Well, well,' Keogh's smile had faded. 'You're not serving the enemy now, O'Riordan, you're among friends. You won't have learned much at Jefferson in the few days you were there, so show me what you learned with the Iniskillens.'

He slid out of the saddle and handed his reins to the trooper. 'This is Comanche,' he said. 'See here,' he pointed to an old scar on the horse's shoulder, 'a Comanche bullet did that and I reckon an animal that could survive that could carry me all his life. He won't let you down.'

Keogh scanned the parade ground. 'Over there,' he said, pointing. 'There's a canteen hanging on the hitching rail. Get it at the gallop.' He flicked a silver-cased watch, a gift, had the men known it, from a *very* appreciative lady. 'I'm timing you.'

'Sir.' O'Riordan snatched the reins and swung into Keogh's saddle. The McClellan was not as comfortable as the leather of the Iniskillens and the stirrups were shorter in the American style, but they would do. He broke into a trot and then a canter as he rode in the opposite direction from the rail. Then he spun the animal around, a tighter turn than any of the recruits had seen before, and thundered across the parade ground, the dust flung up behind him like a devil. As they all watched, O'Riordan crouched in the saddle, then leaned far out over Comanche's neck and flicked the canteen into the air. The recruits cheered; Myles Keogh did too.

O'Riordan rode back to the lines.

'No, don't dismount.' Keogh stopped him. 'Do it again. This time, standing up.' He flicked his fingers and another recruit scurried across the ground, replacing the canteen on the rail.

'It'll be a little slower this time, sir,' O'Riordan said.

'As I would expect,' Keogh said, putting his watch away.

Again, the recruit trotted to the far end, but this time he turned slowly and eased himself upwards, balancing with arms outstretched. He was standing on the slippery leather and had let the reins dangle on the horse's neck. All he had to steady him now was sheer luck, or perhaps a belief in the God he prayed to.

He clicked his tongue twice and Comanche's ears pricked up. The animal broke into a trot, then a canter, while O'Riordan, his cap gone and rivulets of sweat running down his face, teetered on top of him. At the rail, the Irishman suddenly let his feet slide apart, hitting the saddle with a thud that made the other recruits' eyes water in sympathy. Then the canteen strap was in his hand again and there was an even louder roar of approval.

Keogh took Comanche's bridle and stroked his nose. 'Well done, soldier,' he said. 'I'll have a word with the General about some stripes for you. Welcome to the Wild I.'

'Thank you, sir.' O'Riordan saluted.

'Where are you from, by the way?' the captain asked.

'Offaly, sir.'

Keogh's face fell a little. 'Bad luck,' he said, 'but we can't all come from the blessed Limerick, can we? You, soldier,' he spun to face another recruit, 'where do you hail from?'

'Schwabmünchen, sir.' The soldier clicked his heels in the Prussian tradition.

'Mother of God defend us,' Keogh said. 'Well, here you go. Put that canteen back on the rail, as I am sure they taught you to do in the Kaiser's army.'

The German blinked at him.

'Well, look lively, man,' Keogh said. 'Corporal O'Riordan here's got some important sewing to do.'

Grand and Batchelor had been given adjoining rooms in the visitors' block near Officers' Row and they were not half bad. Kellogg, as a journalist and therefore slightly below mule skinner in the fort hierarchy, had a spare bunk in the non-commissioned officers' quarters. He didn't mind; he had had much, *much* worse. Batchelor was just beginning to feel better. Actually, he had to admit to himself, that wasn't absolutely true. He still felt worse than he had ever felt before in his life. Every now and then, the smell of Calamity Jane's ill-cured buckskins would rise up in his memory and envelop him in a nauseous cloud. That would remind him of the rocking and rolling of the stagecoach and then the whole sorry saga would replay before his eyes, in all its gory glory. His brain had wiped much of the detail for his own protection, but he got flashes of dust, rock, cacti and some animal that growled threateningly at him when he walked a little way from the coach in search of just a little privacy so he could die in peace. He lay on his bed and tried to make it stay still.

The door crashed back and he felt the end of the bed sag as Grand sat down at his feet.

'Are you feeling better, James?' It was a cliché, but it needed to be asked.

'Better than what?' Batchelor murmured. 'Better than something that has been dead for a week, yes, barely. Better than anything else you care to name, no, not really.'

'This motion sickness of yours is the devil,' Grand said, with only the barest trace of sympathy in his voice. 'I've brought you a pick-me-up from Cookie. He isn't in Mrs R's league, but the things he can do with buffalo balls can bring tears to your eyes.'

Batchelor looked at Grand from under his lashes and winced. 'Can you sprain your eyelids?' he asked, weakly.

'I guess you can,' Grand said, not listening. 'Here. Take it. It'll do you good.'

Batchelor closed his mouth as tight as his eyes and shook his head, but gently.

'James, you're being childish. Look. It's just a drink.'

Batchelor opened one eye and peered into the light. Yes, it did seem to be liquid. It was colourless and didn't look like too big a dose. But a lifetime of being sold stories of how medicine wasn't nasty left him suspicious. 'Warrisit?'

'Just some . . . natural medicine.'

'Natural?' Batchelor heaved himself up on one elbow. 'What does it taste of?'

Grand sniffed it. 'Seems bland enough to me, James. Try it. It can't do any harm, can it? Cookie makes it up for any of the men who are under the weather.'

'You try some.'

'I'm not feeling sick. Look, just try a little. Libbie had Cookie make it for you. She'll be so hurt if you don't . . .'

'Oh, all right!' Batchelor was carrying a bit of a torch for Libbie. 'Give it here.' He reached out, took it and downed it in one. The taste hit his tonsils just as the smell hit his nostrils. 'Holy Mother of God! What *is* it?'

Grand was uncertain how to proceed. 'You've heard of snake oil salesmen?'

'Yes.' Batchelor was dubious.

'Well, let's just say,' Grand took the glass from Batchelor's numb fingers, 'they're real.' And before Batchelor could respond, he was through the door and gone, with only his laughter echoing behind him.

Whatever had been in the cook's concoction, Batchelor really did feel a lot better the next day. The heat out in the parade ground was just as bad as he had remembered it, but he could bear it now. The smell of the dust was just as strong, but not enough to make him gag. The noise of the bugle still went through him like a knife, but judging from the expressions on other men's faces, he was not alone. The women titupping along on their little kitten heels, their parasols aslant, looked at him with new eyes. True, he wasn't as good-looking as Matthew Grand, son of their own soil and built like an Adonis, but in his own, slightly weaselly way, he was quite attractive.

The ladies with younger sisters made a mental note to mention their single siblings when they were introduced. All Englishmen were dukes travelling incognito; all the books in the library in Bismarck said so!

Custer rode by on Vic as Batchelor took the air. 'You're looking a bit more chipper today, James,' he said. 'Perhaps a ride out this afternoon will perk your pecker up.'

Batchelor was doubtful. Not only did it sound slightly off-colour, but he had never been improved by a horse ride in his life and doubted that it would work this time. He smiled and tipped his hat and Custer rode on.

At the hitching rail of the Dew Drop, a manly figure who looked a lot like Jane Cannary was fiddling with the girths of a horse. Batchelor decided that he wanted to go another way and turned off down a side street leading to the stables. He had never been in a fort before, so was surprised by the amount of activity; men were shouting, smiths were smithing and a whole lot of horseflesh of varying quality was being put through its paces. O'Riordan was triumphantly saddling the best horse in the string, the corporal's stripes on his sleeve glinting in the morning sun. As he had pointed out, with a great deal of blarney, it was no good giving the best horseman in the place the worst mount. The stable sergeant had told him right back that if he was that good, he could ride a table from the Dew Drop and still beat any other trooper, but Keogh had been passing and insisted that the Irishman had the best they had, a lovely sorrel with a sensitive mouth and a high arch to her neck. Reno's and Benteen's horses were steaming under blankets and the men themselves were lounging on stools outside the tack room, each with a foaming tankard, despite it being barely eight o'clock in the morning.

Taking another right turn took Batchelor past the non-commissioned officers' quarters where Mark Kellogg was sitting on the step.

'Morning, James!' he called, raising a hand. 'Come and sit a spell.' Being out West had made him rather homespun.

Batchelor lowered himself gingerly on to the pine boarding. 'Sorry,' he said when he realized Kellogg had noticed him wincing. 'I'm still a bit . . .'

Kellogg laughed. 'The Deadwood isn't for everyone, James. Perhaps, when your visit's over, you can go home a rather slower way. Not so . . .' he waved a hand in front of Batchelor's face '. . . bumpy.'

'*Is* there such a way?' Batchelor's face lit up.

Kellogg pointed with his thumb over his shoulder. 'We came that way,' he said. 'But if you go *that* way,' he pointed ahead of them, 'you come to the railroad again, but in less than half the time.'

Batchelor was dumbfounded. 'You mean . . . the same railroad? The one we were on? The one we got off?'

'The same.'

'So . . . why?'

'Indians.' Kellogg was succinct. 'Indian attacks on about one in every five trains. It doesn't always end in killing, of course. Sometimes, I think they just do it for the sport. You know, like your fox hunting at home. Perhaps they think we like it. Anyway, it's for you to decide. The Deadwood. Or Gall and his men.'

Batchelor narrowed his eyes. It was a tough one to call, but he thought he would rather take the Indians any time.

SEVEN

The officers' mess at Fort Abraham Lincoln didn't get much use as a general rule. There had been the skunk problem, which had made it not very popular for a while. And then there had been that winter when the bear had decided it made a perfect den and no one had cared to dissuade her. But that night, no one would have guessed any of that. Banks of candles down the tables cast a golden glow on the regimental silver and the crested plates. Batchelor had seen this at other military dinners when he was a journalist, but out here, in the heat, dust and danger, he hadn't expected it.

Each place had a card, written in an immaculate copperplate, so that everyone knew exactly where to sit. The ladies of the fort had put endless hours into deciding who was to sit where. Put friends together and of course the evening would go smoothly, but what was the point of that? There was no gossip-fodder to be had when everyone just sat and chatted amicably. Obviously, the table needed mixing up a bit. So it was obvious that Marcus Reno and George Custer had to sit opposite each other in the centre of the table. The flower arrangements were deliberately lower here so they couldn't avoid looking at each other. When Mary Reno was out of earshot, all the ladies were agreed that anyone looking at Reno's face whilst eating would be getting indigestion for sure.

They put Frederick Benteen to Reno's left, separated by the wife of one of the junior officers. She wasn't invited just yet to the ladies' gatherings. They weren't sure whether she ever would be. Whenever she was near enough to be overheard, she was always twittering about how marvellous her husband was, when everyone knew he was just *nobody*. To add insult to injury, the woman was also expecting a child and made no bones about it. Her dresses were flowing, her cheeks were glowing and, all the ladies were agreed, it just wasn't quite

decent. So the ladies had nodded and smiled and put little
Susie Chater between Reno and Benteen.

Libbie went next to George, of course. Then, alternating
with the other upper-echelon ladies came Grand in one direction, Batchelor in the other. Next, in descending order of
importance, the rest of the Custers. Some of the ladies clenched
their teeth around their smiles, just writing the names. Soon,
they murmured to each other, there would be no one but
Custers in the whole fort. Tom came next after Grand, after
a judicious positioning of Mary Reno. Next but one to
Batchelor came Autie Reed, nineteen and as daft as a brush
and not anything like as useful. The Canadian William Cooke
was such a nice feller, all the ladies agreed. So *polite*, like all
Canucks, and if those stupid side whiskers detracted from his
lovely smile, well, at least they made him easy to spot from
a distance. Myles Keogh was always easy to seat – between
any two women, he was as happy as a clam.

Pencils tapped on teeth for a while when trying to position
that dratted journalist, Kellogg. Who, for land's sakes, as Libbie
said, would want to sit next to a newspaperman? In the end,
they stuck him on one end, between the horse doctor and his
wife. They never really mixed with anyone, so they couldn't
inadvertently tell him anything he shouldn't know. The ladies
had finally put away their propelling pencils and sat back, a
job well done.

And now, the seats were filling up as George and Libbie
Custer brought in their guests. The room was heavy with the
scent of flowers and cheap candle fat, the air full of the sound
of people muttering together as they found their seats. Susie
Chater's eyes filled with tears when she saw she wasn't sitting
near her husband. She didn't understand why he had to be *so*
far away! He was sitting next to Belle Custer, Tom's wife, and
everyone knew that she was no better than she should be! Who
knew what she would be doing to her husband's thigh – or
worse – under the folds of the starched damask? Susie looked
right and left and a tear trickled down her cheek. Marcus Reno
and Frederick Benteen. Everyone just *knew* they were *animals*.
How poor Frabbie and Mary *stood* them pawing them, she
just didn't know. Sometimes even her beloved Harold turned

her stomach and he was young and handsome. If she was married to either of these two, she would just *die*, she knew she would.

Marcus Reno turned to her and pulled out her chair. His mess-dress cuff brushed her shoulder and she shrieked as if he had stabbed her. He sighed. Opposite Custer was bad enough, but to be seated next to this little air-headed ninny might be more than he could bear. He would have to have a strong word with Mary – he couldn't believe she had done this to him and, if she didn't know, then she should. She was, after all, senior to Libbie Custer, no doubt a nice enough woman in her way, though clearly not that bright if she could put up with that idiot Custer and his kin.

Benteen looked straight ahead. Perhaps if he stared with enough venom at Custer, he might catch fire, disappear up his own asshole or something similar. He raked the table with his deep-set eyes, glowering from beneath dark eyebrows that were so much at odds with his silver hair. That hair had caused many a trooper to mistake him for a pleasant old gent, a mistaken idea they didn't hold for long.

As soon as everyone was seated, Libbie touched a bell in front of her place setting and the meal began. Grand and Batchelor had become used to the superlative food and rather slapdash serving methods of Mrs Rackstraw and daft Maisie. The meal as it progressed proved to be like those dinners but in a rather different way – the food was slapdash, the service superlative. There was a man in polished and pressed full dress blues for every two diners, so the food was hot, at least that could be said for it. The service was flawless, apart from the awkward moment when a trooper, polished up, but still, after all, just a trooper in this man's army, spilled a drop of soup on Benteen's sleeve.

'What the hell you playing at, Trooper?' he yelled, jumping as if scalded. 'What's your name?'

The trooper bent low and muttered in the captain's ear.

'McGee? Never heard of you. You in my company?'

The trooper was just a boy, smooth-skinned and crop-haired, straight off the farm, unless Grand missed his guess. He squared his shoulders ready to butt in; yes, the lad was a trooper and should learn to take the rough with the smooth. But Grand had been to dinners in the finest places and rarely got home without some extra embellishment on his clothes. Mrs Rackstraw relied on it – otherwise, how could she be sure that he was being fed properly at all those fancy places?

But Myles Keogh was quicker. 'Leave the boy alone, Benteen,' he said. 'A drop of soup won't hurt you none.' To McGee, he flashed a smile. 'Get back to the kitchen, McGee,' he said. 'Change places with Dobbs and make sure you serve me the next course.'

McGee, scarlet to the ears, raced back to the kitchen.

Benteen snarled at Keogh, but a glance from Frabbie made him subside. Sometimes, you let the men have it both barrels. Sometimes, you obeyed your wife.

After the soup, there was a certain sameness about the menu. The soup was a thick, creamy concoction which had no discernible taste other than flour. Grand had eaten its fellows many times on campaign. Usually, the basis was maize and a floating kernel near the bottom confirmed his suspicion. He couldn't see Batchelor from where he sat, but he could imagine his expression and gave a small chuckle. The fish course just didn't happen. There *were* fish in the rivers, of course there were; it was just that by the time the cook had stripped off the spines, the scales like armour plate, and got down to business trying to find the edible bits, he was out the other side. Instead of the fish, Cookie had concocted a savoury on toast that was cut to the shape of a fish; Grand smacked his lips. Did he detect a hint of maize, made more interesting if not more palatable with a good slug of Bourbon half and half with chilli? Once the meat course arrived, the kitchen staff were more at home. A great slab of seared buffalo meat never came amiss, and with a few oven-roast sweet potatoes and some collard greens, it was a feast fit for a king. Some of the ladies pushed the meat around their plates; it wasn't that it wasn't tasty, but it wasn't really *done* in Washington these days for ladies to eat meat too much, or so Libbie had told them. Susie Chater, eating for two, was greasy to the ears by this point, but hardly cared.

James Batchelor had been brought up to eat everything on

his plate. He could usually manage this with no real effort, but his recent travel problems had made his stomach rather sensitive and he was struggling. The careful calligraphy of the place names had not been put to use to display a menu, so he had no idea what was coming next. The buffalo wasn't awful; it was just a lot of work for relatively little reward. He hoped that the next course would be a nice, easy pudding. Nothing fancy. Just some fruit and ice. That would be just perfect.

The pudding wasn't perfect. There was no ice, but how could there be, in the heat and dust that was Fort Abraham Lincoln? Sometimes, in the colder weather, they were sent up into the mountains and brought back some snow which would keep for a while in the broken ice house behind the canteen. If someone was sick – really sick, not just being an Englishman abroad – they would fetch snow to cool them down. But it was too dangerous just for a pudding. But there was fruit. Batchelor didn't know *what* fruit, except that it was probably out of season as it was clearly bottled. Mary Reno saw him poking at it and called across to him.

'It's boysenberry, Mr Batchelor,' she explained. 'Libbie bottles them in the fall. Isn't it just *delicious*?'

Batchelor was startled. Poisonberry?

Mark Kellogg, almost out of earshot, saw the problem at once. He nudged the horse doctor to his left. 'Tell Mr Batchelor that it's boysenberry, will you?' he asked. 'I think he thinks it's poisonberry.'

Dr Madden worked it out almost without moving his lips and passed the message on. He was of a rather sullen disposition; from dreams of being Surgeon General to the President of the United States to horse doctor at a fort in the ass end of nowhere was a big leap – a downward leap – but Madden was used to it by now. His wife was still bearing a grudge, but that woman could bear a grudge at a professional level. She could also bear children; eight, when Dr Madden had last looked, and probably room for more. They'd lost a few; he had mourned them but she scarcely seemed to notice. When it came to being a rugged pioneer woman, Martha Madden didn't believe in doing things by halves.

Reassured, at least partly, Batchelor dipped his spoon and

tried the fruit. It wasn't delicious but it wasn't horrible either and as it was bottled by Libbie, he thought he had better do it justice. At least it signalled the end of the meal and, with any luck, the brandy would be circulating soon and he could at least drink some as medicine. Slowly, the coffee pot came round, then Libbie rose and led her ladies out into the next room, where a fire burned despite the hot weather and more coffee and some iced biscuits waited for their delicate constitutions.

Martha Madden threw herself down on the sofa, which groaned under her weight.

'If I don't unlace these stays soon,' she grunted, 'I may well go off bang.'

Libbie looked at her reprovingly. 'Don't tell me you're expecting again, Mattie,' she said. 'Land sakes, I do declare you don't know when enough is enough.'

Martha gave her a look from under saturnine brows. 'I declare right back at you, Elizabeth Bacon Custer,' she said. 'What do you know about it? You have a handsome husband who adores you. You don't need to keep him off your back . . .'

'As it were,' Mary Reno whispered to Frabbie Benteen.

'When I'm knocked up, he leaves me alone. So, that gives me a year off in between having to put up with his . . .'

'Martha! Really!' Libbie was secretly rather fond of the woman, who she preferred to the mealy-mouthed Frabbie and Mary, whose husbands, she knew, hated hers. But there was a limit. 'You're upsetting Susie.'

Susie Chater was looking rather aghast. She had her views on that kind of thing but could never imagine having the bare-faced cheek to discuss them with her husband, let alone the ladies of the fort. Her pregnancy was advanced and she was dreading the end of it; when she had asked her mother in a letter when she announced her condition what happened, the reply – it comes out where it went in – was less than helpful, as she wasn't at all sure where that was, having her eyes closed and fists clenched at her sides the whole time.

The ladies fluttered around her and left Martha to her own

devices, hauling up her bodice to unloose her stays by herself. She looked down at her belly; it was looking a bit bigger, now Libbie came to mention it. But . . . she cast her mind back . . . no, it couldn't be. Her husband had been hanging round the mule skinner lately and he didn't do that unless he had to, so obviously nothing had happened lately that had slipped her mind.

The ladies gathered around Susie Chater were asking Libbie about the guests. A few of them vaguely remembered Matthew Grand from their younger days. Hadn't he been spooning at one point with Arlette Ross McIntyre? Oh, my dear, I had forgotten. But didn't she end up with . . .? And didn't he . . .? Voices dropped, venom flowed. Oh, the ladies of the fort knew how to assassinate a character, all right.

'What about Mr Batchelor?' Mary Reno asked Libbie, pointedly.

She coloured prettily. 'Mr Batchelor is a friend of Captain Grand's,' she said. 'And of course, Captain Grand is a great friend of my husband.'

The ladies knew better than to progress that line of questioning. They knew that anything George Custer did, anyone he knew, was perfect in Libbie's eyes and she would never think any differently.

'Well,' Frabbie Benteen muttered to Mary Reno, 'that's us told.'

'And Mr Kellogg?' Martha Madden piped up. 'He seems an interesting man. He sat between Madden and me at dinner.' Her words were pointed – she knew that they had been given the pariah.

'A newspaperman,' said Libbie and shut her mouth with a snap.

'How disgusting.' Belle Custer spoke for the first time. 'If there's one thing I can't stand, it's a journalist. Do you know, last spring, Tom and I went to a society wedding in Washington – my dears, *quite* the occasion – and the idiot writing it up for the *Post* didn't even mention us.' She looked around the room and was so high on her horse she didn't notice the several seconds' delay before the ladies of the fort shook their heads and murmured in her support.

Susie Chater suddenly clutched her protruding stomach in what Mary Reno and her clique thought a very unbecoming way. 'Harold!' she cried. 'Harold! I am in such pain. I need my husband.'

Martha Madden, the acknowledged expert in everything childbirth, elbowed her way to the front. She looked down at the girl, leaning back dramatically on the chaise longue. She poked her just below what had been her waist. 'Wind,' she announced. 'What you need, young lady is a damned good f—'

Just in time to save everyone from embarrassment, the door opened and George Custer strode in. 'May we join you, ladies?'

The Dew Drop Inn was not the most salubrious watering hole that James Batchelor had ever drunk in, but when in Rome . . . The shanty town that had grown up around the fort was technically off limits to the men, but George Custer, like every other commanding officer worthy of the name, was prepared to turn as many blind eyes as it took. One thing he did not allow was Indians drinking there, which was why the scout Bloody Knife was still kicking his moccasined heels in the fort's lock-up.

Now it had to be said that Batchelor was not much of a card sharp, but in the Dew Drop of a Dakota evening, if you didn't drink yourself into a stupor, what else was there to do? The game had been going on for an hour or so and the pile of crumpled paper money, a few rings and a gold nugget was in the middle of the table. The candles in the candelabra fashioned from a cartwheel, which hung just above their heads, dropped desultory stalactites of wax, which occasionally broke off and joined the heap below. Eyes squinted at the greasy cards in their hands, teeth clamped on the short ends of cigars which had once been elegant Coronas but which had become distorted by many pinchings-out.

'I'm out.' One of the NCOs, two months' money already on the table, pushed his chair back and went over to the bar.

'I'll raise you . . .' Grand looked again at his cards and at the stash of money still in front of him, 'ten dollars.'

A few more men threw in their hands but stayed to watch the play.

They were an assorted bunch around the table. Matthew Grand sat opposite Batchelor, with Mark Kellogg to his left. Isaac Dobbs, bugler of Keogh's I Company, was next to him. The others were troopers, whose names Batchelor hadn't caught in the introductions, and Lonesome Charley Reynolds, the chief scout. Had Batchelor known what a rare presence he was, he might have paid more attention. Reynolds hadn't got the moniker from nowhere; he liked his own company best. Drinking with somebody was a rarity; playing cards unheard of. Dobbs and his comrades eyed him suspiciously.

'I'll see you,' Dobbs said, pushing forward the money. He had just had a birthday and his ma had sent him a card with a couple of bills in it, so he was feeling flush. Batchelor looked once more at his cards to see if they had improved when he hadn't been looking; no, they were still the same. He threw them in and crossed to the bar, glad he had kept a little change in his pocket. He ordered a beer, but before he put his moustache into the froth, he caught a disturbing scent he had smelled somewhere before. A short, wiry figure in buckskins slumped at the bar next to him, elbows on the mahogany.

'Calam,' the barman twitched his handlebar moustache. He hadn't smiled in years – the quiver of his facial hair was as good as it got. 'You got any money?'

'I have when this feller gives me his laundry to do,' she said, jerking a thumb in Batchelor's direction.

Batchelor tipped his hat. 'Whatever the lady's having,' he said to the barman.

'Rye,' she growled, and downed it in one almost as soon as it hit the counter. She raised the glass again and waggled it at the barman, smiling at Batchelor. He smiled back and nodded. Calamity's glass was full again. The Englishman looked across at Grand. If he wasn't careful, this mule-skinning, scouting laundress would drink him dry. Grand, however, was concentrating on the game in hand. Between Dobbs and Charley Reynolds, he'd have to be *extra* careful tonight.

Calamity leaned over so that she could whisper in Batchelor's ear. 'Wanna see a real-live Injun, Mister?' she hissed.

Batchelor had seen a few around the fort already, shrunken shadows wrapped in blankets, making mementos for the folks back east, and while he had never seen anything similar in the Haymarket or along the Strand, he couldn't say he was particularly impressed. It was as though Calamity had read his mind. 'I ain't talkin' 'bout no fort Injun,' she muttered. 'There, in the corner. Don't look now.'

When Grand and Batchelor, Enquiry Agents of the Strand, had first set up in business, the words 'don't look now' were the sign for James Batchelor to spin round and stare goggle-eyed. But now, he knew different – he waited a good three seconds before turning slowly to look at the card-players while using the corner of his eye to look in the relevant direction. Near a side door, a tall Indian stood draped in a buffalo robe. His neck was heavy with beads but he wore no feathers and seemed content to stand in the shadows, as still as death.

'That's Gall,' Calamity hissed. 'Hunkpapa chief. If the General know'd he was here, he'd have him shot.'

'Who's that with him?' Batchelor murmured, as good as the next mule-skinner at sotto voce conversations in bars.

'That's Jim Thompson, what I guess you Limeys'd call the proprietor.' She glanced sidelong at Batchelor, suddenly uncertain. She'd heard most Englishmen were none too smart. 'That means he owns the joint.'

'He doesn't object to Mr Gall being here, then?' It took an Englishman to come out with that observation.

'Jim Thompson'd do a deal with the devil himself if he thought gold was involved.'

'Gold?' Batchelor's question was a little louder than he would have liked, but the moment had gone and nobody seemed to notice.

Calamity drove a sharp elbow into his ribs. 'Tell the world, why doncha?' she hissed. She sipped her whiskey in a surprisingly ladylike gesture. 'They've been findin' gold in the Black Hills since I was a girl back in Missoura. But now,' she crept even closer to Batchelor, who was grateful for the pervading smell of old alcohol and tobacco of the bar; it cancelled out some of Calam's natural aroma. 'Now, they've found the mother lode. Or so they say. The General himself come across it.'

'Just like that?' Batchelor asked. To both the journalist and enquiry agent who were at constant war within him, it seemed a little too pat.

Calamity stood up to her full five foot three, meagre chest puffed out. 'You callin' me a liar, mister?'

'No, no.' Batchelor was quick to defuse the situation, flicking his finger desperately for the barman to refill her glass. He had already noticed the pistol butt jutting out from her hip, and although the chances were she couldn't hit a barn door, he *was* standing only inches from her. 'It's just that . . . well, I'm a stranger . . .' He waited until the barman had gone. 'And I don't fully understand how things work around here. Are you telling me that Mr Gall knows where the gold is?'

Calamity shrugged. 'It's his land, ain't it?' she said. 'And what's with this "Mister" shit? He's just Gall is all.' Batchelor took another sideways glance, but the silent chief and the proprietor had gone, slipping out, Batchelor assumed, by the side door.

There was a kerfuffle at Grand's table and Batchelor turned to see Charley Reynolds ostentatiously laying his army Colt down on the pitted wood.

'Is there a problem, Mr Reynolds?' Grand asked.

'Not with you, Captain Grand,' Reynolds said. He was looking hard at the soldier across the table from him. 'Let's just say I'm warning you, Dobbs.'

'Atten-shun!' A roar came from nowhere and two troopers in forage caps and night capes crashed through the saloon's doors. In their wake, equally dressed for an evening stroll, sauntered George Custer.

'Mr Thompson,' he said once all noise in the room had stopped. 'I'd like a word.'

Batchelor hadn't seen the man come back in but there he was now, without his Indian companion, standing at the end of the bar with his hands in his waistcoat pockets.

'What do you have to say, General?' he asked, spitting something or other out of his mouth.

'In private, if you please,' Custer said.

'Anything you gotta say, you can say it here. Among my friends.'

Custer looked around the room. Some of the card players and barflies were his own men, his boys in blue. Others were miners from Deadwood, panhandlers, mule skinners and buffalo hunters. Most of them were drunk and all of them, Custer guessed, were armed.

'Very well,' he said. 'It is my understanding that against my explicit orders, you have been serving drinks to Indians in this establishment.'

Thompson's eyes swivelled sideways. His two barmen looked like choirboys at a Temperance meeting. Briefly, his gaze fell on Calamity and the fancy Dan she was drinking with. 'I think you've been misinformed, General,' he said.

'Trooper.' Custer called over his shoulder without turning his head. A large soldier burst into the Dew Drop, a small Indian in shackles under his arm.

'Have I been misinformed, Bloody Knife?' Custer asked.

The Indian was wearing a blue jacket with a corporal's stripe on his sleeves. He scowled at Custer, saying nothing.

'You got drunk the other night,' the General said. 'Who gave you the whiskey?'

Still nothing.

Custer bowed his head so that he was staring the dishevelled scout in the face. 'Who was it, Bloody Knife?'

'Him, Custer,' the scout barked in the best English he could muster.

'Let the records show,' the General had faced courts martial before and knew the drill, 'that the witness is pointing to Mr James Thompson, formerly sutler to the Seventh Cavalry.'

Thompson straightened. 'Formerly?' he bellowed. 'You got no right . . .'

Custer marched forward, as always to the sound of the trumpets in his head, straight at the guns. 'I have every right,' he said, 'as officer commanding Fort Abraham Lincoln, to dispense with the services of civilians acting – or, rather, not acting – in the service of the army. You're fired, Thompson. If I see you on army property again, I'll have you hanged.'

'Ah,' Thompson knew a loophole when he saw one, 'but the Dew Drop's not army property, is it? Now, you get the hell off *my* property. Come in here again . . .' he grinned at Calamity, 'and I'll get Calamity Jane Cannary to breathe all over yer.' There were guffaws all round, mule skinners thumping the tables and buffalo hunters whooping with delight. Calam didn't see the funny side.

Custer spun on his heel, kicking Bloody Knife out of the way. At the door, he turned back. 'Any man of the Seventh who isn't within the fort perimeter in the next five minutes will be carrying out double drill with full pack until hell freezes over.'

There was an unseemly rush for the door, led by Bugler Dobbs who swept his ill-gotten earnings into his campaign hat before hurtling past Custer, saluting as he went. The General took one lingering look around the saloon and left.

'Georgie's getting soft,' Grand said as Batchelor joined him at the depleted table. 'In my day, if an enlisted man saluted a senior officer without his cap on, there'd be hell to pay.'

'Have I got this right?' Batchelor asked him. 'Custer just closed down the sutler's store?'

'Removed the manager,' Grand corrected him. 'The store will go on – it has to in a place as remote as this. Means a hell of a lost income for Thompson.'

'That's what you get if you don't play by the rules.' Mark Kellogg pulled up a chair and poured himself a large one from the bottle that seemed to have appeared from nowhere.

'Bloody Knife, you mean?' Batchelor said.

'The General's made it clear, apparently,' the newspaperman said. 'No Indians in the saloon.'

'Good thing he didn't see Gall, then,' Batchelor said.

'Gall?' Grand and Kellogg chorused.

'He was over there in the corner, chatting to Thompson as if they were old friends. Weren't they, Calamity?' But the woman of the greasy buckskins had gone and the three men at the table suddenly felt very alone.

'I trust we'll read all about this in the Bismarck *Tribune* any time soon, Mr Kellogg.'

'Count on it, Mr Batchelor.' Kellogg raised his glass.

'Well, gentlemen.' Grand took up the abandoned pack of

cards, thick with grease and bent on every corner from where players had had a go at cheating; the occasional bloodstain, mostly on the aces, paid testimony to that. 'Do you think we can turn this lot into Happy Families?'

EIGHT

James Batchelor *had* ridden a McClellan saddle before but that was all of eight years ago back in Tennessee and he had to admit he'd lost the knack, had he ever had it in the first place. Everybody told him that he couldn't say he had actually ridden the Plains until he'd been on an Indian patrol. Tom Custer, whose company he rode with, told him there was no need to worry; they were as likely to see a hostile as a basking shark.

The little platoon wound its way west towards the Rosebud River, the day hot and sticky. The winds that could freeze a man's blood in the winter up here were warm too and brought no relief. Batchelor had borrowed a battered old campaign hat from W.W. Cooke and was not at all surprised when Custer halted the dusty column and rolled up his shirtsleeves. The tattoo on his forearm said it all – the stars and stripes floating over the goddess of Liberty and his initials – TWC.

'That's in case he forgets who he is,' Charley Reynolds muttered. The scout was enjoying this. At the command, the troop dismounted, much to Batchelor's relief, and they walked their horses along a high grassy ridge. Reynolds and a handful of troopers stopped to pick the spring flowers, fashioning them into bouquets and nosegays or twining them into their hats, pinned there by the crossed-sabre badge of the Seventh.

Batchelor had never seen skies so vast. As far as the eye could see, great thunderheads rose in menacing silence, dwarfing the rocky outcrops of the Black Hills and the Rosebud mountains beyond. The horses raised their heads, sniffing the wind with the scent of distant rain mingled with the smell of dust and hot rocks and hotter men.

'Chaw!' Custer shouted back, and the column halted their horses, unlashing the tethering posts and hobbling their horses to them. Reynolds did the honours for Batchelor, who seemed to have difficulty knowing which end of the piece of wood was which.

A ragtag line drew itself up alongside the covered wagon that brought up the rear and a makeshift stove was placed over a portable fire pit. As the men received something indescribable from a large cooking pot and sat down on the unforgiving ground to eat it, Tom Custer joined Batchelor and Reynolds.

'Captain Grand not joining us today, Mr Batchelor?' Custer was tucking in to what might have been reheated stew with gusto.

'Maybe he'd read the lunch menu,' Reynolds growled, doing the same.

'Ha, ha, think yourself lucky, Mr Batchelor.' Custer noted the look of disbelief on the Englishman's face. 'If this was the campaigning season, there'd be no fires and you'd be chewing hard tack.'

Batchelor looked none the wiser.

'That's sort of like saddle leather,' Reynolds explained, 'but not as tasty and harder, so's you're likely to break your teeth.'

'Keeps Surgeon Madden busy, though,' Custer observed. 'When he's not gelding horses or cauterizing clap sores. Where's that coffee, Cookie?'

A wizened corporal in a greasy apron was still doling out the stew to the drag riders, those two unfortunates who rode behind the wagon, eating everybody else's dust. Out of sight of the captain, they could just about manage a cigar, but the constant dust blowing into their scarved faces made even that secret luxury unlikely.

'What's your take on all this, Charley?' Custer asked the scout. 'Is it me or is there something building?'

Reynolds looked out across the rolling hills of grass, waving slightly in the warm breeze. 'Your guess is as good as mine, Captain,' he said with a shrug, not meaning a word of it. 'I had a word with Bloody Knife the other day, who'd heard it from a squaw over in Medicine Trail. Sitting Bull's been having visions.'

'Sitting Bull?' Batchelor had heard that name somewhere.

'Hunkpapa medicine man,' the scout said, as if that said it all.

'As far as the Lakota have a leader,' Custer said, 'it's Sitting

Bull. He has visions like you and I have shits, but he's got a following among his people. And the Cheyenne.'

'Cheyenne?' Batchelor was finding it very hard to keep up with all these strange names. He was at home with the Hoxton High Rips and Old Nicol Gang, but the tribes and their complex allegiances were all Greek to him.

Custer swept off his campaign hat and mopped his brow with his forearm. 'They've been quiet for a while,' he said to the scout.

Reynolds shrugged; quiet wasn't necessarily good news when it came to the Cheyenne. 'The Cheyenne's a whole different kettle of fish from the Lakota,' he explained to Batchelor. 'They're all Injuns, and they spend most of their time killing each other . . .' He held up his tin mug as the harassed corporal came round with the coffee.

'. . . which is good news for us,' Custer chipped in.

'. . . until now,' Reynolds went on, ignoring him. 'Look, let me put it this way. I don't know too much of the history of your home country, but you're English, right?'

'Right,' Batchelor confessed.

'Well, it'd be like the Irish and the Welsh and the Scotch all ganging up together against you. That'd be a war and a half, wouldn't it?'

'It would,' Batchelor had to admit.

'It's like that out here. We've got to keep the Plains peaceable. And while it's the Hunkpapa and the Miniconjou and the Oglala and the Teton – and that's just the subdivisions of the Lakota people – while it's just them, in kinda isolation, we can keep picking away at 'em. But if those painted bastards join forces . . . well, you catch my drift.'

'And that's all we're likely to catch at this rate.' Custer stood up, knocked the dust from his hat and put it on his head. 'Rain by five, Charley?' He nodded in the direction of the thunderheads.

Reynolds lifted his head from his mug and sniffed the air, raising a finger to test the breeze. 'Make that four.'

'All right, you saddlebums,' Custer shouted. 'Make your mothers proud. Column of twos.'

*   *   *

The clouds grew blacker as the column rode west, yet the sun still gilded the mountaintops and a rainbow, brighter than any Batchelor had seen, arced through the clouds, its ghost on its shoulder. If what Calamity Jane had told him the other night at the Dew Drop was even half true, there might well be another mother lode at the point where the colours reached the ground.

Suddenly, Custer's hand was in the air. 'What's that, Charley?' He was pointing to a stand of pines on the hillside, where a makeshift platform of buffalo skins was supported by four upright poles.

'Grave,' Reynolds muttered, a sense of unease in his voice.

'Help yourselves, boys,' Custer called to his halted column. 'Get your souvenirs here.'

'Not this one, Captain,' Reynolds shouted, and Custer reined in his men.

'Why not this one?' The captain was clearly irked to have his instructions countermanded by a mere scout.

'Let's take a look.'

Reynolds and Custer spurred their horses forward. Out of sheer curiosity, Batchelor did the same.

All three had to stand in the stirrups to see the corpse that lay on the buffalo skin. The body was small, no more than a child.

'It's a boy,' said Reynolds. 'Can't be more'n ten, I'd say.'

Batchelor gasped in disbelief. The boy was wrapped like a mummy in buffalo hide but some of it was disintegrating, pecked or gnawed by birds and vermin, and it flapped loose in the wind. The boy's eyes were closed and his face had been painted bright red. His hands and feet were bent upwards and backwards where the hide had shrunk in the rain and sun.

'So, what's the problem?' Custer sat in his saddle again and turned to his men. 'Corporal . . .'

'Look at the poles,' Reynolds said, a hand on his arm. 'What do you see?'

Custer looked them up and down and shrugged. 'Red and black. Bound with feathers . . . umm, what am I supposed to see?'

'That's all you should need,' the scout said, dismissively.

'The sign of a warrior, and a brave one too. How many ten year olds do you know would merit a grave marked like that?'

Custer was confused. 'What's your point?' he asked.

'This is somebody's son,' Reynolds said, walking his horse around it. 'Look at those beads. Hunkpapa.'

The scout waited until he had Custer's full attention. 'This is Gall's boy,' he growled. 'Better leave it alone.'

'Gall?' Custer repeated. 'That horse thief? Corporal, tear it down.'

'At least bury the body,' Reynolds snapped.

'Tut, tut, Charley,' Custer clicked his tongue. 'You know that's not the Indian way. Corporal!'

The column spurred forward, throwing lariats around the poles and pulling the whole structure down. The body bounced as it hit the ground, pieces of bone and feather flying in all directions. Batchelor was sickened. The troopers dismounted and helped themselves to anything that had a resale value – a small bow, a quiver of arrows, a little knife, beads.

Almost as though heaven were acknowledging this outrage, the thunder rolled for the first time and the rain could be seen driving in from the northwest, perhaps an hour away. The air smelled of wet ground and burning tin; the horses snickered and pulled at their bits; it was as if the defiled boy had called this down.

'All right, boys,' Custer called his scavengers to order. 'Time for home.'

'I'll be along presently, Captain,' Reynolds said. He was hauling a shovel out of the chuck wagon.

'Please yourself,' Custer said, and wheeled his horse to lead the column back.

'I'd count it an honour, Mr Reynolds,' Batchelor said, 'if you'd let me help you.'

The scout looked up at the Englishman who was dismounting already. 'I'd count it an honour to let you, Mr Batchelor,' he said, and he threw down his hat and started to dig in the dry sand of the hillside.

Batchelor steeled himself to pick up the rotting body and whatever remains of a young life he could find. He rewrapped the skin as best he could, tucking in the loose ends with gentle hands; he found himself humming a lullaby as he put the boy back into a peaceful sleep. 'How do you know that this is Gall's son?' he asked Reynolds when the scout had finished scraping a shallow grave.

'I don't,' Reynolds admitted. 'Just a gut feeling I've got. Gall's wife and kids were killed by Arikara scouts working for Reno a while back. I guess this little 'un died protecting his ma.' He reached around behind him and pulled out a Bowie knife, tucking it into the buffalo shroud. 'Here,' he said, with tears in his throat. 'This'll keep you safe, kid.' He wiped his nose with the back of his hand, but couldn't stop the tear from falling, splashing a dark circle on the dusty hide. Charley Reynolds wasn't lonesome for nothing, people said, and James Batchelor had just seen further into his soul than any man alive.

Batchelor cleared his throat and sniffed back his own tears. 'Is that . . . is that usual practice?'

Reynolds picked up his shovel and started to backfill the grave. 'I was reading in the paper the other day,' he said. '"The stand of the Plains Indian is just an episode in the inexorable westward march of the Caucasian."' He looked Batchelor in the eye. 'That's just fancy speak for we're gonna wipe out every Injun west of the Missoura, Mr Batchelor. You may not like it. I sure as hell don't. But it's gonna happen, anyway.' He patted down the sandy earth. 'Now, we just need a few stones to tuck this little fella in tight and we'll be on our way.'

The two men rode in silence, neither of them in a hurry to catch up with Tom Custer's column. The thunder followed them, and by the time they reached the foothills, the rain was falling in huge drops, bouncing on their hats and soaking through their coats. The day, which had been unpleasantly hot, had turned cold and the rain was in their faces.

'Whoa!' Reynolds's arm was in the air and he had reined in his horse. 'What do you see there, Batchelor?' he asked.

Batchelor followed his pointing finger. Through the driving rain, he could make out a horse, reins dangling, munching the lush grass yards ahead. Near it lay a body, half-hidden in the undergrowth.

'It's a horse.' Batchelor could think of nothing else to
say.

'Not just *a* horse,' Reynolds told him. 'That's Vic, General
Custer's mount.'

Reynolds was glad of the darkness as they reached the fort.
Vic and Dandy, Custer's horses, were the best-known animals
at Abraham Lincoln. Reynolds hoped that the miserable soaking
night would disguise the animal at least for a while.

'Carpenter!' the scout hissed at the duty sergeant at the
main gate.

'Charley.' The sergeant was chewing tobacco and stamping
his feet in an effort to keep out the cold. He was glad that the
stripes on his arm gave him carte blanche to avoid the worst
of the weather. He only did his rounds every hour, on the hour.
For the rest of the time he was safely in the warm and the
dry, hands encircling a mug of hot coffee. 'Is that . . .?' He
caught sight of Vic's blaze and white stockings.

'Yes. Get him quartered, will you? And get a message to
the Doc. Tell him . . . tell him his life's about to change.'

Sergeant Carpenter frowned. When a man like Charley
Reynolds says something like that, it's best to jump to it and
ask questions later. He did.

Somehow, the scout and the enquiry agent carried the corpse
across the parade ground, going the long way around, keeping
to the shadows. There was no moon tonight – too many clouds
– but the guttering torches on the walls took some evading.
Batchelor was still reeling, if truth be told, because of the
events of the day, but his concentration now was on getting
to the sanitorium without dropping his dripping burden which
seemed to get heavier with every step.

Doctor Madden had the rank of captain, which was guaranteed to give him a sort of gravitas with the men. In fact, he
had no medical qualifications other than those he had picked
up as an orderly in the Wilderness when Americans killed
each other in their Civil War and men like Madden were in
short supply. Nevertheless, he knew what was expected of
him, and was already hauling on his white coat, complete with
epaulettes, when the arrivals laid the body down.

He looked at the corpse, then at the two men who had delivered it. Charley Reynolds he had known for years. James Batchelor was the visiting Limey at the General's mess the other night. It all looked decidedly odd.

'Who's this?' he put on his pince-nez.

'That's kinda what we hoped you'd tell us,' Reynolds said.

'What?'

'Take a look,' the scout said, unfolding the corpse's cape. 'Take a *good* look.'

Madden moved the candle nearer the body. 'Looks like . . . looks like Trooper McGee,' he muttered. 'I Company.'

'Look again,' Reynolds insisted.

The doctor did, beginning with the face and moving down the body where the blue jacket had been slashed and ripped. 'Mother of God,' he whispered. And his candle went out.

Sergeant Carpenter hoped he knew how to do his duty. He took Vic to his stall and rubbed him down with a wisp of straw, muttering words of comfort to him as he unbuckled his girth and lifted the saddle from his sodden back. He undid his bridle and smoothed the mane back from his eyes. He stepped back from the animal, checking him in the candlelight for any injuries.

'What in the name of tarnation?' A hand flew out from under the deep litter in the stall and grabbed Carpenter by the balls. The sergeant yelped and kicked and before he knew where he was, he had a knife to the throat.

'Sergeant!' Jane Cannary stepped back and sheathed her knife. 'What are you doing here?'

'*Me?*' The sergeant was still fighting the flashing lights in front of his eyes and the temptation to be sick right there in the straw. 'What are *you* doing here, Calam? You could have killed me. I could have had a heart attack right there!'

'Sorry, Sergeant. I was . . .' she paused and looked the man in the face. He was one of the better ones. He hardly ever made fun of her and he seemed like a man she could trust. 'I was waiting for someone.'

Carpenter was indeed a nice man. But no one could call

him quick. 'You weren't waiting for the General, surely?'
Carpenter had heard the rumours; negro cooks, Indian squaws
but . . . *Calam*?

Jane was as insulted as Custer would have been. 'Hell, no.
He's no prize.' She quickly sketched in the skinny, gangling
frame, the receding chin and freckles and Carpenter smiled in
spite of himself.

'Reilly, then?' That was also a surprise. Although Reilly
had no wife at the fort, there was something about him that
suggested that, somewhere, he had a hearth and home. But
only Reilly and the General rode Vic, so who else could it
be? 'I hope you're ready for this, Calam, but if you're waiting
for Reilly, you've got a long wait ahead. Vic's rider was
. . .' he looked into her deep-set eyes, her mouth already
hanging open in pre-emptive shock, '. . . hurt. He's in the
sanitorium.' But he was talking to himself. Calamity Jane
Cannary was running for the stable door, out into the wet
night, into horror.

Madden fumbled with his matches and relit the candle, passing
it over the body again, to make sure his eyes were not playing
him tricks. He turned to Batchelor. 'Is this some sort of joke?
A trick?' he asked. Yes, that was it. This damned Limey had
come from Washington. He was in the pay of the Surgeon
General, checking credentials. They had done this to . . . no.
That was plumb crazy. There were simpler ways than this to
check up on a man.

Reynolds answered. 'A *joke*? Where are you from, man?
The funny farm? What's funny about this? First off, Trooper
McGee has been killed by hostiles, the first in weeks. Months,
even. But more than that.' He snatched the candle from the
surgeon's wavering hand. 'Trooper McGee . . .'

The door slammed back and Jane Cannary stood in the
room, sodden, dripping on the tiled floor. She took two steps
forward and elbowed her way in between Batchelor and the
surgeon. 'She's a woman, yes. Have you seen enough?' She
took the edges of the trooper's shirt and breeches and pulled
them together, covering the dead woman's modesty. 'I can't
believe you boys ain't never seen a woman's bits before that

you need to stare at hers.' She glared at the three men. 'It's
men like you as make women like her behave this way. She
was as good a soldier as any in this fort. Better than most, I
would say. She was brave. She was fearless. She was loyal.
She was . . .' the mule skinner was oblivious to the tears
mingling with the raindrops that carved clean streaks down
her face, 'she was my *friend*.' And she gave in to her sadness,
hiding her face in Batchelor's chest and crying like a child.

Batchelor was methodical. First, he traipsed through the rain
and took Calamity to the Dew Drop and put a good few dollars
behind the bar for her personal use. He warned both barmen
that she was drunk as a skunk and anything she said was likely
to be so much hogwash. He was secretly proud of his mastery
of American as he went out to find Matthew Grand. He hadn't
expected to find him in his room but, against the odds, he was.
Grand was beginning to worry about his partner and had got
fed up with being told how Charley Reynolds hadn't lost
anyone in his care for nigh on two weeks and everything would
be all right in the end, despite the fact that they had stayed to
bury an Indian child which would almost certainly enrage any
hostile in the territory. So he was trying to look calm and
collected and engrossed in his book when Batchelor put his
head round the door.

Grand leapt to his feet. 'Where in God's name have you
been, James?' he exploded. 'Have you no idea what time it
is? How dangerous it is out there? Have you forgotten, you
don't know anything about this country? Surely, you haven't
forgotten the bear? If . . .'

Batchelor shook himself like a wet dog and sparkling drops
flew from the shoulders of his coat. The campaign hat had a
drooping look and he took it off and hung it on a peg behind
the door. 'I've been out with Captain Custer and latterly with
Charley Reynolds. I actually have no idea at all what time it
is. I haven't known with any certainty for weeks. I think I
know as well as the next man how dangerous it is; perhaps,
after today, more so. And I know nothing about this country,
that's true. And as for the bear . . . I may never sleep with
both eyes closed again. So, that's the obvious questions

answered. Would you like to know why I am so late, wet, exhausted and terrified or not?'

Grand stood where he was, feeling rather chastened. Now he looked more closely, he could see that Batchelor was actually soaked to the skin and looked like death had laid his hand on him. He shepherded him to a chair, helping him off with his coat. When he was seated, he turned to the sideboard and poured him a stiff brandy. Batchelor took it with both hands and took a hefty swig. He put his head back on the antimacassar and sighed. 'Today has been a bit trying, Matthew, if I'm honest.'

'It is very wild out there,' Grand acknowledged. It wasn't as if they didn't have thunder in London, but somehow it didn't get into your head and rattle your soul like it did out west.

'It isn't the weather,' Batchelor said, draining his glass with another gulp and holding it out for more. 'It's the rest . . .'

Grand pulled up another chair and leaned forward. James had the heart of a lion, he knew that, but he doubted he was really ready for the unadulterated West, unfiltered through the pen of his favourite writers. He patted his knee. 'Tell me,' he said, gently.

Grand was still rather in shock when he and Batchelor got to the Sanitorium. Madden had cleaned Trooper McGee up and dressed her in a shroud. He had put a nosegay on her breast and crossed her arms decently. With her severe haircut, she still looked totally male, though in the candlelight it was very clear that she didn't have even a hint of stubble and, more importantly, no Adam's apple. But many of the boys in this man's army were hardly out of diapers so, even so, she would have fitted right in. Madden looked up from his contemplation of the body as the door swung shut.

'Gentlemen,' he said and stepped back. 'Come to pay your respects? I guess when the story gets out there'll be a rush of people here for the thrill.'

'We're not here because Trooper McGee is a woman,' Grand said, sharply. He had been living in the city which was home to Boulton and Park and all their many and various friends; if men in women's clothing didn't cause a stir in London, why should this girl in a trooper's shirt bother him here? 'We're here because she was riding General Custer's horse and died for it.'

'Surely not!' Madden was shocked. 'A coincidence, wasn't it?'

'No one rides Vic except the General,' Grand said. 'Or Reilly. But I suppose while they were away, Vic and Dandy needed their exercise, yes?'

The doctor's eyes widened. 'Of *course*,' he said. 'It was entrusted to that young idiot Autie, but he isn't so much a horseman as . . .'

'. . . a complete waste of air,' Batchelor finished for him. 'Yes, I gathered that much at the dinner. So, he asked McGee to do it for him.'

'McGee was good on a horse,' the doctor agreed. 'Good hands. Good seat.' He realized what he was saying and flushed unevenly. 'I mean . . .'

'We know what you mean, Madden,' Grand said. 'But since the General and Reilly have been back . . .?'

'They have been the only ones to ride him. I guess this poor young thing missed the thrill.'

The enquiry agents looked down at the face, closed in death, full of secrets they would now never know. 'But was it a thrill worth dying for?' Grand asked, gently.

'I'm surprised the hostiles killed her like this,' the doctor said.

'Well, after Custer's little display in the saloon,' Batchelor said, 'I suppose you could say they held a grudge.'

'But who could mistake this girl for the General?' the surgeon pointed out. 'Sure, he's skinny, but he's six foot if he's an inch. Kinda gangly. And he has long hair. This girl had hers shaved to the bone.'

'From a distance, though?' Grand suggested. 'And the weather was dark. Raining.' But he didn't sound as if he convinced even himself.

'No,' Batchelor suddenly remembered. 'The ground under the body was dry. She was killed before the weather turned.'

Grand looked at him. 'I did not know that,' he said smoothly, inwardly seething. When would Batchelor ever remember everything first time through? 'So, all right then, there was reasonable visibility. In any case, in my limited experience of tribal warfare, they don't wait to ask questions. I know.' He clicked his fingers. 'Have you checked for an arrow wound? A spear?'

'Not as such,' Madden said. 'But I have washed the body and laid her out, as you can see. And apart from a few knife slashes, I couldn't see anything untoward. Nothing *fatal*, if you take my meaning.'

Grand leaned forward and reached out his hand for Madden's candle. 'James, hold this for a moment, would you?' Batchelor leaned in as well, directing the light as Grand indicated. 'What's this?' Grand pointed to a dark mark in the stubbled hair.

Batchelor peered at it. 'Is it . . .?'

Grand probed it with a matchstick. 'Yes, James, it is,' he said. He straightened up and addressed the doctor, who was looking worried. 'Congratulations, Dr Madden,' he said. 'You didn't find a spear or an arrow wound. You didn't find a bullet hole either, and yet,' he gestured, 'here one is. What does that mean, do you think?'

'Hostiles have rifles,' the doctor hedged.

'So I hear,' Grand agreed. 'But unless I miss my guess, this bullet,' he held the twisted lead slug up to the light, 'is from a Springfield Carbine. Cavalry issue.'

Jane Cannary was making the most of Batchelor's kind contribution to her drinking fund and was sitting at the bar of the Dew Drop, her head cradled in one elbow while her other hand spun her glass round and round on the wet surface. She was smiling at it. After a while, she raised her head a little and looked around. Seeing no one but Dobbs in earshot, she spoke to him, though she had never really taken to him. Rumour was he did his own laundry. 'Look here, Dobbs,' she said, spinning the glass some more. ''S pretty.'

Dobbs nodded politely and finished his drink. It was always a good idea to make yourself scarce when Calam got maudlin. She would start by crying over you and end by trying to shoot you; it was as inevitable as night following day. And drunk or sober, she could outshoot most men on the post. The news about Trooper McGee had spread but only partially. They knew that one of their number was dead and that was – so far – it. Obviously, as soon as the ladies of the fort got hold of the rest of the news, everyone would know, but for now it was only Calamity who was weeping for the little girl lost. The others had raised a quick glass to the lad and got on with their evening.

'Where're you goin', Dobbs?' The mule skinner's voice was gravelly and designed to grab a man by the balls.

The bugler stopped and half-turned. 'Just off to my bed, Calam,' he said, hoping it didn't sound like an invitation. Everyone had known how tight she and McGee had been but surely she wasn't looking for a replacement beau so soon? 'Hard day tomorrow.'

'Hard day?' The woman was still spinning the glass, but now she was looking beyond it, right into Dobbs's soul.

'Well . . .' he could hear himself walking into it, but couldn't stop himself. 'Burial party.' He paused. One arm was still under her head, the other hand spinning, spinning, spinning. Perhaps he was all right after all.

'Burial party?' Her voice sounded too light for his liking. The barman had suddenly found something vital to do out back and the hog-ranch drunk in the corner of the room slid bonelessly down below the table. 'Party?' Slowly, she straightened up, her hand no longer spinning the glass but resting casually on the butt of her Remington. 'You think Trooper McGee being killed is worth a party, do you?'

Dobbs's eyes widened and he felt for his own firearm and just found an empty space. He knew where it was. It was on his bunk. But that wasn't much help to him now. 'No! No, Calam . . . come on, you know we always call it a burial party . . .' He could have kicked himself for saying it again, but the words just didn't seem to be under his control any more. 'Detail. Burial *detail*, then.'

'So, Trooper McGee was just a detail, was she?'

She? Dobbs nearly passed out with fear. If Calam didn't even know her lads from her lasses, she must be liquored up even beyond her usual. He was a dead man, for sure. He said a silent farewell to his bugle, to his ma, to his friends, to his life and closed his eyes.

'I've always known you hated her, Dobbs.' Suddenly, the voice was much nearer, brought to him on a blast of whiskey and worse. He opened his eyes and nearly swallowed his tongue. Silently, against all the odds without falling over, she had covered the ground between them and had her gun pointed at his midriff and just inches away.

Dobbs decided to get this conversation on an even keel again. 'I didn't hate McGee,' he said. 'He was a first-class soldier. Always said so.' He looked at her through lowered lashes; Calam in this mood had a trigger finger itchier than a skunk in a drought.

'Firs' class. Y're right,' she said, and the gun sagged a little in her hand. Then, she pulled it back up and pressed it against him, just under his breastbone. His heart was beating so hard that the gun bounced along in time. 'So, why'd you kill her, then? Eh, Dobbs?' Her thumb pulled back the hammer and Dobbs began to silently pray. He had never felt so alone in his life.

Suddenly, on a gust of fresh air and rain, there was someone else in the saloon. A large hand clasped over Calamity's and eased the gun away, throwing it on to the bar. The barman reappeared, gingerly looking around the edge of the door and the hog-ranch drunk crawled from under his table and took up his drink again. The newcomer was a head taller than Dobbs and could have tucked Jane Cannary under his arm and carried her off without turning a hair. But all he did was sit her down on a bar stool and gesture to the barman to top up her glass. Dobbs recognized the Irishman from his bravura ride; he had already divided the troop into camps, one of which thought he was a hero and the other of which thought he was an asshole. Dobbs had been in the latter but he was never afraid to change allegiance.

'O'Riordan,' he gasped. 'Thank God . . .'

'Don't take His name lightly, son,' the Irishman said. 'You were in no danger. She wouldn't have shot you.'

Dobbs raised his eyebrows and mentally sat O'Riordan on the fence between hero and asshole. 'When Calam thumbs the hammer, it usually ends up with somebody shot,' he said. He might not be able to ride like O'Riordan, but he knew Calamity Jane Cannary better than the Irishman and it had, after all, been his heart in her hand.

'Why was she picking on you, anyway?' O'Riordan was trying to sort out all the loyalties and cliques in the fort; it was the best way to stay alive, in his experience.

'She thought I'd killed McGee.'

'McGee? Oh, the trooper the hostiles got a-hold of today.'

'Hostiles? Is that the story? Well, in that case, what was she going on about? She was roaring drunk, that I know. She kept calling McGee a she not a he.'

O'Riordan looked at him. 'You got Irish blood in you, Dobbs?' he asked. 'That sounded like some blarney to me.'

Dobbs shrugged and straightened his hat. Calamity was banging her glass on the bar for more drink and he saw no need to hang around. 'No. No Irish. Just pure Philadelphia for as long as I know.'

'I knew a Dobbs back in Offaly.'

'Dobbses are all over. But my Dobbses come from Philadelphia.' Dobbs didn't know quite why that was important, but it was. He was feeling a bit stupid that he had let Calam – drunk as a skunk as she was – get the drop on him like that, so he needed his dignity. And Philadelphia was about as dignified as it came, as far as Dobbs was concerned. 'I'll be back to the bunkhouse, then.' Dobbs wheeled and made for the door, then turned. 'Oh, and . . . thanks, Corporal.'

'You're welcome.' O'Riordan sketched a salute and turned back to Calamity, who was back to spinning her glass. He clicked his fingers at the barman. 'One more for her, then I'll see her home. A double for me as well, if you will.'

The barman, glad that order was restored, made it on the house.

NINE

'Gentlemen,' Myles Keogh was off duty and lounging in an expensive smoking jacket when Grand and Batchelor knocked on his door. 'To what do I owe the pleasure?'

'Trooper McGee,' Grand said. 'One of yours, I believe?'

'Well, now,' Keogh's smile was tight. 'In the light of what we now know, I'm not so sure.'

'She *was* a member of I Company?' Batchelor's face was stony. Keogh looked at him.

'She was,' the captain said, 'and already I'm having difficulty with that concept.' He ushered them to comfortable seats. 'I'll be looking at all my troopers more carefully from now on.'

'It goes without saying, I assume, that you had no idea?' Batchelor had to raise the question.

'That McGee was a woman?' Keogh handed round the cigars. 'Of course not.' He rang a little silver bell on the table and Bugler Dobbs appeared, ramrod straight and ready to serve. 'Coffee, gentlemen? I don't approve of anything stronger at this hour of the morning – you've had breakfast, I presume?'

'We have,' Grand said. 'And thank you.'

'Three coffees, Dobbs,' Keogh said. 'Then make yourself scarce. These gentlemen and I have things to discuss.'

'Very good, sir.' Dobbs saluted and scuttled off into the kitchen, clattering pots and pans. Buglers like him were in short supply – a man whose job it was to communicate, but who knew when to shut up and when not to hear. Buglers like him were all three wise monkeys, rolled into one. At least, that was how Bugler Dobbs saw himself.

'What do you know about McGee?' Batchelor asked Keogh.

The captain twirled his cigar for a while, then said, 'I'm intrigued to know your interest in all this, Mr Batchelor – other than the prurient, I suppose.'

'Prurience has nothing to do with it, Captain,' Batchelor

snapped. 'I happened to be with Charley Reynolds when we found McGee, out on the prairie.'

Keogh narrowed his eyes. 'You don't much like the Irish, do you, Mr Batchelor?' He was smiling, but Grand felt uneasy.

'The Irish, Captain Keogh,' Batchelor said, 'spend a lot of their time blowing up parts of my home town, not to mention Manchester. You'll forgive me if I'm a little partisan in such matters.'

'I will,' Keogh said, 'but I'm not sure I'll forgive you for the potato famine.'

'You were telling us about Trooper McGee.' Grand thought it was time to intervene.

Slowly, Keogh turned his gaze to the American. 'So I was. Ah, Dobbs, thank you. Find Lonesome Charley for me, will you? Tell him I'd like a word.'

'Yessir.' Dobbs saluted and left.

'Reynolds doesn't say a great deal but what he does say is worth listening to.' Keogh poured the coffee. 'I'll be mother,' he said, winking, 'with all due respect to Trooper McGee.'

'How long had he . . . she . . . been with the Seventh?' Grand asked.

'Joined in '73 if memory serves,' Keogh said, 'in Kentucky. A paper-hanger before that. Apprentice and all.'

'Why the army?' Batchelor asked.

Keogh laughed. 'Do you want me to answer that one, Captain Grand?' he said. 'Or will you?'

'For me, it was a means of getting out from under my father's business,' Grand shrugged. 'Number crunching was never my idea of a career. Then, of course, the war came along. So before long, the choice would not have been mine to make.'

'True enough. I was ADC to General Stoneman, among other things. You were with the Third Cavalry, I believe?'

'Among other things,' Grand nodded.

'But to answer your question, Mr Batchelor; Other Ranks enlist for reasons different from officers. The rye, the pay, the rough life – who knows? It's not a bad life – comrades, three squares a day, a dry billet. And if you like horses, it's made for you. And what girl doesn't love a man in uniform?'

He stopped, hearing what he had just said but it was too late to backtrack now. He was saved by a knock on the door. 'Come in!' he bellowed.

Charley Reynolds stood on the threshold with his rifle slung over his shoulder. 'On my way to Bismarck,' he grunted. 'What is it you want?'

'Set a spell, Charley,' Keogh patted the sofa alongside him. 'We're talking about Trooper McGee.'

The scout hauled the rifle-strap off his back and sat on the floor, cross-legged. He liked Myles Keogh, as much as he liked anyone, but he'd no more accept his hospitality than fly to the moon.

'You didn't know, I suppose.' Keogh raised an eyebrow.

'What a cuss hides under his breeches is his concern, I reckon,' Reynolds said. 'It's no business of mine.'

'I agree,' Keogh said, 'but it is, apparently, of Mr Batchelor here.'

'I just want to know who killed her,' Batchelor said.

'Oh, well, that's easy.' Keogh was pouring himself another coffee. He hadn't offered one to Reynolds. 'Gall.'

Grand and Batchelor looked at each other.

'The Hunkpapa chief?' Grand checked, though it was unlikely there would be two with that name.

'Chief, horse thief and murderer,' Keogh shrugged. 'Take your pick. Gall is all things to all men.'

'He don't shoot troopers for target practice,' Reynolds grunted, looking Keogh in the face.

The captain of the Wild I looked at him, then at Grand and Batchelor. 'Gentlemen,' he said, 'I think we're all missing the point here.'

'Which is?' Batchelor asked.

'This has nothing to do with Trooper McGee,' Keogh said, 'but it has everything to do with the General.'

Again, Grand and Batchelor exchanged glances. Nobody spoke.

'Think about it. McGee, God rest her soul, was nobody. God alone knows what possessed her to join this man's army, but Charley here's right. Gall wouldn't waste his tomahawk on a *wasichu*, but . . .'

'A what?' Batchelor thought he'd misheard.

'Dog-face,' Reynolds said. 'It's what the Lakota call us whites on account of our whiskers.'

'. . . but Custer, now, that's different,' Keogh went on. The others still looked suitably blank; Grand and Batchelor from years of experience; Reynolds – who knew why? 'McGee was riding Custer's horse,' Keogh explained, as though he was talking to the fort idiot. 'It wasn't until Gall got close enough, he realized his mistake. McGee wasn't scalped, was she?'

All three shook their heads. It was hard to see how she could have been; there would have been nothing to grab hold of but stubble.

'That's because there'd be no point,' Keogh went on. 'But Long Hair, now. *That* would be a prize Gall couldn't resist.'

'It's not Gall,' Reynolds said defiantly.

'I know you've got a soft spot for the Indians, Charley . . .' Keogh started.

The scout was back on his feet, slinging the rifle over his shoulder. 'It's not a soft spot,' he said, 'it's plain justice. We've broken every goddamned treaty we ever made with the Indians. White men don't make promises, they make progress.' And he swept out.

Keogh's cigar had gone out and he relit it. 'He has a point, of course,' he said, 'but in my view, that only underlines Gall's motivation. The word in the lodges is that he has sworn to kill Custer. Poor old Charley's turning into an old woman.'

'What kind of rifle does Gall carry, Captain?' Grand asked.

'Any he can get his hands on,' Keogh shrugged. 'Why do you ask?'

'And who does he know back in Washington?'

Keogh frowned. 'Gall?' he said. 'In Washington? Man, that might as well be the far side of the moon. What a strange question, if you don't mind my saying so. I know you haven't been here long, but surely, it's been long enough to know that if hostiles aren't welcome in the Dew Drop Inn, they sure as hell aren't welcome in the White House.'

Grand leaned forward. 'Because, I think you're right,' he said, 'about Custer being the real target here, not McGee. It's happened before.'

'What has?' Keogh asked.

'Attempts on Custer's life,' Batchelor said.

'In Washington?'

'A runaway cab near the Capitol building,' Grand said. 'Killed a senator by mistake.'

Keogh clicked his fingers. 'Hal Maitland,' he said. 'Yes, I read about that in the *Tribune*. But surely, that was a political thing, wasn't it? Jealousy; it's rife in Washington, or so I hear.'

'And Custer was attacked by roughs in the Division,' Batchelor said. '*Irish* roughs.'

Keogh laughed. 'I wouldn't expect there to be any other type,' he said. 'And I won't even ask what the General was doing in the Division either. Did Libbie know?' He looked from one man to the other. 'Of *course* she did. Libbie knows everything that Georgie does and thinks it's wonderful.'

'So, you'll agree,' Grand went on, 'that the chances of Gall being involved in that are pretty remote.'

'On the face of it, yes,' Keogh had to admit. 'Assuming you're right, of course – about the Washington attempts, I mean. And if you are . . .'

'If we are,' Batchelor said, 'then we're not looking for a Hunkpapa Lakota, are we?' And he felt proud of himself for even being able to say that out loud.

'I must admit,' Keogh said, lolling back on his sofa, 'that the Washington connection has me stumped. The list of people with a grudge against the General must stretch to the Mexican border, but who's got the links east and west? All right, so Reno and Benteen can't stand him . . .'

'Reno and Benteen?' Batchelor repeated.

'You must have met them,' Keogh said. 'Of course you have – at the dinner the other night. I thought everybody knew . . . a fort like Lincoln has its cliques, gentlemen. Grand, you know how this works.'

'We had other priorities in the Wilderness, Captain,' Grand said. 'Scuttlebutt wasn't high on the list for spare-time activities. It was more a case of staying alive.'

'Fair enough,' Keogh nodded, 'but out here . . . Apart from the occasional hostile and somebody's drunken antics in the Dew Drop, the overriding atmosphere is one of stultifying boredom. I daresay you've even heard gossip about me being a womanizer.'

'You *are* a womanizer, Captain,' Grand pointed out.

'Granted, but I think you would be surprised to learn how little of what they say about me is true.' He paused and stared into the distance. 'Most of it isn't true.' Grand stared at him, unblinking. 'All right, most of it *is* true, but it's just as well for them that I give them something to talk about. People have too much time on their hands here. They become . . . introspective, I guess you'd say. When you're thrown back on your imagination for long enough, nothing seems too unlikely to spread as gossip.'

'Is that what Reno and Benteen do?' Batchelor asked.

Keogh laughed. 'You make them sound like some sort of double act on the stage,' he said. 'Technically, Marcus Reno is my superior officer, so I shouldn't, of course, be saying a word . . .'

'But if we overlook technicalities?' Grand persisted.

'Then the man's an asshole. Took him years to get through West Point because of the number of demerits he'd racked up. Never quite got over Custer getting the Seventh; he thought it should have gone to him.'

'What about Benteen?' Batchelor asked.

'Never trust a man whose hair is a different colour from his eyebrows.' Keogh patted the side of his nose. 'He may look like everybody's favourite uncle, but he's an utter shit when it comes down to it. Ask anybody in D Company.'

There was a silence and, during it, Myles Keogh grew serious. 'But, gentlemen, if you're suggesting that either of those officers – comrades of mine, remember – wants to see Custer dead, I'd have to say you were barking up the wrong tree.'

The fort was humming with activity, much of it of the useless variety designed to keep men busy who might otherwise sneak off for a snooze in the fast-increasing heat of the day. Buttons and buckles were polished, scabbards burnished. Bales of fodder were moved from one stable to another. Buckets of water were hauled from the well to fill horse troughs and the water from the horse troughs was collected and tipped down the well to keep the water sweet. Dust was swept. Stones were whitewashed and if the men chafed under such treatment, they didn't let it show. There were even outbreaks of singing, mostly of old Irish ballads, and if the words were not always for ladies' ears, well, the ladies were as yet not really stirring.

Libbie Custer never rose before eleven. Before she had gone out West, her mother had warned her that the early morning sun was death to a peaches-and-cream complexion like hers, as was the moist heat of noon and the dry heat of the afternoon. As for the icy cold of the desert night, it must be avoided at all costs. In short, *any* sort of weather they didn't have in Monroe, Michigan, was an unmitigated disaster. Libbie ignored her mother's advice by and large, but she had never been an early riser, so adamantly believed the bit about the early morning.

She was lying back in bed, cocooned in lace-trimmed pillows, when Georgie looked in. She held out her hands to him and patted the bed. Land, but didn't he look handsome this morning? 'You look solemn, Georgie,' she said, turning down her pretty mouth.

'I've had some news, Libbie,' he said, in his most portentous tone, the one he used in front of the mirror when he was accepting the Presidency. 'And you must brace yourself.'

She put her hands up to her mouth. 'Oh, Georgie!' Her eyes were wide. 'Not Bleuch?'

He shook his head, and before she went through the list of all the animals she knew, he cut in quickly. 'It isn't the dogs or the horses.'

'Not . . . Mama?' The tears were already in her eyes.

George didn't share her distress in the event of something fatal happening to his mother-in-law but he let it pass. 'No, Libbie, it's Trooper McGee.'

She let her hands fall and she frowned. 'Who?'

'Trooper McGee. I Company. You must have heard the commotion last night?'

She pulled a sulky face. 'There's *always* a commotion, Georgie. Land, sometimes I wonder how I sleep at all. And I didn't see James all yesterday. Or today, for that matter.'

'Well, in a way, Mr Batchelor was involved. You see, he and Charley Reynolds found Trooper McGee, dead out in the Plains.'

'How *dreadful* for poor James! Is he all right?'

Custer didn't often get angry with his wife, but sometimes he really wanted to give her a good one upside the head. While he admitted he wouldn't want her to *look* like Martha Madden, a bit more of her pioneer grit would come in handy. 'James is fine, I'm sure. He just found the body, he isn't dead. Anyhow, he and Charley found McGee and . . . well, Libbie, this is hard for me to speak of, even as a husband to a wife, a man who has . . .'

'Thank you, Georgie,' she said with a blush. 'I don't think we need to have too much detail on that score.'

He patted her hand. 'I'm sorry, my love, but . . . I am trying to prepare you. You see, it turns out that Trooper McGee was . . . a woman.'

Libbie looked at him with an eyebrow raised quizzically but said nothing.

'Did you hear what . . .?'

'Of course I heard you, George,' she said, with asperity. 'I'm not deaf, even though it is barely dawn. I'm just wondering what you think will upset me. I am as upset at Trooper McGee's death as I would be at anyone's passing. Land, I hope I am not heartless. But that she was a woman . . . I think it's fair to say that we all knew that.'

'We? All?' This wasn't going at all the way the General had expected. He had expected tears. Fainting. Tears *and* fainting.

'All we ladies. Well, possibly not Susie Chater, who hasn't the sense God gave sheep, but the rest of us, yes.' She leaned forward and took her husband's hand and patted it condescendingly. 'There are times for a woman, George, of which you may be aware, when her . . . health . . . is precarious. Martha Madden used to help poor Tilly out at those times.' She gave a merry little laugh. 'It wasn't as though she could ask her bunkmate, was it?'

'Tilly?' Custer was floundering.

'Tilly McGee. I can't say that I knew her. I thought in my

position it was best I stayed aloof. But yes . . . most of the ladies knew about her. Oh!' Her hand flew to her mouth again. 'How is Calamity taking it? They were great friends, you know.'

Custer took in a deep breath but let it go again without speaking. He had taken his little mouse out of her milieu and dropped her miles from anywhere and sometimes he wondered how she had survived. And then, along came a conversation such as this, and he had no doubt that whatever life threw at her, she would rise above.

'But, how did Tilly die?'

'She was shot. Riding Vic.'

'Vic?' The question was a scream. 'Then . . . they meant to kill . . . you!'

He nodded, solemnly, aware of how his golden hair caught the sun streaming through the blind. 'I have wondered, my dear.' He used the Presidential voice again; it seemed the most appropriate to the occasion.

Then Libbie Custer played to her strength and fainted dead away.

The mindless non-activity in the fort had stopped. Even the dogs lying in the shade seemed quieter. The horses stopped flicking their ears and tails at the flies which buzzed around. The air seemed heavier, the silence like a stifling blanket over everything. Not a creature was stirring. Then, almost beyond the limit of hearing, came the sound of distant shovels, breaking a hole big enough for a man in the dust of the burial plot. Trooper McGee was going to her reward. No one called attention to her sex. No one looked away. Her comrades in arms stood in silent ranks as she was lowered into her grave and if anyone noticed a weeping mule skinner at the back of the lines, they said nothing. The chaplain intoned the words over the coffin, the dust was replaced on her dust and Bugler Dobbs blew 'Taps' as best he could. He wasn't note perfect – no one would ever accuse him of being musical – but it was heartfelt and, if Trooper McGee could hear it where she had gone, she would indeed have been proud. Soon, the grave would level with the winds from the Plains and just a wooden cross would mark the place. And everyone knew, it wouldn't be the newest grave for long. Twelve troopers, six each side, fired their rifles into the air and the regiment was dismissed. Soon, bales would be moved from place to place, water drawn and poured back down the well and Fort Abraham Lincoln would return to its usual gentle, insular pace.

Later that day, Grand and Batchelor sat on the veranda of their quarters. The afternoon heat made everybody drowsy. Custer's dogs lay sprawled on the edge of the parade ground, in the shade. Only his pet porcupine risked the direct sun, but he, outlawed by Libbie from the General's bedroom, had the run of everywhere else and made a point of such perambulations.

Grand was idly tossing a silver dollar in the air. 'Heads or tails, James?' he asked.

Batchelor looked at him. He'd done this before, many times, and it never ended well. 'Tails,' he said.

The coin flashed as it turned in air and Grand caught it expertly. 'It's heads,' he smiled, showing it to his doubting partner in crime.

'So?' Batchelor, defeated again, waited for the inevitable.

'So, I'll take Frabbie Benteen. You can have, in the nicest possible way, the horse-doctor's wife.'

The horse-doctor's wife wasn't used to visitors, especially interesting, foreign visitors from thousands of miles away. Martha Madden's many children were all away at school, bar the youngest who was out back with the nursemaid who doubled up as maid and sometimes surgery assistant. She missed them, but while her husband was in the Fort Lincoln post and she was a captain's wife, she had little to do for much of the time. She could – and did – embroider for America, and the walls of her parlour were crammed with uplifting texts and associated pictures. Currently, she was working on 'Nearer My God to Thee' with an ecstatic angel in one corner. Occasionally, she was called upon to chase the rabbit, as the common parlance had it; helping to deliver the babies of soldiers' wives.

'Mr Batchelor!' Her face lit up as he had hoped it would. 'What a nice surprise.'

'Am I interrupting, Mrs Madden?' he asked, sweeping off his hat.

'Land, no.' It was an irritating expression she'd picked up from Libbie Custer and she had no idea just how annoying it was. 'Come in. Can I offer you a raspberry tea?'

Batchelor had little idea what that might *actually* be made of, but he accepted gratefully. The Maddens' quarters stood at the end of Officers' Row, nearest to the Suds, which were the Other Ranks' married accommodation, and the babble of children and the wailing of babies wafted in through the open windows. It was an incongruous sound in a frontier fort but James Batchelor, to whom the Wild West had, until now, been Wimbledon Common, didn't know that.

'I hope you don't mind,' he said, perching on furniture that was nowhere near as comfortable as Myles Keogh's, 'but I'd love to hear all about frontier life, from a woman's perspective, I mean.'

'Pity you couldn't have asked Trooper McGee that,' she said, waspishly. When Tilly McGee had been her special protégée, that was one thing. Now she was public property, quite another.

'Indeed,' Batchelor said, impassively.

'We women who actually wear frocks,' she went on, 'have a pretty hard time of it, I can tell you.'

'Are you from the West, Mrs Madden?'

'No, no. I hail from Virginia,' she trilled, although if she was trying to emulate the daughters of the Confederacy, she was failing abysmally. 'Madden is Pennsylvania through and through. If this country of ours had used *our* experience, a mingling, as it were, of North and South, there might never have been a Civil War in the first place.'

'Indeed not,' Batchelor smiled. 'It must be nice, though, to have friends like Mrs Custer and Mrs Benteen.'

She looked oddly at him. 'That depends on which Mrs Custer you mean,' she said.

'Well, Libbie,' Batchelor explained. He had momentarily forgotten about Tom's wife, but even Tom did that most of the time.

'Libbie is all right,' Mrs Madden nodded. 'She's the
commandant's wife and she handles it well. Belle, on the other
hand, is a snob who preens over the rest of us 'cos she's the
General's sister-in-law. And don't get me started on Frabbie
Benteen!'

'Mrs Benteen,' Matthew Grand swept off his hat and stood at
the entrance to the villa.

'Why, Captain Grand,' the woman gushed. 'This *is* a pleasant
surprise. I'm afraid Frederick is on outpost duty with his
company.'

'Well, actually,' he said, 'that's sort of why I'm here.'

'Won't you come in?'

'Thank you.' He stepped inside and almost gasped. He
wasn't ready for the wallpaper or the zebra-skin rug on the
living-room floor, but he was a man of the world and took
such things in his stride. 'You know I was with the Army of
the Potomac during the late war?'

'In a place like this, Captain,' she said, ushering him to an
armchair, 'word gets around. So, yes, I had heard.'

'I'm sure I've met your husband before, but for the life of
me, I can't remember where. I didn't like to ask.' He smiled
deprecatingly. 'It's not very polite to admit that you've
forgotten someone, especially someone as obviously able as
your husband.' He felt his stomach flip over as he laid it on
with a trowel.

'His family were music publishers,' she said. 'Raspberry
tea?'

'Thank you.' He smiled at the sudden appearance of a silver
pot.

'He did various jobs before the war, but of course, it's during
the war that you'll have met him. So, let's see . . . he joined
the Tenth Missouri soon after Fort Sumter. It broke his father's
heart. My father-in-law, Mr Grand, was a son of the South
through and through. The last letter he wrote to Frederick
ended with "I hope the first Goddamned" . . . oh, excuse my
French . . . "bullet gets you".'

'Delightful,' Grand said.

'Yes, he was a delightful man,' Frabbie went on. 'Oh, it's

so difficult to remember Frederick's campaigns. Let me see
. . . were you at Bolivar?'

Grand shook his head.

'Milliken's Bend?'

Likewise.

'Selma?'

Nothing.

'Little Osage?'

The list droned on through the afternoon, not helped by the
sweet warmth of the raspberry tea and the warm winds wafting
in from the Plains outside.

'Major Reno is another matter.' Martha Madden, already flattered by Batchelor's gushing, was warming to the occasion.

'In what way?'

She leaned forward, checking to see that there was no one
in actual earshot. 'Drink,' she mouthed.

'Really?' Batchelor sat back and did his best to look appalled.

'Disgustingly so, on several occasions. I wonder General
Custer doesn't kick him out. He's brave enough, I suppose –
led a cavalry charge against Fitzhugh Lee near the Rappahannock
and had his horse shot from under him. All he got out of that
was a hernia.'

'Dreadful,' Batchelor commented, grimly.

'After that, it was rebuffs all the way. To hear him tell it,
of course, it was all somebody else's fault – Custer's in
particular. I think it rankles that the General is younger than
he is and got all the plaudits.'

'Do you know,' Batchelor asked, forcing down a second
cup of raspberry tea, 'if he has any links with Washington?'

When the list of the minor skirmishes of Captain Benteen
was over, Grand accepted another raspberry tea and said,
'Does he have any connection with the capital? My father
has offices there; perhaps that's where . . .'

Frabbie Benteen frowned, then shook her head. 'Well, he
was hoping for some sort of post there,' she said. 'You know,
via Belknap, but it never happened.'

*   *   *

'Well,' Mrs Madden became even more confidential. 'I do know, because Corporal Dobbs, who is the regiment's telegrapher told me, that Major Reno was in touch with William Belknap. That, of course, was before he resigned as Secretary for War. And please, Mr Batchelor, don't tell a *soul*. I was told it in strictest confidence!'

'Belknap!' Grand and Batchelor chorused when the door closed on their quarters that evening. It really came as no surprise that he would be in the mix somewhere.

'So that's it,' Batchelor said. 'Reno can't stand Custer and Benteen's no big fan either. On their own, they wouldn't so much as break wind, but together, and spurred on by Belknap, who has a real motive . . .'

'One of the oldest in the book,' Grand said. 'Revenge.'

'And it's as sweet out here in the Black Hills as it is in DC. The next question is – and I'm looking to you for soldierly advice here, Matthew – how do we proceed?'

TEN

James Batchelor had never had a particularly friendly feeling towards wildlife, but the wildlife of the American continent seemed to him to be less deserving of his friendship than that at home. At home there was the occasional mouse in the wainscoting, sometimes the sound of a fox rifling kitchen scraps in the area. Kestrels would sometimes attract his attention high in the London skies, fighting a losing battle to minimize the number of pigeons that daily planned to shit on his head. But in this country, there seemed to be no limit to the critters, and he was loath to go out in search of any more. General Custer's porcupine had wandered in while he was having his breakfast this morning, and Grand had annoyed him by giving it a piece of his toast. Skunks, rattlesnakes, even scorpions lurked outside the perimeter of Fort Abraham Lincoln and Batchelor had no intention of mixing with any of them. But Myles Keogh had arranged a hunt to entertain the fort's guests, so it seemed only polite to go along.

'So, what are we hunting?' he asked Grand as he got ready that morning. He had been lent some trousers with leather inserts to make the chafing a little less terminal and a warm coat for when the night turned cold. He had Lieutenant Cooke's broad and shady hat to ward off the sun and a neckerchief to stop his neck from burning, cavalry, for the use of. He had canteens to hang from his saddle and a rifle in a nifty bucket. He had leather gloves to stop the reins from cutting his hands. And yet still he looked like an ex-journalist now turned enquiry agent from just off the Strand.

'Well,' Grand was pulling on his boots. 'I was hoping it would be buffalo. I haven't been on a buffalo hunt for years. But it is a bit of a hot potato at the moment. Hunters are bringing down buffs along the Rosebud in their thousands; the Lakota don't like us hunting their food supply, which I suppose is fair enough, and anyway, it is a bit dangerous for . . .' The sentence petered out.

'For?' Batchelor knew he was hardly a backwoodsman of repute, but a man had his pride.

'Well, for you, James, not to put too fine a point on it. Your riding has come on in leaps and bounds, but I still don't see you surviving a buffalo hunt in anything like original condition. So we're hunting gazelle. Or bighorn, depending on which we scare up first.'

'Bighorn?' Batchelor didn't like the sound of that too much. 'How big?'

'It's just the horns that are big in relation to the animal,' Grand comforted him. 'The antelope stands about, oh,' he extended an arm, 'about yay high. That's a buck. The does are smaller. You'll want a buck, though, for the head.'

'The *head?*'

'You can have it mounted. Shipped home. Everyone does it.'

Batchelor had visited country houses adorned, if that was the word he wanted, with heads of every kind, and hated both the look and the subdued smell of moulder and death that seemed to go with them. 'I'll forgo the head, Matthew, if that's all right with you. I'm not sure Mrs Rackstraw is ready for a bighorn head on the wall.'

'You may be right.' Grand jumped to his feet. 'Ready?'

'As I'll ever be.' Batchelor had one last look round for anything he had missed. An excuse for not going was the only thing he couldn't put his hand on, so he followed his colleague out into the morning sun.

On the veranda, they bumped into Mark Kellogg.

'Hunting today, Mr Kellogg?' Grand asked.

'No, no,' the journalist smiled. 'On the face of it, I'd rather eat buffalo shit. No, I've got to earn my keep with old Sam Lounsbury. As editors go, he's not a bad old stick, but I know he'll be itching for a story about now. I thought, something for the ladies – life on the Plains, *à la* Mrs Custer. What do you think, Mr Batchelor?'

Batchelor found himself blushing but chose to interpret Kellogg's question another way. 'It's been a long time since

I had to please an editor,' he said, 'but I'm sure the ladies of Bismarck would be fascinated.'

'Something for the ladies it is, then,' Kellogg smiled and tipped his hat.

Even Batchelor had to admit that the company looked splendid drawn up in twos in the parade ground, the light glancing off their buttons and buckles, the jingling harness throwing rainbows as the horses tossed their heads.

Batchelor looked along the line. 'There's no provision wagon,' he muttered to Grand.

'Well, no, James. We're going into the foothills. We're not going for a stroll in Hyde Park. We all carry what we need behind our saddles – look, see, everyone has a bedroll and some food. We're only out for a night. We don't need much.'

Batchelor still looked fruitlessly along the ranks. 'But what about tents?'

'No tents. Just the stars for a roof and the ground for our bed.' Trust Myles Keogh to come up with something poetic. You can take the man out of Limerick, but you can't take the Limerick out of the man. Keogh looked down from the saddle of Comanche and continued. 'Come on, Mr Batchelor. You'll enjoy it. A nice ride in the sun and a hunt; it's a holiday for us and some fresh meat for dinner. The General is joining us today – he always seems to bring us luck.' Everyone had heard of Custer's luck. It had never deserted him through four hard years of the war; nor, again, chasing hostiles along the Washita. Keogh turned over his shoulder and whistled. O'Riordan trotted up, leading two horses, accoutred like the rest. 'Here are your mounts. I've . . .' he coughed discreetly and lowered his voice. 'I've given you a nice quiet one, Mr Batchelor, so you'll be comfortable. For you, Captain Grand, something a bit livelier. I know you'll enjoy the challenge.'

O'Riordan handed Grand the reins of a roan with a rolling eye. Her hoofs danced in the dust and she curled a lip in disdain. Grand looked at her and tried to get her measure. She would be a challenge, that was no doubt, but he had missed his riding; going round in circles in the park was not really what he called a ride. He slipped one foot in the stirrup and bounced easily on to her back. She rewarded him with a backward kick and an infuriated snicker.

'Let her know who's boss, Captain,' O'Riordan said. 'I rode her this morning and she's a nice enough temperament if she knows who's on her back.' He gave Batchelor the reins of his horse and went round to the side to hold her still while he mounted. 'Nicely done, Mr Batchelor,' he said, trying to keep the surprise from his voice.

'I can *ride*,' Batchelor said, peevishly. 'I just don't choose to do it that often, that's all.'

'To be sure,' O'Riordan said and wheeled away to his place in the line.

Custer, with Reilly at his side, took his place too and raised an arm. He was riding Big Dandy this morning, a corporal carrying the General's personal guidon close behind. The company moved off, into a trot, and were soon through the gates and on their way across the Plains to the foothills. The heat was intense, making the air shimmer. Batchelor was glad of his kerchief which mopped up much of the sweat that was running from under his hat. The men also began to look less bandbox fresh, with darker patches appearing on their already dark blue bib shirts. Only Bloody Knife looked unfazed by the heat, despite the fact that he was wearing twice the amount of clothing of any other man present. The stripes on his sleeve were all that linked him with the Seventh in terms of appearance.

'How does he do that?' Batchelor asked Keogh. 'He hasn't a bead of sweat on him, though I can count at least three layers of . . . what is that he's wearing?'

'Doeskin,' the Irishman answered. 'It reflects the heat and also soaks up the sweat. That cools a man down.'

'Why don't we all wear that, then?' Batchelor asked. 'I'm melting.'

Keogh looked horrified and Custer turned to look at the Limey riding at his back.

'Mr Batchelor, would you have us dress like Indians?' he asked, shocked.

'Why ever not, if it stops you dying from heatstroke.' James Batchelor had never heard anything so stupid.

Custer blinked for a moment and then turned away. He had

never heard the like! 'Bloody Knife!' He called the scout over. 'Any sign of anything to hunt? As this is a hunt, and all?'

'What say, Custer?' The scout didn't stand on ceremony.

'I said,' Custer had tired of trying to train this man. He had once given him a medal in the fond hope that it would make the man proud enough to behave. It didn't. He would do what he wanted anyway. 'I said, any sign of anything to hunt. Bighorn? Anything?'

Bloody Knife pointed ahead. On a rock standing clear of the grass and stunted pines stood a magnificent buck, with one of the best spreads of horn Custer had seen in years. Around him, cropping the sweet grass in the shade, was his harem, probably twelve does, with last year's young on the edge of the group.

'Well . . . why didn't you say so?' Custer blustered at the man.

'Didn't see the point,' the scout said, turning to ride back at the rear. 'You ain't blind, far as I c'n see.'

No one was ever sure how good Bloody Knife's English was because he rarely said enough to judge, but what he did say was usually to the point and it was true that the buck was hard to miss. He was poised now on his flat-topped rock, staring with his cat's eyes at the men, stationary now at Keogh's signal. The captain lowered his raised hand slowly, oh, so slowly, and the men slid soundlessly from their saddles, some stroking their mounts' noses to keep them quiet. Custer remained mounted, reaching for his custom-built rifle slung on his saddle. He raised it slowly to sight the buck and the men of the company did the same. They all knew that if the buck fell it would be Custer's kill. If he got away, it would be someone's fault for making a noise. The best outcome was that the magnificent animal died because that would mean good eating and also a happy General. Slowly, slowly the General squeezed the trigger and, in the potential last seconds of the buck's life, Batchelor gave vent to an enormous sneeze.

The buck's head came up, the bullets flying wide, and he leapt from his rock to the ground beneath, his women clustering round him, cavorting in panic. With a flash of bunched buff muscles and a clatter of hoofs they were off, jinking through the rough scrub, leaping from rock to rock and rebounding like so many rubber balls. The herd stayed together, the laggards taking off at angles to increase their odds, the leaders heading straight for where the rocks were steepest, the inclines more impossible for men on horses. Soon, the company were as spread as the herd, their horses being held in threes and fours by some of the less sure-footed of the men. O'Riordan led a posse up into a gully after the buck, tactfully hanging back so that Custer could appear to be in front. Soon, shots were ringing out and the few men left with the horses began to shield their eyes looking into the sun, waiting for their comrades to come back, carrying antelope strung on poles.

Batchelor sat in the shade and got ready for the aftermath of his sneeze. Grand had gone off up the gully with Custer, but Dobbs was not slow to make him feel worse.

'The General won't be too pleased with you, Mr Batchelor, with that sneeze and all,' he remarked.

'No, Dobbs, I don't suppose he will be.' Batchelor wasn't too sure himself whether he had done it on purpose or not. The buck was certainly a very beautiful animal, and far nicer to look at outlined against a sun-kissed rock than on a plaque on a wall.

'Mind you, if he gets him after a chase, likely he'll forgive you.'

Batchelor gave a wan smile.

'But he's a great one for a grudge, is the General.' Dobbs gathered the reins of his charges more securely in his hand and sat down next to Batchelor. 'I've known him bear grudges for the littlest thing. Why, once, there was a captain . . .'

'Yes, Dobbs. Thank you. Let's hope he catches his buck then, shall we? I wouldn't like him to bear a grudge against me.' Batchelor just wished the corporal would go away. He was a nice enough lad, but the conversation was a tad one-dimensional.

'He'll catch him for sure,' Dobbs said, cutting a wad of tobacco and offering a piece to Batchelor, who shook his head. 'Or he'll think he will. I guess O'Riordan will do the shooting. The General can't hit a barn door. Common knowledge.'

Batchelor was intrigued. 'I thought he was something of a crack shot.'

Dobbs looked conspiratorial. 'Well, you would do. But I heard it from Bloody Knife that he shouldn't be let loose with no weapon when anyone is within range.'

'I see. Well . . . let's hope he *thinks* he bagged the buck, then.' Batchelor lifted his head. The shooting had stopped and the sounds of men's voices filled the void. The voices got closer and into the little valley, floored with sand worn through long years of wind through the rocks, came the company, some empty handed, others with their prey. Custer led his party, the buck, head down, horns dabbled with the blood that ran from a wound right between his eyes.

'Mr Batchelor!' Custer called. 'I nearly lost him, but here he is. Thank you for your sneeze – you gave us some good sport.' The men laughed and clapped Batchelor on the back. 'You shall have the head.'

Batchelor raised a hand. 'No, really, it's . . . well, it's yours by rights, General.'

Behind him, he heard Dobbs give a little snort.

Soon the air was thick with the smell of blood and guts as the men cleaned the carcases. The flies came thick and fast and, high above, turkey vultures and kites spun lazy circles on the updraughts and waited to eat their fill. The company moved off with the kill slung between two horses, the feet tied together at the ankles and the headless necks dragging the ground. The skins were tied in neat parcels on the backs of saddles and the flies were hard put as to whether to follow them or stay where the pickings were even sweeter.

As they moved higher into the mountains, the heat grew less until, at dusk, it began to get chilly and the flies fell back and left them alone. As dark began to take over, Keogh ordered the column to halt and they made camp, with a fire in the middle to roast one of the yearling does, tender eating with no need to hang the meat. Soon the men were sitting round telling tales and singing songs of home. Keogh and O'Riordan made a formidable duo and Grand whispered to Batchelor that they were a loss to the Halls. Up here, the tensions of the fort didn't seem to exist, and if any cliques were represented around the campfire, they were impossible to distinguish. The coffee pot went round and round, followed by the whiskey bottle and, before long, men wandered off to find a place to lay their head, tucked into the gnarled roots of a tree clinging to the hillside or, failing that, in the lee of a log. Soon, the only sound to be heard was soft snoring and the occasional passing of wind. Two guards patrolled in silence, patting their sleeves to keep warm. After all, this was potentially hostile territory. It wouldn't do to be careless.

James Batchelor was not keen on sleeping outdoors. Where he came from, it meant that you hadn't anywhere better to lay your head and didn't have so much as fourpence for a doss. But here, it seemed, it was just another place to be, the same as a room or a house or a mansion. Custer bedded down the same as the men. In fact, Batchelor could see him now in the dying light of the fire, back to back with the faithful Reilly.

Grand could see that Batchelor was unwilling to bite the bullet and find somewhere to sleep. He unrolled his blanket and tapped his friend on the shoulder. 'Custer and Reilly have it right. We'll sleep back to back over there and we'll keep each other warm. No draughts when you have someone with you.'

Batchelor looked doubtful. 'Does sleeping back to back stop scorpions, snakes, things of that nature?'

Grand shrugged. 'Too cold up here at night for that,' he said. 'Nothing dangerous except what you see.' He waved a hand.

'What?' Batchelor scanned his surroundings by the light of the embers. 'What? All I can see is the men.'

'And they're all that's dangerous. I'd rather face a rattler than Bloody Knife with some whiskey in him. So let's bed down. Tomorrow night, you'll be sleeping in your own bed back at the fort. Just keep that in mind and you'll sleep like a baby. Look, here we are, a nice scoop in the dirt. Someone's slept here before, I reckon.'

Batchelor made a note to himself to check when they would be setting off for home. When Grand started to get homespun, it was time to get him back within the sound of Big Ben.

*   *   *

Like everyone who didn't sleep outside on a regular basis, Batchelor tossed and turned for a while before getting the knack of it. He tucked his saddlebag tight under his chin rather than trying to use it like a feather pillow, crossed his ankles and bent his knees, tilted his pelvis into the ground and, just as he was feeling surprised that it was so comfortable, he drifted off. The snores and explosions of wind got further and further away and he felt he was in a little boat on a fathomless sea, under a starry sky, rocking gently into the unknown. He smiled to himself and let his mind go, deep into sleep, the residual warmth and faint light from the campfire the last thing he remembered.

He woke some time later in the cold and dark and it took him a while to work out where he was. It wasn't his bed, of that much he was certain. It was pitch dark; there were stars in the sky but the branches of the pines overhead more than blocked them out. Slowly, Batchelor remembered he was in the Black Hills, on the ground under a blanket. He reached a cautious hand behind him and encountered a leg, clad in serviceable denim and leather. It had all come back to him now. He was lying back to back with Matthew Grand, in a scrape in the ground. Somewhere in the dark were men of the Seventh Cavalry, the Wild I. If he wasn't safe here, where would he be safe?

Although still by no means comfortable, he started to drift off to sleep again. Grand shifted in his sleep and muttered. The snores and wind reached a crescendo and then, as suddenly as if he had gone deaf, Batchelor could hear nothing but the beat of his heart. Then nothing at all except a footfall, regular and soft, which began somewhere up the hillside and came on down, not disturbing so much as a pebble, just pace, pace, pace, as if a guardsman was parading in carpet slippers. But the guards were yards away, below the bluffs with the horses. He heard it go out of earshot down the hill and realized he was holding his breath. He let it out with a sigh and pinched himself to make sure he was awake. Then it came again, as regular as a clock, the unmistakeable sound of someone in soft shoes, pacing heel to toe down the slope and away beyond the bluff below the camp.

On the third repeat, Batchelor could stand it no longer and poked Grand in the thigh with a trembling finger.

'Wha—?' Grand sat up with commendable speed, his hand on his gun.

'Hush, Matthew,' Batchelor hissed. 'There's someone in the camp.'

'Of course,' Grand began, but got an elbow in the ribs for his pains.

Batchelor put his mouth close to his ear. 'I don't mean one of us. I mean, someone else. Listen.'

Both men froze and strained their ears so they could almost hear the click of rocks cooling in the night air. Then, just as Batchelor was beginning to fear he had imagined it, the footfalls came again, soft as a thought, down the hill and away around the bluff.

Grand and Batchelor sat silently, shoulder to shoulder, not speaking. Finally, Grand broke the silence.

'What the hell was that?'

'You're asking me? I thought you were the seasoned camperout? I don't even go for a walk in the park after dark, so I am probably the last man alive you should ask.' Batchelor was now cold and tetchy as well as frightened out of his wits.

'It must be . . . a hostile, I suppose. But why would he just walk through the camp like that? They go for horses, if anything. And in fact, it can't be just one, can it? How would he get back up the hill so fast? How many of these have you heard?' Grand was beginning to think practically.

Batchelor thought. 'I don't know. Five?'

'In that case . . .' Grand stopped to listen as the footsteps went past again. He interrupted himself. 'Did you notice anything?'

Batchelor turned in the dark to look at his colleague. 'Apart from the footsteps sneaking through the camp, do you mean?' he hissed.

'Yes, I mean apart from that. No breathing. No creak of leather, clothes rustling. Just the footsteps. That's weird.'

'Do you fellers mind shutting the hell up?' The voice in their ears made the enquiry agents jump. 'Some of us're trying to sleep here.'

The blast of whiskey made them pretty certain it was Bloody Knife.

'It's . . . it's the footsteps,' Batchelor began.

'Consarn it,' the scout said, sliding back into the darkness almost as silently as he had appeared. 'If'n you can't sleep for the Nightwalkers, then you shouldn't'a come on a hunt. They're just watching the sacred places, is all. Go to sleep and if you can't sleep, shut the hell up, like I says.'

The two men sat back to back for a while, like bookends. Then, by common consent, they slid down into sleeping positions and stayed like that, wide-eyed, until dawn.

He could see them clearly now through the sights he'd had fitted to his Sharps buffalo gun; two men out for a ride on the High Plains. From time to time, they stopped to swig from their canteens; one of them bent in the saddle to pick flowers.

Charley Reynolds clicked his teeth and shook his head. Lambs to the slaughter. He slid down the rock to where his mount chewed the long grass and swung into the saddle, spurring westwards behind the mountain ridge. His pinto knew this ground as well as his rider, and when Lonesome Charley wanted to, he could ride for miles, making no sound at all. He knew the pair would reach the bluffs and, long before they did, he was waiting for them, rifle in hand, hammer cocked.

'Hello, boys.'

The cavalrymen pulled up sharp, one of them all but dropping his canteen in surprise.

'Easy, now,' the scout said. 'I could have picked you assholes off at any point along the ridge, but chose not to. Don't make me plug you now. Might spook the horses.'

'Come on, Charley,' the younger trooper said, wiping his mouth, 'Give us a break. We was just out for the ride.'

The scout looked at the pair. Tomlinson was in Benteen's company, a blond, gangly, awkward boy who looked too young for this man's army. His fellow-deserter was the Prussian cuss, the one from Schwabmünchen whose name Reynolds couldn't pronounce.

'Out for a ride?' the scout smiled. 'Well, ain't that nice? Turn your mounts around, boys. We're going back.'

'*Nein*,' the Prussian said. 'You have no authority over us, Herr Reynolds; you are only a scout.'

'You're absolutely right,' Reynolds said, 'but this is a Sharps rifle that'll blow a hole in you the size of a bull buffalo's pizzle, so that sort of gives me authority, don't it? Now, very gently, I want you to lift those side irons out of your holsters and drop them on the ground.'

The pair looked at each other. Tomlinson had known Reynolds for a couple of years. He knew him to be a fair man, but not one to cross if the wind was in a certain direction. Baumgartner didn't know him at all, but he knew what a buffalo gun could do at close quarters. Gingerly, they eased their Remingtons out of the leather and threw them on to the grass.

'Now the carbines.'

The rifles followed suit.

'Now, let's see how much drill you soldier-boys have mastered during your time with the Seventh. Twos right!'

The horses' heads and ears pricked up and Tomlinson half-turned, taking his mount with him to wheel in formation. Baumgartner hadn't moved, however, and merely sat there, folding his arms.

'*Nein*,' he said again.

'Well, ain't you a stubborn son of a bitch?' Reynolds muttered, and blasted a shot with the Sharps. The bullet whizzed high over Baumgartner's head, but it served its purpose and the Prussian somersaulted over his horse's rump in surprise, landing in the tall grass with the air knocked out of him.

'You too, Tomlinson.' Reynolds had recocked his weapon. 'Dismount.'

For a moment, the trooper hesitated, then, seeing the cold light in Reynolds's eyes, obeyed the command. The scout swung into his own saddle and trotted forward, bending to pick up the reins of the troopers' animals. He began to lead them away.

'Hey!' Tomlinson shouted. Baumgartner was still fighting for breath. 'You can't do that!'

'Do what?' Reynolds called back over his shoulder.

'Take our horses,' Tomlinson said. 'We'll be sitting ducks for hostiles out here on foot.'

Reynolds swung his horse around to face the deserters. 'You stupid little shit,' he hissed. 'You're sitting ducks for hostiles whether you're on foot or in the saddle. Like I said, I could have picked you off at any time in the last half-hour. So could a Lakota. Anyhow, I'm doing you cusses a favour. Deserting from the United States cavalry is one thing. Stealing government-branded horses is altogether another – they'd hang you for that. And I *have* left you your guns, given you an even chance against hostiles. Oh, sure, an Oglala or Hunkpapa warrior can loose three arrows before you've so much as cocked your rifle, but, hey, that's life, ain't it?'

'No, no,' Tomlinson shuffled forward.

'*Nein*,' Baumgartner had found his voice too. 'What will they do to us?' he asked Reynolds, 'if we go back?'

'A lot less than *they'll* do to you if you don't,' Reynolds pointed to the rocky horizon.

Both soldiers followed his fingers but saw nothing.

'Who?' Tomlinson asked. 'I can't see nobody.'

Reynolds chuckled, 'My point exactly,' he said. 'Mount up, boys. It's a long ride back.'

'Good morning, good morning, good morning!' George Custer was up and about and making sure everyone knew it. He had slept like a log and was bright eyed and bushy tailed. 'You look tired, Mr Batchelor. Bad night?' He didn't mean to poke fun at the Limey but really – he had never visited London but was pretty sure that if he did, he would sleep soundly.

Batchelor hugged his coffee mug and looked up. 'A bit disturbed,' he muttered. 'Footsteps, you know . . .'

'Footsteps?' Custer roared. 'Fetch me the outposts!' Two troopers appeared as though by magic. 'Footsteps, the man says. Did we have intruders in the night?'

The guards snickered. 'No, sir!' they chorused.

'Then . . . dreaming, eh?' Custer was suddenly avuncular.

'Nah, Custer.' Bloody Knife wandered past, a hunk of cold meat in his hand. 'Just the Nightwalkers is all.'

Custer looked doubtful. 'Nightwalkers, here? How so? I haven't heard of them this far north.'

Bloody Knife shrugged. 'You dog-faces keep disturbing

Lakota land, the Nightwalkers will have more ground to protect.'

Reilly stepped out from behind a thorn bush, pulling up his braces and hitching the crotch of his britches. 'I heard 'em,' he said. 'Went past a time or two.'

Custer was crestfallen. 'I wish you'd woken me, Reilly,' he said. 'I haven't heard a Nightwalker in years.'

Batchelor followed the conversation with goggling eyes. 'You mean . . . ghosts?'

Reilly laughed. 'Not like you think of them, Mr Batchelor, no. They don't rattle no chains, nor have their heads under their arms. You can't see 'em. They're the spirits of the place, looking out for their own. They won't hurt you.'

'You'll just have to let this one go, James,' Grand said from the edge of the campfire. 'I doubt any of us will ever understand this place.'

Reilly started kicking sand over the fire. 'If you's all have finished drinking and eating,' he bellowed, 'Captain Keogh wants all men saddled in five minutes.'

Captain Keogh had had no such intention. He was content to let the morning sun warm the night chill from his bones, but he could tell an order filtered down from the General when he heard one and tipped the remains of his coffee on to the ground. 'Yo, men,' he called. 'Let's get your asses in those saddles and we're off in five.'

From a crowd of men all dressed the same and lolling round a smouldering fire, the hunting party was suddenly transformed into a unit of crack fighting men. Still more used to the uniforms of the British army, Batchelor suddenly saw the cavalrymen with new eyes. Despite the apparent casual attitude to soldiering, in fact they could whip any fighting force that could be thrown at them; there was a true camaraderie there. It made him proud to be an adoptive American, even just for a while.

A trooper brought his horse to him and he even remembered to get on from the right side. This cavalry thing must be catching.

The company wound its way through the foothills, heading down all the way but taking a circuitous route. Keogh had some new men with him and this was an opportunity to get some training under their belt that they would never have had at Jefferson Barracks on the Missouri. There was nothing quite like on-the-spot action and, as they meandered through the scrub and brush, clinging to life between the towering rocks, he rode up and down the column, pointing out places where hostiles could be lurking, hidden clefts in the rock which could open out into a space where a complete raiding party could lurk in ambush.

'Smoke ahead!' One of the outriders had spotted a faint plume against the unbroken blue of the sky.

'Now,' Keogh said to his men, 'we all know that this is probably just a prospectors' campfire, but it might not be. O'Riordan? How should we proceed?'

'Dismount, sir. Split into groups, circle round and check. If it's hostiles, clean them up. If it's prospectors, say howdy and move on.'

A wave of laughter rippled down the rank and Custer made a mental note to watch this man, who was a bit too clever by half.

Keogh nodded and raised an arm. 'What he said.' He spoke low but his voice carried, ricocheting off the rocks. 'Quiet now.' He backed down the line and spoke to Grand and Batchelor. 'It probably *is* prospectors,' he said, 'but if you gents would rather . . .' he wasn't sure how to word the next bit. He knew Grand had some cavalry miles under his saddle, but the Limey was a civilian, through and through.

Batchelor spoke for them both. 'If we won't be in your way, Captain Keogh, we'll come along.' He had learned already that safety lay in numbers. Waiting behind a rock while the rest of the company moved off was the best way of getting an arrow in your back, or worse.

'Then if you would follow Sergeant Reilly, gentlemen,' and Keogh rode off to check the rest of his men.

Leaving the horses hobbled in the narrow cut between the rocks, the men swarmed over the hot boulders in all directions. To a Lakota they would have sounded like a herd of buffalo playing war horns, but for a cavalry regiment they moved like snakes. Soon, they had the source of the smoke surrounded and yes, the first thoughts were the right ones; it *was* a prospectors' fire. What no one had predicted, though, was that the prospectors in question – three of them, though from a distance it was hard to tell – would be lying dead and bloody, surrounded by clouds of flies. One had a turkey vulture pecking in a desultory fashion at his chest but it looked at first glance as if the best pickings had already been had.

Keogh pointed silently at three of his most hardened men. This was no scene for the new recruits. Keogh was finding it hard not to throw up – he didn't need men incapacitated for the ride home. And he would need a burial party. He pointed to six more. The men climbed down the rocks into the little dried-out gully. It was clear that the prospectors were greenhorns. No one with even a day's experience would have camped there. A storm like they had had the other night would have washed them and their camp away, to dash them on the rocks on their way down to the Rosebud river.

Custer raised a buckskinned arm and gathered the other men to him. He spoke in low tones because it was impossible to be too careful. 'It's clear, men, that this is a hostile attack. From here, it looks as though it happened early this morning, as they were getting up. So they are probably long gone. But even so, we must sweep the area. If one of them is still here, just one, we will hunt him down and make him pay for what he did to those innocent men down there. If we find the entire party, so much the better. So, men, mount up and let's go. No quarter, not to man, woman nor child.'

Batchelor turned troubled eyes to Grand who raised a hand.

'No, James. This isn't the time for the "is that fair?" speech. No, it isn't. But if you want to live to get back to the fort, you will have to put yourself in Custer's hands. Don't forget, that child you helped Reynolds bury was equipped for war. Trust no one.' He caught Batchelor's eye. 'Except Custer.'

Down in the valley, Keogh's men worked in silence. There was nothing taken from the camp but it was as though a whirlwind had passed through it, with blankets, shovels, picks and tents hurled every which way. One of the prospectors had a pick through the back of his head, the others were peppered with arrows. All had been scalped. Their heads were matted crimson with their own blood and their thighs and arms had been slashed. None of them would ever dig again for the yellow metal the white man craved. There was nothing but sand washed through in floods, just inches thick on rock, so the burial party made the men decent and left them to the elements. They didn't want to do it, but there was so little left that it would not even have been possible to sling them across a saddle to get them back to the fort. Using the details from their wallets, torn apart, with dollar bills fluttering in the breeze across the sand, one of the party scratched their names on the wall of the gully – it seemed a shame that a hunt for gold had ended like this, but Keogh had lost count of the number of hopefuls who stopped off at the fort asking directions. Some of them, for God's sake, still wearing the brand-new duds they had picked up in some Mom and Pop in Bismarck, without a grain of dust on them, the bright shiny shovels strapped to their backs with a triumph of hope over experience. Keogh found a book, clotted with blood, but he could still read the title; *Prospecting for Beginners*. He shook his head, chuckling grimly; you couldn't make it up. It should be against the law, in his opinion, to encourage the poor cusses. And now, the General would have to write home to three grieving families, to tell them that their men wouldn't be coming home with pockets full of gold; that they wouldn't be coming home at all, not even in a box.

Custer's detail rode silently through the foothills until they were almost back on the plain. They all knew that once the raiding party were in the open, they would be gone and would never be identified. Their only hope was to find them still among the rocks where they couldn't move much faster than the cavalrymen. After a mile or two, Reilly nudged Custer and, without moving his head, cast his eyes up and to the left. Sure enough, just visible above the edge of the highest rock, silhouetted against the sky, was a dark head which bobbed down almost immediately. Custer nodded imperceptibly and put a hand down by his side to halt the column. They knew what to do, even the new recruits and the civilian; self-preservation is a wonderful teacher.

As one, they slid down from their saddles and crept along, shielded by their horses. Losing a horse was serious; losing your own life was worse, and every man knew they were in danger of doing just that. They all walked along, listening for the hiss of an arrow through the air and hoping it wasn't headed for them. The rumour was that you didn't hear the one that killed you, but who could possibly ever prove it if no one lived to tell that tale?

'Long Hair!' A voice rang out from above and the General looked up. Against the sky, a magnificent figure rose up, with a feathered war lance in his hand. He shook it in the air and, almost as soon as the men below him had realized he was there, he was gone again, whoops and cries from his men filling the echoes. No hissing arrows followed his appearance and soon there was nothing but the whickering of nervous horses to be heard. Custer stood up and looked around. Could it be that Gall – because he couldn't believe it wasn't Gall – would be content with counting coup on this occasion? Perhaps his men had slaked their thirst for dog-face blood with the prospectors. Reilly, not to be outdone, stood beside him, perhaps an inch or two taller and what looked like twice as broad. Slowly, one by one, the rest of the men uncurled themselves too and began to remount. They hadn't caught the hostiles, but then on the other hand, they hadn't been caught either.

'Three cheers for the General,' one man cried. He didn't know why, but it was better than going hysterical, which was more the way he felt.

The rest of the men let rip. Being a soldier in this man's army didn't mean you couldn't be scared to death most of the time. The echoes did funny things to the cheers. The third one sounded very like a gunshot and a few small pebbles fell from the height.

Then all was chaos. Custer was shouting and the Limey and the captain from out east were running to the front of the column.

'Stretcher!' someone shouted, and the orderly at the back

of the column started to untie it from his saddle. He ran forward
with his kit. He didn't know what had happened, but his
training kicked him in the pants like a mule and he just did
what he had to do. At the front of the column, Sergeant Reilly
lay in the dust, a pool of blood spreading and soaking into
the ground. In his shoulder, a gaping hole showed where the
bullet had passed clean through. The orderly pulled out some
wadding from his pack and pressed it into the hole. Reilly's
eyes flew open.

'Steady there, soldier,' he muttered. 'That smarts.' Then his
eyes rolled up into his head and he went into blessed oblivion.

ELEVEN

Charley Reynolds wasn't a bad man. He chatted to the deserters on the way back to Fort Lincoln. It was probably the most he'd said in a whole year. And by the time they reached the hog-ranches, he'd determined to keep his mouth shut about the little matter of desertion and allow the pair to slip into the fort unnoticed. Captain Frederick Benteen had other ideas, however.

He stood like an ox in the furrow that afternoon, arms locked behind his back. It didn't help that Frabbie had been boring the pants off him over some trivial family matter and the colic from which he routinely suffered had returned with a vengeance.

'Charley Reynolds,' he hailed the scout as he rode up to the fort gates. 'You've got a couple of snowbirds there, I understand.'

'Boys just out for a ride, Captain,' Reynolds said, glancing at the men behind him.

'You,' Benteen pointed at the Prussian with his riding crop. 'Sauerkraut, you're in Captain Keogh's company, aren't you?'

'Yes, Hauptmann, sir.' Baumgartner sat upright in the saddle.

'Hauptmann, sir,' Benteen spat. 'Won't you Goddamned foreigners ever learn English?'

Charley Reynolds happened to know that Benteen's family hailed from Holland back in the day, but it was hardly his place to say so.

'You men,' the captain clicked his fingers, 'get them to the guardhouse. I want Companies D and I assembled to witness punishment at four o'clock sharp.'

Reynolds swung his leg over his horse's neck and approached Benteen direct. 'Couldn't you go easy, Captain?' he asked. 'Prussian cuss hasn't been with us long . . . and Tomlinson . . .'

'Tomlinson is an enlisted trooper in my own company, Reynolds,' Benteen turned on him. 'A disgrace to the uniform. I'll thank you to keep your civilian nose out of army affairs.'

Having got the answer he more or less expected, Reynolds fired the only salvo he had left. 'I shall have to report this to the fort commander,' he said, loudly. Soldiers standing around heard it with glee. Anybody who stood up to Benteen was all right in their book.

The captain was already marching away but he spun on his heel and went nose to nose with the scout. 'Very well,' he said, 'if you want to make a drum-head court martial out of what is actually a minor incident, so be it. Corporal Allen.'

The man leading away the deserters halted halfway across the parade ground. 'Sir?'

'Take these men to Major Reno's quarters. At the double.'

The little squad wheeled away.

Benteen saw the momentary surprise on Reynolds's face. 'The General is out hunting today,' he said, 'so Major Reno is acting commandant.' He let the silence speak for itself. Then he closed to Reynolds. 'Cheer up, Charley,' he murmured. 'If Custer had been here, he'd have had those two cowardly bastards shot.'

The party carrying Reilly had by necessity to travel slowly. He had lost a lot of blood and jolting could only make it worse. The orderly had slung the stretcher like an Indian travois behind his horse, but nobody could claim the Indian way was painless. Reilly woke up from time to time and anyone within earshot learned a lot of new words, many of them in Gaelic but all clearly very derogatory about horses, stretchers, men who couldn't march straight and, occasionally and when the slugs of whiskey which were his only painkiller began to really kick in, Custer.

'Where did that shot come from?' Batchelor asked Grand as they walked along in the line.

'Behind,' Grand said, simply.

'So . . . from the ranks, then?'

'Not necessarily,' Grand answered. 'Without knowing exactly how Reilly was standing when he was hit, then we can't tell the trajectory. But that seems to be the most obvious answer. Who could have done it, though? Surely, anyone would see if their neighbour suddenly shot the sergeant.'

'You would think so, certainly. *Could* it have been one of Gall's men? They had us surrounded, after all.' At least, that was the civilian Batchelor's understanding of what happened.

'The bullet has long gone, so we can't check that. But . . . I wouldn't like to be the brave who tried to pick off Custer. Gall has him earmarked for himself, if I am any judge. But in a fair fight, not underhand like this.'

'Custer? You think this is another shot at him?'

'Why not? Who would want to shoot Reilly?'

Batchelor fell silent. 'It seems a bit . . . complicated.'

'Complicated?'

'Well, how could anyone have arranged this? The prospectors, the raiding party? It must have been just a random piece of madness from a brave.'

Grand shrugged. 'You may be right. But I think we're going to need to look into a whole lot of alibis when we get back to the fort.'

'And question Reilly, see if he can think of anyone who bears him a grudge.'

'Question Reilly? Is that going to be . . . likely?' Grand couldn't help remembering the pool of blood soaking into the sand.

Batchelor shrugged. 'Trying to look on the bright side,' he murmured. And the little column wound its way across the grassy plain, to the accompaniment of Irish tunes of doubtful accuracy, as Reilly sang his way home.

Marcus Reno wasn't pleased to have his post-prandial drink interrupted. An army doctor had told him once that, in moderation, Scotch whisky was good for the body as well as the soul. That sounded like good advice to a man so far under the influence he sometimes didn't know what day it was. And the arrival of a punishment detail, all tramping boots, clicking heels and stiff salutes, was not designed to put any man at his ease.

'Yes, Captain Benteen?' Reno addressed the most senior man present.

'Snowbirds, Major,' Benteen answered, peeling off his white gloves and flinging himself down in a swivel chair in Reno's office.

'Names?' Reno narrowed his eyes, trying to focus on the pair in front of him. These days, most of the men looked the same to him. It would have been helpful if at least one or two had distinguishing features, such as a wooden leg, though even he would concede that wouldn't make for a first-class regiment.

Corporal Allen nudged the younger of them and the boy stepped forward. 'Tomlinson, Ezekiel, Number 45308, D Company, sir.'

Reno looked at the other man, fighting the urge to close one eye.

'Baumgartner, Manfred, Number 61842, I Company, Major.'

Reno didn't recognize the last word at first but a glance across at the writing of the clerk who was recording all this made it perfectly clear.

'The Wild I,' Reno smiled. 'I trust Captain Keogh will have some sort of explanation for this.'

He was looking at Benteen, a glance that expected an explanation from him too; after all, Tomlinson *was* in his company. In the event, nothing was forthcoming. There was a smugness about Fred Benteen that no one, not even Frabbie, could stand for long.

'Reynolds,' Reno called to the scout, leaning against his doorframe. 'You caught these men?'

'I did,' Reynolds said.

'They had taken army horses, weapons?'

'Well, now . . .'

'Yes or no, Reynolds?' Reno barked.

'Yes,' the scout sighed. None of this was going the way he wanted it.

For a moment, Reno contemplated the options. Then he pushed a ledger away from him on his desk and rested his hands on the scarred and ink-stained mahogany. 'I won't bore you gentlemen with the number of deserters we have in the army every year,' he said, 'or what it does to a regiment's morale. For the theft of horses and equipment, it's within my rights to have you shot. But,' he stood up and had to hold on to the edge of the desk for a moment while the room settled down and stopped spinning, 'it's well known that I am a generous man. Captain Benteen, Corporal Allen. Companies D and I to witness punishment. Branding and the lash. Oh, and give the band something to do. "Rogues March", slow time.'

It was the tune the band liked least, but an order was an order and they mounted their greys and struck up. The ladies of the regiment, officers' wives and the Other Ranks' women, preferred not to watch. The whole of D Company, and the remnants of the Wild I who had not gone on the hunt, stood with arms reversed, carbine butts against their shoulders in hollow square. On a dais under a makeshift awning, Major Reno and Captain Benteen were officiating.

'It goes without saying,' Reno bellowed so that everybody in the fort and beyond could hear him, 'that desertion and horse stealing in the United States army will not be tolerated. Forward, Troopers Tomlinson and . . .'

The clerk muttered in the major's ear.

'. . . Bormgarden.'

The men stepped forward. Neither of them wore his cap and their braces dangled from their breeches.

'Think yourselves lucky,' Reno said, 'that this is all you get. In another mood, on another day, you'd be facing a firing squad.' He nodded and everything happened at once. Two burly soldiers grabbed the deserters and forced them to their knees. Then they flipped them over sideways so that they were lying on their right sides. As a further indignity, their breeches and combinations were hauled down so that they were naked between waist and knees. There were whistles and guffaws from the watching civilians, grim faces from the soldiers of the Seventh. The fort Indians looked on solemnly, mesmerized by the barbarity of the dog-faces. Calam, the mule skinner, was the only woman to witness the scene. She'd seen a man with his trousers down before and no doubt would again. She spat a wad of tobacco into the Lincoln dust, fondly imagining that she had just spat at Reno and hit him full in the face.

'Farriers of the regiment,' the major called, 'do your duty.'

The blacksmiths had been stoking their fires for the past hour and the irons were ready. Two farriers, their trademark spur badges glinting on their sleeves, approached the men pinned to the ground. There was a scream from Tomlinson and the hiss of burning flesh as the first iron struck home. He twisted and writhed in the agony of the metal cutting into his skin just below the hip bone. The stench of the branding wisped up into the air and not a few troopers had to stifle their retching. When Reno was in this mood, throwing up could have them next for the burning. Baumgartner was made of sterner stuff. Although the tears trickled down his cheeks and his nose ran, his body barely reacted to the pain.

Reno noticed this and shouted, 'Again, farrier.'

The man hesitated, then reapplied the glowing 'D' in the same place.

Both men were hauled upright and given the choice of wriggling back into their breeches or not. Both took the option so that at least some of their dignity was intact, though the pain was even worse with the rough cloth chafing their new wounds. They stood shakily between their guards who were, in effect, holding them up.

'Farriers,' Reno's voice brought the thump of 'The Rogues March' to an end. 'One hundred lashes.'

The only officer on the dais who was not in the Reno–Benteen camp was Lieutenant Chater. He was young and still decidedly damp behind the ears and, at West Point, had gone through the pain and humiliation of hazing with the best of them. But, in the presence of a superior officer or not, he couldn't keep silent.

'Major Reno, in the name of God, enough is enough.'

Reno spun round and prodded the man in the chest. 'Chater,' he snarled, 'until you've earned another bar on your shoulder, you'll keep your Goddamned mouth shut. Do I make myself clear?'

Chater blinked. Reno on the charge was as terrifying as Custer. A nerve jumped in his cheek. 'Perfectly, sir,' he said, 'but the conditions of war . . .'

'What the hell do you know about the conditions of war? I was killing Confederates along the Shenandoah while you were still shitting yellow. Go to your quarters, sir, before both of us say something we'll regret.'

'But . . .'

In the event, it was the band that ended Chater's sentence
for him. 'The Rogues March' had suddenly given way to the
wholly inappropriate 'Garryowen'. Reno was outraged, his eyes
whirling everywhere for insubordination. He'd put the entire
band on a charge for this. Then his eyes locked on the fort
gates and the change of tune made sense. He saw the red and
blue guidon flapping, the buckskin, fringed jacket and the horse
with the white blaze. Custer and the Seventh Cavalry had
arrived.

'Officer commanding!' somebody roared above the band and
the whole square came to attention.

Custer rode up to the dais, steadying Dandy as he cara-
coled alongside the platform. 'Reno,' he returned the major's
salute. 'What's going on here?'

'Punishment for desertion, General,' Reno said.

Custer looked at the snowbirds standing forlornly with their
braces still dangling. 'Branding?' he asked Reno.

'I was about to follow up with the lash, sir,' the major said.

Custer's cold blue eyes flashed. 'Were you involved in this,
Benteen?' he snapped.

Myles Keogh eased his left leg out of the stirrup and hooked
it over the pommel, the position he usually adopted when he
was about to enjoy himself.

'It was my decision, General,' Benteen said. 'I merely
consulted my superior officer.'

'And it's a pity, Major Reno, that you did not consult yours.'

'Sir?'

Custer swung out of the saddle and bounced up the steps
to stand level with his insubordinate subordinates. 'The next
time you decide arbitrarily to try to run this fort, I'll have you
court-martialled.'

Reno's mouth hung open. 'In your absence, General,' he
blustered, 'I *am* in command.'

Custer closed to the man, looking him straight in the eyes.
'Reno,' he said, 'your trouble is you have delusions of gran-
deur. *I* wear the stars here, sir, and don't you forget it. Tell
me, are you determined to end your career as ignominiously
as you began it? We don't give West Point demerits here,

Major, we give insubordinate drunks a loaded revolver and the chance to do what's right and proper, for once.' Reno was speechless. Custer's eyes swivelled to the right. 'Don't stand there like you've shat yourself, Benteen. If one of those snow-birds is in your company, you'd better do something about it. Something more constructive than beat the bejasus out of him and burn him to death. You!'

Corporal Allen was next in the General's line of fire and he snapped to attention.

'I've got a man here injured. Get him to Dr Madden. Then, these two. I want them patched up post-haste.'

'Very good, sir.'

Custer jumped down on to the parade ground and, without bothering to turn round, called back to Reno and Benteen, 'Keep out of my sight, gentlemen, for your own sakes.' And he marched off to his quarters.

Grand was still sitting his horse as Keogh dismissed the hunting party. 'And that, James my boy,' he said, 'is how to win friends and influence people.'

Batchelor winced as his buttocks reacted to a change of position out of the saddle. 'He was on your side in the war, wasn't he? Custer?'

'Holy Jesus and Mother of God!' was one of the milder of Sergeant Reilly's expletives as he lay on the hard boards of Dr Madden's operating theatre that night.

'There's no need for blasphemy, Sergeant,' Madden upbraided him, dabbing at his wound with a swab.

'There might not be,' Reilly grunted, 'from where you're standing.'

From where he was standing, Madden could tell that the soldier would live. He had the constitution of an ox and the orneriness of a mule; it was a winning combination out West.

'Jenkins,' the doctor summoned his orderly, 'your eyes are younger than mine. Sew up this hole, would you? I'm low on laudanum, so any rotgut the sergeant has in his belongings'll do.'

'That's just grand!' Reilly groaned. 'I've got a hole in my

shoulder serving Uncle Sam and I've got to find me own whiskey to staunch the pain.'

'You're fine, Sarge,' Jenkins said. He had already patched the man up, strapped him on to the travois and got him back safely to the fort. All in all, he might have expected Reilly to be a little more grateful.

'I'll be the judge of that,' the sergeant grunted. 'And go easy with that blanket-stitch, you bastard. As long as I've got one arm left, I can flog a little shit like you into line.'

'It'll be my pleasure, Sergeant,' Jenkins said. 'Delighted to be of service. You'll thank me later and so on.'

Madden chuckled. It was when men didn't make jokes like this that he worried. He wiped his pince-nez on a piece of bloody cloth and made for the door. Here, he paused. 'I'll look in on you in the morning, Reilly,' he said.

'Can't wait,' the Irishman muttered, and let rip with another string of invective as the needlewoman in Trooper Jenkins went to work.

'Oh.' Madden caught sight of the snowbirds still waiting for treatment. 'I'd forgotten about you two.'

'Doctor.' Matthew Grand stepped into the surgery, followed by James Batchelor. 'Could we have a word?'

Madden adjusted his pince-nez. 'Not fort fever, is it?' he frowned. 'We haven't had a case in weeks.'

'No,' Batchelor said. 'It's . . . personal.'

Madden gave him a strange look. He didn't take either of the visitors for men who would frequent My Lady's Bower, but you could never tell. But he was pretty well stocked with mercury, as it happened, so Cupid's Measles should cause few problems.

'In private,' Grand nodded towards the deserters.

'Er . . . oh, yes, I see. Drop your britches, gentlemen. Don't be shy. I am a medical man, after all.'

Grudgingly, Tomlinson and Baumgartner obliged. Madden bent down and peered at both hips. 'Hmm,' he said. 'You've been burned.'

Tomlinson rolled his eyes. It never ceased to amaze him how precise medical science had become, and in only several thousand years too.

'Here,' Madden rummaged in a desk in his outer office, angling the oil lamp so that he could see what he was doing. 'Put some of that on. A poultice would be good. And no riding for a day or two. Can't pretend it won't hurt.'

The men hitched up their trousers and saluted. At the door, Madden stopped them. 'And next time,' he said, suddenly toeing the military line, 'perhaps you'll think twice about deserting. Now, gentlemen, to business.' He offered Grand and Batchelor chairs and sat snugly behind his desk. 'What seems to be the trouble?'

'Reilly,' Grand said.

'What about him?'

'Will he live?' Batchelor asked.

'God, yes. For as long as any of us, anyway. I'm sure he'd be touched by your concern.'

'Did you find the bullet?' Grand asked.

'No,' Madden admitted. 'Must have gone straight through.'

'In which direction?' Batchelor pitched in.

Madden frowned at him, then at Grand. 'Look, what's going on?' he asked.

'Humour us, Doctor,' Grand said. 'Did the bullet hit Reilly in the back or the front?'

'The back, definitely,' Madden said. 'That was the entry wound, as we medical men say. To the right of the spine, bounced off the shoulder blade and exited . . . about here, just down from the . . . er . . . clavichord.'

'Shot from behind,' Batchelor was thinking aloud.

'Yes,' Madden said. 'Not what I would expect from a man like Reilly. He's more the sort to be standing four-square up to a savage, not running away. Course, I know they're sneaky sons of bitches, always creeping up on a fella unexpectedly.'

'Yes,' Grand said, getting up. 'Yes, that must be it.'

'But . . .' Batchelor was on his feet too.

'When will Sergeant Reilly be well enough to visit?' Grand asked, genially.

'He's been taking slugs of whiskey to dull the pain,' the doctor told him. 'But when that wears off, then I don't see why you couldn't drop in. It's good of you to take the trouble.'

'No trouble,' Grand assured him. 'We'll be back in the

morning. Meanwhile, we'll let you get on. You must be busy.'

Madden looked around. The snowbirds had flown. Reilly hadn't uttered an oath in perhaps five minutes. He supposed he was busy, by his usual standards, but he was going home to his dinner, nonetheless.

The back room of the Dew Drop Inn was not for everyone. The barman had strict instructions to never let Calamity Jane Cannary in no matter how much she begged. No Other Ranks. No mule skinners. No drunks – no drunks on admission, that was. They could get as drunk as they liked once they were inside and in fact, as far as Jim Thompson was concerned, the drunker the better. He had often been heard to say that the colour of a drunk's money was the same as everyone else's, except that it got spent easier.

Tonight the company was very exclusive. Thompson had taken up residence at his usual early hour. Losing the sutler concession had put a crease in his income, it was true, but it hadn't dried up altogether. He still had My Lady's Bower bringing in more than a man could spend in a six-month and, as he was the first owner who didn't take his rent in kind, he was not only richer than his predecessors but also in noticeably better health. The Dew Drop Inn would never let him down, he knew that. A saloon in a fort was like having your own private gold mine, without the digging. He sat in his favourite chair, blowing gently on the end of his cigar to make it draw and having a manicure from one of the cleaner ladies.

There was a discreet tap on the door and the barman put his head round. 'Beg pardon, Mr Thompson, sir, but Major Reno and Captain Benteen are asking if they may come in.'

Shaking off the attendant lady, Thompson waved a lordly hand. 'Send 'em through, Fergus, send 'em through. I could do with some company.' He flicked a half-dollar at the manicurist and sent her on her way. As forty-five cents of it was coming back to him anyway, he didn't consider it over-generous.

Benteen and Reno slunk in like two caned schoolboys. Thompson swivelled in his chair to watch them approach his table.

'Join you?' Reno said. His eyes were bloodshot, but then they usually were. The best that most people could do when assessing Reno's sobriety was to say that he was drunk. Thompson, something of an expert, could do better; he assessed him as being half a bottle from being unconscious. Never mind; there was a back door so he wouldn't need to be carried out feet first through all the men having an evening drink.

'Be my guest.' Thompson pushed out a chair with a foot and gestured to Benteen to take the other. 'What are you gentlemen drinking?' This evening probably wouldn't be a great one as regards profit margins, but there was a lot to be learned about Custer from these two, who exuded malice like a bad smell.

Before either of them could answer, there was another tap at the door. 'Mr Kellogg says . . .'

'Send him in,' Thompson said, magnanimously. 'And send in a fresh bottle when he comes through, there's a good feller.'

Mark Kellogg was noticeably more sober than either of the officers. In fact, he hadn't had a serious drink in months and was consequently clear-eyed and alert. 'Gentlemen,' he pulled over a chair from an adjoining table, 'mind if I join you?'

Reno looked at him and tried to remember who he was. 'Free country,' he muttered, then looked around. 'Where's the drink?'

'I have it here,' Kellogg said, placing it on the table. He fished out a complicated-looking knife from his vest pocket and chose a corkscrew from its many blades. With a deft movement he cut the wax and extracted the stopper. Thompson reached behind him and grabbed three more glasses from the sideboard and Kellogg filled them to the brim. 'Your good health, gentlemen,' he said and sipped genteelly. Reno downed his in one, Benteen in two. Like Kellogg, Thompson took a sip.

'Nice to see you gentlemen,' the ex-sutler said. 'It isn't often I have such stimulating company in my humble parlour.'

'Don't wanna drink at home,' Reno slurred. 'Mary don' like me drinking inna house.'

As far as Thompson had heard, that was about the only place on the face of the earth that Reno didn't drink. But he could see Mrs Reno's point. 'Well, we're all friends here,' he topped up Reno's glass, 'so feel free.'

Reno knocked back the drink again and sat back, staring into space. Benteen was already looking worse than Reno though he had drunk far less; he just didn't have the head for it.

'I hear you gents had a bit of a run-in with the General this afternoon,' Thompson said, quiet as a snake in Eden.

Benteen raised a hand, palm down, and wobbled it.

'Fair enough what you did, I'd say,' Thompson pursued. 'Deserters need a whipping, otherwise how would any of them learn?'

''S true!' Benteen came suddenly to life and made everyone jump. 'I've known him shoot deserters.'

'Really?' Kellogg looked mildly at Benteen. 'Is that story true?'

'True's I'm sitting here,' Benteen said. 'During the war, I knew officers who he sent out to round 'em up and shoot 'em like dogs.' He slumped into his chair again and dropped his chin on to his chest. 'Like dogs.'

'But in wartime, that's different, I guess.' Thompson was probing the problem like a tongue in a sore tooth.

'*This* is wartime!' Reno suddenly said. 'If this isn't war, I don't know what is. Those troopers, they ran off with horses and . . . and . . . guns and who knows what else. Thieves and deserters. They deserved more'n they got and that's the truth.'

Another tap on the door made everyone turn. The barman was by now beyond apologetic. He didn't have to disturb the boss this many times in a week as a rule. 'It's a Mister . . .' he put his head back round the door to speak to whoever it was in the front room '. . . Grand and a . . .'

'Show 'em in, show 'em in. The more the merrier.' Thompson hadn't met the famous visitors to the fort. It would be amusing to see what the Englishman made of his Special Brand Whiskey, made out on the prairie by a couple of renegades he had employed for the purpose. While Grand and Batchelor came in and greeted the men already present, Thompson busied himself pushing two tables together.

'More friendly,' he said, as he put the bottle and glasses

back down. 'Let me call Fergus to bring some hog crackling
And some peanuts. Chat goes better when there's something
to chaw.' He raised his chin and his voice. 'Fergus!' The
barman scuttled in. 'A bottle of Special Brand and some vittles
Some chittlins, some crackling, some goober peas and . . .
why not, some pickles.' He smiled around at his guests. 'Let's
make a night of it, shall we, gents?'

'How's Sergeant Reilly?' Kellogg asked politely.

'Alive,' Grand said, shortly.

'Only, I couldn't help noticing you coming out of the sanitorium a while back,' the journalist explained.

'Well, as we were there when he was shot,' Batchelor said
'it seemed only civil.' He turned to Benteen and Reno. 'You'l
probably be glad to hear that your men are both on the mend
as well.'

Thompson almost rubbed his hands. It was going to be
one of *those* evenings. He hoped the furniture would stand
it – he had had some corking fights in his parlour, but i
could come expensive in mahogany.

Benteen smiled but only with his teeth. Reno didn't seem
to have heard.

'Indeed,' Kellogg said, 'I must speak to you gentlemen after
this evening's entertainment to ask for your views. For my
readers, you know.'

'You'd write up the branding?' Batchelor was surprised
Although it was news in a way, equally, it wasn't, and he couldn't
imagine any editor of his ever allowing the story to run.

'Not for the *Tribune*,' Kellogg said smoothly. 'But I might
be able to syndicate it to some of the papers back East. No,
I was thinking of the shooting of Sergeant Reilly.'

'Reilly deserves all he gets,' Reno suddenly exploded.
'Trailing around with a piece of garbage like Custer. Lie down
with dogs, get up with fleas, that's what I say.'

'Reilly got a bit more than fleas,' Grand observed. 'He
almost bled to death.'

Reno shrugged. 'Whatever. If he kept away from that skunk,
he wouldn't get shot and beaten up.'

'Reilly's been with the General a long time,' Thompson
said. 'Loyalty is a wonderful thing, I say.' As if on cue, Fergus

the barman came into the room, balancing a tray of food and with a bottle of Special Brand under his arm. There was a silence as he spread it all out in front of the guests.

Grand and Batchelor had never met a buffet they didn't like – except perhaps that one time when they had done some work for Bert Bosomworth the Cowheel King – and were soon nibbling nuts and pickles while they watched Benteen and Reno get more and more morose. Grand decided to poke the anthill.

'Custer can be a difficult cuss,' he remarked. 'Why, when I was at West Point with him . . .'

'West Point, West Point,' muttered Reno. 'I'm tired of the very name. You'd think none of us had done anything since. West Point ain't everything, you know. Benteen's a lucky son of a bitch – he never went there. Besides, that skunk Custer didn't do so well, if memory serves.'

Grand shrugged. 'No, he . . .'

'So, how'd he get to be commanding a fort? How'd he get to *still* be commanding a fort after he had it stripped off him?' Reno was gathering momentum now. 'Because of people he *knows*, that's how. He fills the darned place with his family, idiots every consarned one of them. Tom's an asshole. Autie Reed belongs in some kind of home. He surely shouldn't be lieutenant. I've got fleas on my dog with more brains'n him.'

Kellogg smiled and patted Reno's arm. 'Again with the fleas, Marcus. They're persistent little critters, I'll give them that.'

Benteen weighed in. 'I think something ought to be done about the cuss. He couldn't run a store – begging your pardon, Thompson – let alone a fort. That wife of his is no better than she should be, neither. Sucking up to that Limey . . . ow, what?' He jumped and looked under the table, to where Kellogg's boot had fetched him a nasty one on the ankle. Then he looked up and saw Batchelor, who was putting down a handful of peanuts on the table and seemed to be squaring his shoulders prior to giving him a darned good whupping, if he was any judge. 'Begging your pardon, Mr Batchelor, I . . . well, I clean forgot you were there, to tell the truth.' He looked round the table and got up, unsteadily. 'I think I'm going now. I . . . need to sober up a bit before I go back to Frabbie. She doesn't like it when I drink.' Stifling a hiccough, he wove his way across the room and out the back door.

Thompson looked on indulgently. 'If all the wives didn't mind the men drinking in the house, I would be bankrupt,' he said.

Reno looked at the chair where Benteen had lately been sitting. 'Where's Fred gone?'

'Home,' Kellogg said. 'And I don't mind telling you, Marcus, perhaps you should join him.'

Reno looked out of one eye, then the other. It still made no sense. 'I don' think Frabbie would let me in,' he said, suddenly wise. 'She don' like drinking in the house.' Nevertheless, he got up and followed Benteen, but not until he had fallen over two chairs and an occasional table.

Thompson got up and righted the furniture. Then he strolled back to the others. 'Why are those things called occasional tables?' he wondered aloud.

'That's one question,' Batchelor said. 'The other is why do those two hate George Custer so much?'

'Reasons as listed,' Kellogg said. 'He has been promoted above his station, he is vain, autocratic, pretty stupid in the scheme of things. Do they need more?'

'Would they try to kill him, though?' Grand wondered.

'*Kill* him?' Thompson's eyebrows rose. 'Kill Custer?' He mused on the idea for a while. 'I don't like the cuss any more than they do. He took my sutler's store away from me and if it wasn't for my . . . other interests . . . I would be starving in a gutter for all he feels. But I want to break the cuss, not *kill* him. Killing is too good for him, ask my opinion.'

Grand and Batchelor both felt he was protesting a little too much. 'Where were you this afternoon, Mr Thompson?' Batchelor asked the question for them both.

Thompson pursed his lips and looked at the ceiling, then at Batchelor. 'Why?'

'I was just wondering,' the enquiry agent said. 'It was when Reilly was shot.'

'I've got no argument with Reilly,' Thompson said.

'He was just inches from Custer,' Grand pointed out. Did he really have to paint a picture?

'Oh, I see. You think that not only did I shoot Reilly, but that I couldn't hit a barn door at a hundred paces. Well, in the latter, you would be right.' Thompson spread the sides of his coat to reveal nothing more threatening than a pair of rather greasy trousers. 'I don't even carry a gun because it would be an invitation to disaster. So, that covers the first bit; no, I didn't shoot Reilly. I was here, stocktaking.' He called out. 'Fergus!'

The barman appeared like a rabbit from a hat. 'Yes, Mr Thompson?'

'Where was I this afternoon?'

Fergus looked a little hunted. Questions like that could have so many answers.

'Really, where was I?'

'You mean *really*, Mr Thompson?'

'Yes. Well, after the bit with . . . you know, Mrs . . . you know. After that.'

'Oh.' Fergus sagged with relief. No point in meeting trouble halfway. 'After *that*, you were stocktaking here, with me.'

Thompson spread his arms. 'There you are, gentlemen. That was my afternoon. A little recreation and then stocktaking.'

'I suppose,' Kellogg said suddenly, 'that you want to know where I was too, gentlemen?'

'If you wouldn't mind,' Grand said politely.

'I won't ask again why you want to know,' Kellogg said. 'Anyone would think you were enquiry agents or some-such. But in answer to the question you haven't asked me, I was not enjoying recreation with Mrs – or even Miss – anyone. Nor, of course, was I stocktaking. I went for a walk.'

'A walk?' Grand and Batchelor had heard some poor alibis in their time but this one was so bad it almost had to be true. 'Did you meet anyone?' Grand asked.

'Not a soul. I watched some squaws weaving blankets. A couple of dogs. That was all.'

'How did your article go? The one on the ladies' point of view?'

Kellogg shrugged. 'Didn't write a word.'

'Won't your editor mind?'

'Old Clem is an understanding old cuss. He'll be glad of anything I send in, when I send it.'

Batchelor sighed for all the times he had been shouted at by an editor for a single spelling error in par ten and wished he knew Mr Lounsbury. Something was niggling him, though, and he couldn't put his finger on it.

'So, I didn't shoot Reilly either, gentlemen. Though I could if I wanted to.' Suddenly, with no warning, the journalist threw a dollar in the air and drew a gun in the same breath. The dollar clattered back on the table, a perfect hole drilled through it. The smoke drifted through the room, weaving brief patterns in the air.

Fergus popped his head around the door, scattergun under his arm, but his boss shook his head and the barman went away. Thompson decided to overlook the hole in his ceiling and the faint dusting of plaster raining down over the room. This would be a story he could use; a bar needed something to amuse the drinkers on a slow night. He reached for the coin. 'Nice shooting,' he said. 'Can I keep this?'

'Sorry,' Kellogg said, pocketing it. 'Trick coin. But I *can* hit a barn door at a hundred paces or a sergeant at whatever distance you care to name. I just didn't.' And throwing a handful of nuts into his mouth, he pushed back his chair and made for the door.

TWELVE

The talk that day and all the next was the fate of the prospectors rash enough to venture out from Bismarck in search of a new life. First of many, the old sweats said. If the *Tribune* kept sporting its 'Come West, young man' articles, then anybody who could chew Adams New York Gum would be out on the prairie, just begging to have their skulls smashed and their scalps taken. Whatever happened, the Seventh were likely to be kept pretty busy in the weeks ahead.

The weeks ahead weren't what concerned Bugler Dobbs. What concerned him were the next few seconds, whether Calamity Jane Cannary had come back to finish the job she'd started a few days ago. He saw her at the far end of the bar in the Dew Drop, a clear foot shorter than most of the boys in blue, but just as mean looking. Actually, that wasn't quite true. The battered old hat she habitually wore had gone and there was a slightly wilted bunch of prairie anemones in her hair. There was another on her left breast and she was wearing a blue bolero coat over a pair of army trousers, tapering at the ankles. She *did* look like someone earning her last dime in My Lady's Bower or Washington's Division, but she didn't look like Calamity Jane. Nor did she smell. Nor – and for this, Dobbs thanked his God – was she packing iron.

She approached the bugler, sitting alone at a side table and sat down next to him.

'I'd like to buy you a drink, Dobbs,' she growled. No amount of lye soap and laundry starch could soften that voice.

'No call, Calam,' he said, feeling his way carefully, as he always did in conversation with the mule skinner.

'Oh, I reckon there is,' she said, sliding back a chair and sitting down. 'Unusually, the drink was on me the other day. I said some pretty stupid things about Tilly McGee. And I'm sorry.'

This was a real red-letter day in the Dew Drop Inn. Not

only was Calamity Jane done up like a dog's dinner, she was being *nice*. 'Well,' said Dobbs, 'that's mighty gracious of you, Calam. But the one you ought to be apologizing to – and thanking, I reckon – is Corporal O'Riordan over there. What he did that night saved my life – and yours too. Without him, you'd be looking at a rope, for sure.'

Calam peered through the cigar smoke to where a group of soldiers sat playing cards at a nearby table. The corporal there was tall and kinda good-looking in an Irish sort of way. She thumped Dobbs playfully in the shoulder, forgetting momentarily that it was his bugling arm, and crossed the floor.

'Corporal O'Riordan,' she grunted. 'Can I have a word with you?'

There were whistles and guffaws from the others at the table and Calam's dark eyes flashed thunder. If ever there was a bad time to leave her Remington and Bowie knife at home, this was it.

'Get lost, Calam,' one of them sneered. 'We'll be along Thursday with our long johns.'

More laughter. Slowly, Calam turned and walked away.

'Miss Cannary.' The strangeness of the salutation hit her like a wall. She turned to see the handsome corporal standing up, his hat in his hand. 'I'd be pleased to have a word with you,' O'Riordan said, 'but not here.' He glanced down at his comrades. 'The company is too unpleasant.'

And, to more whistles and brays, he led the woman out of the room, opening the door and ushering her through like a real lady. Dobbs breathed a sigh of relief. There was a God, after all.

'You know, you didn't have to talk to me,' Calam said after a while. She sat with O'Riordan on upturned straw bales in I Company's stables, the stalls gleaming with polished saddlery and tack.

'And you didn't have to apologize to me,' he said. 'For all I knew, Bugler Dobbs had coming whatever you'd planned for him. I didn't want to see you hang, is all.'

'Well,' she said, unsure what to do in the company of this new man, 'that's nice.'

'I saw a woman hanged once,' O'Riordan said.

'Did you?'

'Back in Offaly – that's where I come from, in the Old Country. She wasn't afraid to die. All that bothered her was her modesty. She asked the hangman not to hang her too high so that the crowd couldn't see up her skirt.'

'Did he?'

'Oh, he was a decent sort of a man – if a hangman can be such a thing. He tied a rope around her dress and she died quiet. Even so, it took her . . . what . . . five minutes to pass. Twisting and jerking at the rope's end.'

The mule skinner looked up into his face. It was set like granite, the eyes far away. 'Did you know her?' she asked, quietly.

'Oh, yes.' O'Riordan returned from wherever the story had taken him and he looked her in the eyes. 'Yes, I knew her. She was my mother.'

'Your . . .?'

O'Riordan looked away again, but he could feel her eyes on his face, could sense her trying to find the words which would help, not hurt.

'What had she done?' she asked.

'Nothing,' he said, softly. 'That's just it. Nothing. She owed rent. Everybody did in those days. The gael, they call it in Ireland. The English landlords charge an exorbitant gael and if a man – or woman – can't pay, they're evicted, sent out on to the roads with only the clothes on their backs. That's what happened to us. My Da died years ago, of the cholera. So Ma, with us six kids, she tried to do what she could. Sell her body in Dublin to keep food in our mouths.'

'They hang women for that in Ireland?' Calam was outraged.

'No, no,' he smiled. 'Not for that. No, one of her clients, a bailiff called Murphy, accused her of robbing him. Believe me, Miss Cannary, a more honest woman than my Ma never lived. He trumped up the charges.'

'Why?'

O'Riordan found himself laughing, despite his memories. 'Because he knew her name was O'Riordan,' he said. 'And in that particular part of Ireland, the Murphies and the O'Riordans have hated each other with a passion for generations. It's in our blood.'

'There's a Murphy in B Company,' Calam remembered.

'There is.' O'Riordan's Irish twinkle had returned. 'I've met him. Nice feller.'

She frowned. 'Don't you want to kill him?'

O'Riordan laughed. 'I left Ireland to get away from all that,' he said. 'If I went around killing every Murphy I met, I wouldn't get very far. Not in this man's army.' His smile faded. 'No, there's only one man I blame for my Ma's death. When Murphy accused her, no one stood up. No one spoke for her. There was one man who could have, should have, but he was a Murphy too, so he colluded in it.'

'Who was he?'

'The bailiff's son. I know for a fact that *he* stole his Da's money and was happy to pin it on my Ma.'

'Did you face him down?'

'I was a child at the time, maybe thirteen, fourteen. He was ten years older. Anyway, by the time it was all over, he'd emigrated, left the sacred soil for good.'

'Where did he go?'

O'Riordan sighed. 'To hell, for all I know or care. One thing I've learned in life, Miss Cannary, is that you can't go through it carrying a grudge for ever. It will break your back, break your soul.' He looked at her. 'You know, here I am, bleating on about me. I must have bored you stiff. Come on, back to the Dew Drop; I'd like to buy you a drink.'

She smiled, something that few men had ever seen. 'I'd like to let you,' she said.

Grand had inveigled Batchelor into going for a ride. Nothing too strenuous. Hopefully, no bodies littering the path, just an amble along some of the well-worn tracks from the fort. And Batchelor had to admit, it was very pleasant. Without a column in attendance, there was no dust, just the waving grass almost as far as the eye could see. The wind soughing through the distant rocks was almost the only sound, apart from the dull thud of the horses' hoofs in the grass and the occasional shout from the fort and the odd bugle call. It was still hot, but somehow, without the dust, bearable.

After a while, Batchelor spoke. 'Something's been bothering me,' he said.

'I know.' Grand extended both arms, something Batchelor would never be able to do while riding a horse, no matter how placid. 'That's why I suggested a ride. A nice wander on a horse, going where the fancy takes you, is a wonderful way of unstopping mental constipation.'

'It's something Kellogg said.'

'He is as twisty as the Rosebud, I agree,' Grand said, 'but apart from that trick with the coin, I don't remember . . .'

'I've *got* it!' Batchelor punched his colleague on the shoulder. It would have unhorsed a lesser man. 'I've *got* it, by God. You know his editor is Clem Lounsbury.'

'Um . . . yes. Probably.' Grand had never really taken that much interest in the newspaper business.

Batchelor waved a hand at him. 'I always notice editors' names, whenever I read a new paper. Can't help it, I suppose. So, take it from me, that's his name.'

'All right. Kellogg's editor is Clem Lounsbury.' He smiled. 'Is that it?'

'No. Well, yes. When we were heading out on the hunt, we bumped into Kellogg if you recall.'

'Yes. You and he talked about an article he was planning.'

'Correct. And *he* said that *Sam* Lounsbury was a good old stick, something like that. But that he would be wanting some copy around about now.'

Grand cast his mind back. 'I believe he did. But Sam . . . Clem . . . it's an easy slip.'

'Not for a journalist talking about his editor. The editor is *God*. The editor has to be obeyed, no matter how crazy his idea. If he is sending you to do your fiftieth funeral in two weeks, you go. Dog shows. Baby shows. You just do it. So, you don't forget his name. Or the name of his wife, his children, his butler. You remember his birthday, his wedding anniversary, his favourite colour . . .'

'I get it. So, you're saying . . . what *are* you saying, exactly, James?'

'I'm saying that if Kellogg is a journalist – which is by no means certain in my book – then he isn't a journalist on the Bismarck *Tribune*.'

They rode along in silence for a while.

'Is the Bismarck *Tribune* the sort of paper you would lie about working for?' Grand asked. 'If you, for example, were pretending to be a journalist, would you choose that paper?'

'God, no. I would choose something like the *Washington Post*, or if I was still at home, the *Telegraph* or *The Times*.'

'So, there you are, then. Doesn't that prove it was just a slip of the tongue?' Grand was trying not to start too many hares – the situation was fuzzy enough at the edges as it was, without introducing more confusion.

Batchelor was thinking. 'Actually, now I really give it some thought, perhaps I would choose the *Tribune*. The journalists on the big papers are quite famous in their own world. So pretending to be on a little provincial might be safest; hiding in plain sight. You could ask a thousand people to name a writer on the *Tribune* and you probably wouldn't get a single answer.' Batchelor wheeled his horse in a determined fashion, which surprised both him and Grand, but perhaps the horse most of all. It had been making all the decisions thus far.

'Back already?' Grand fell into step.

'I think a telegraph message might clear this up,' Batchelor said.

'Why not just ask Kellogg?' Grand always had found the obvious solution to be the best.

'Is he likely to admit it?' Batchelor said. 'Who is he, after all?'

'Probably just a carpetbagger,' Grand said. 'Out for a free ride, free food, free lodgings. And you must admit, he hasn't put his hand in his pocket since he got here. Apart from that dollar he shot a hole in – or didn't shoot a hole in – last night, I have no reason to assume he *has* any money.'

'That's the usual state of affairs for a journalist,' Batchelor had to concede. 'But I'll feel better when I know. Who's the telegrapher in the fort?'

Grand shrugged. 'I don't know. Probably Dobbs. He seems to do everything else.'

Back at Fort Abraham Lincoln, Batchelor put his head around the door of Myles Keogh's office. From the room behind came the sound of muffled giggling. Batchelor coughed loudly and, after a few moments, Keogh appeared, looking both a little tousled and also rather pleased with himself.

'Yes, Mr Batchelor? You must excuse me. I was buffing my accoutrements.'

'I feel sure you were, Captain,' Batchelor said, smothering a smirk. 'But don't you have people for that? Can you tell me where to go to send a telegraph?'

'If you find Bugler Dobbs, he will be able to help you. He does all the communications at Fort Lincoln.'

'Thank you. And . . . he would be . . .?'

Keogh glanced at the clock on the wall. 'Meal break. In the Dew Drop, I would imagine.'

Batchelor nodded his thanks and left the man to continue his buffing.

'Dobbs?' The bugler looked up and nodded at the Limey. His so-called meal break was turning out to be rather busy, what with Calam and now this. But he was a pleasant sort of man and so he smiled and said, 'Yes?'

'I want to telegraph someone. Captain Keogh tells me you're the man to help me.'

'I sure am.' Dobbs wasn't called upon to send telegraphs very often, except when there had been a hostile attack or something of that nature. Mrs Custer sometimes telegraphed her ma, but he wasn't supposed to let anyone know about that. 'Is it fort business, though, sir? I'm only supposed to send telegraphs on fort business.'

Batchelor didn't hesitate. 'It's more than fort business,' he said, solemnly. 'It could involve national security.'

Dobbs's eyes opened wide. 'In that case, sir,' he swigged his beer and stood up, putting on his hat and tugging his bib-front straight, 'follow me. We'll do it right away.'

The telegraph office was on the ramparts of the fort, not

for security purposes but to make slinging the wires easier. They were cut from time to time by hostiles, or occasionally just as a drunken prank. But as the only means of communication, Custer had two men patrolling the wire at all times and total breakdowns were rare. Today, everything was in order. Dobbs replaced his campaign hat with a kepi and, rather unexpectedly, wound the wire arms of a pair of spectacles over his ears.

'Just for close work, sir,' he said, interpreting Batchelor's rather surprised look. 'I'm a bit long-sighted if anything. Fine for shooting, don't you worry. Now, what's the message and who's it to?'

'It's to the editor of the Bismarck *Tribune*,' Batchelor said. 'Let me know when you're ready.' He had seen people telegraphing before and it never ceased to amaze him. He had just managed to come to terms with the typewriting machine and that had taken him an age to master. Seeing Dobbs, whom he had secretly docketed as none too bright, hammering away at the little key, seemingly at random, impressed him all over again.

Dobbs enjoyed playing with his toy. He was the only one in the fort who understood how it worked and he would be the first to admit that he didn't actually *know* how it worked, just that it did, most of the time. His favourite messages were the ones in code which he sometimes had to send for the General. It was all something to do with letters from a certain book, turned into numbers. They were hard to send and even harder to receive because you couldn't second-guess what the word would be. But it was a challenge Dobbs enjoyed and he flattered himself that he had the job because the tempo of telegraphy was not unlike music. He would have been disappointed to know that he had the job because he was the next man to arrive when the previous telegrapher had been shipped back East, a hopeless drunk who had begun running round the fort with his pants on his head shouting 'Dit Dit Dit' at the ladies.

Dobbs keyed in the address and looked up expectantly. He had forgotten, in the excitement, that this was meant to be government business at the very least. 'Message, sir?'

'Sir,' Batchelor began. 'Do you have a journalist named

Kellogg on your staff. Query. Most important we know. Stop. How old Clem Lounsbury. Query. James Batchelor. Stop. Fort Abraham Lincoln. Stop.'

Dobbs's tongue hung out slightly as he sent the message. It seemed a bit of a waste of time to him. Mr Kellogg was here as large as life and twice as natural in the fort, so why ask? Finally, the last syllable was sent.

'How long does it take for a reply to arrive?' Batchelor asked Dobbs.

'Depends,' he said. 'When we send to another fort, it's generally more or less instantly. Depends on hostiles leaving the lines alone, that kinda thing. But pretty much straight away, yes. Other times, it can take hours. Days, even. If the other end can't be bothered, don't see the message . . .'

'In other words,' Batchelor said, 'there's no point my waiting here.'

'Probably not, sir,' Dobbs said. 'A bell rings when a message comes. I'll come get you. You in your quarters?'

Batchelor suddenly felt a pang that he was a bad guest. 'I may call on Mrs Custer,' he said. 'I haven't visited her lately.'

Dobbs smiled but only slightly. Everyone liked Mrs Custer and he hoped this Limey wasn't dallying with her. 'Sure enough, then, Mr Batchelor, I'll call for you at the General's.'

'Thank you.' Batchelor was halfway down the ladder already. 'Thank you, Dobbs.'

Dobbs shook his head. The way folks carried on here, it made your hair fair curl sometimes, it really did.

Batchelor put his head round the door of the quarters he shared with Grand. As usual, the American had his head in a book. Batchelor was never sure how much reading he ever got done, but it was better than many other ways he could pass the time so he let it go.

'Sent the message?' Grand asked.

'Yes. Surprisingly easy, as a matter of fact. Dobbs is like lightning on that key.'

'Talented cuss, that Dobbs,' Grand said. 'Not so much at bugling, but he seems to be able to turn his hand to most other things.'

'He says the answer may take a while. I was . . . er . . . I thought I would just drop in on . . .'

Grand waved a hand. 'Go,' he said. 'I'm sure Mrs Custer will be delighted to see you.' He swung his legs down from off the bed. 'I think I'll finish my ride, if that's all right with you. These big skies – I need to store a few away for when we're back in London.'

Batchelor was suddenly homesick. 'When are we going home, Matthew?' he said. He tried, for now, to forget about the thousands of miles which lay between here and there.

'Soon, I think. The General doesn't have any need to keep us here and he's just being polite. *We* know that someone is trying to kill him, but he's too vain to see it; he thinks everyone loves him. One part of him believes he is the only person in the world, therefore the obvious target of everything, good or bad. The other part thinks he will live for ever. At least one of those views is wrong.'

Batchelor laughed. The thought of home was suddenly flooding his mind and he could hardly stop himself from beginning the packing. Once he had exposed Kellogg, he knew, the puzzle of why everyone around Custer was beginning to die – or in the case of Reilly, almost die – would be solved, he was sure. He walked off down to Officers' Row, humming what snatches he could remember of 'The Judge's Song' from *Trial By Jury*; what could be more English than that?

Because of the humming, Batchelor missed some clues which he might have found useful, most notably, the twitterings coming from the parlour of Libbie Custer's house on Officers' Row. So he was ushered in by Libbie's maid into what at first sight was a scene from *Macbeth*; then the crones crouching over a cauldron resolved and became Frabbie Benteen, Mary Reno and Libbie, gathered around a teapot.

'James!' Libbie jumped to her feet and tripped over to him, hands in their tiny cotton gloves extended in welcome. 'Come in, come in. You know Mrs Marcus Reno, of course, Mrs Frederick Benteen?'

Batchelor nodded to them, smiling.

'Well, land, we were just talking about you and Mr Grand, weren't we, ladies?'

The two women looked at Batchelor as if he had just dropped from the ceiling and was not a welcome addition at that.

'What have you boys been doing today? Frabbie saw you ride off and then, not half an hour later, you were seen in the saloon with Dobbs.' Bright though Libbie's voice was, there was an undercurrent of disapproval.

Batchelor couldn't help thinking that with these three on the payroll, he and Grand wouldn't have to stir a hand to have the best enquiry agency in London. 'Well, we *do* have a business to run at home, ladies,' he said, at his most smarming.

Frabbie Benteen's lip curled. *Trade!* She knew it. That story about the Other One being related to Andrew Grand of Washington and Boston was so much hogwash, then. She couldn't wait to tell the others.

'Land sakes!' Libbie clutched a hand to her lace-covered bosom. 'No trouble, I hope.' She winked at Batchelor, so quickly he thought for a moment he had imagined it. 'But, come and sit a spell. You have had *such* a time of it, what with one thing and another. Those *poor* prospectors. And their poor *wives*. Such news to have!'

Frabbie and Mary made sympathetic noises, although if either of them had been told of their husband's terrible demise that afternoon, they would have wasted few tears. They were curmudgeonly men at the best of times but, nursing a skinful of booze like they currently were, they were worse. Reno hadn't gone home at all; Mary bore it with fortitude when almost every wife on the place told her he had been seen sleeping it off on the porch of My Lady's Bower, but inwardly, she wished them all to hell.

'It was not a pretty sight, ladies, I will admit. And then, of course, Sergeant Reilly . . .'

'Poor Reilly,' Libbie echoed. 'And a bullet clearly meant for my Georgie.'

Frabbie Benteen scarcely bothered to stifle a sigh. Even someone's near death was grist to Libbie's mill. 'I don't see why you assume that, Libbie,' she said, caustically. 'Not *everything* is about Georgie, you know.'

Libbie bridled and looked at the woman quizzically. Of *course* everything was to do with Georgie. Why did no one understand that?

'It was probably just an unfortunate accident,' Batchelor said, trying to pour oil on waters so troubled he might as well have saved himself the bother. 'A random bullet from an over-excited trooper. A hostile who had circled round behind. We probably will never know.' No one listening to him would have guessed that, actually, he was lying through his teeth.

There was a rap on the door and the maid stepped in, remembering just in time that they had company and she mustn't address the missis as Libbie. 'Caller for Mr Batchelor, ma'am,' she said.

The enquiry agent smiled at her and she blushed. He wasn't as handsome as Captain Grand, but she wouldn't kick him out of her bed on a cold Dakota night.

'It's Dobbs, sir,' she said. 'Shall I send him away? He says it's important. A message, or some such.'

Batchelor grabbed the chance like a drowning man will clutch at a straw. 'Ladies,' he bowed himself out. 'This is a message I have been waiting for. À *bientôt*.' He bit his lip as he pulled the door to behind him. À *bientôt*? What was he thinking? They had him on their lists as a peculiar Limey. Now he was there as a *very* peculiar Limey, with a strange accent. He couldn't have been more wrong. None of the women knew what he had said, but a man who could speak French; land, whatever next? They all twittered into their handker-chiefs; it would keep them going all day!

'Dobbs,' he gasped, out in the tiny garden out front. 'What news?'

Dobbs looked this way and that, then slipped a piece of paper into Batchelor's hand. 'Message came right back, sir,' he said. 'Looks like you were right. Want me to arrest the cuss?'

Batchelor skimmed the reply. 'No one of that name stop impostor stop old Clem Lounsbury fine how you just a joke stop am thirty-seven. Lounsbury stop.' He pocketed the slip and then beckoned Dobbs closer. 'I need another message sending now, Dobbs. Just for confirmation. Do you have a . . .?' Before he could finish, Dobbs had a pad and pencil in his hand. 'Right. Take this down. To the principal . . . um, actually, Dobbs, I'm not sure who it is to. It's to a college in Northfield, Minnesota.'

'I'll send it to the station, Mr Batchelor. That's what I always do when I don't have an address. They know everything, the train guys.'

'That's very enterprising of you, Dobbs.'

Dobbs grinned from ear to ear. In this man's army, you didn't get much praise.

'Well, to the principal of a college to be identified for young ladies. Do you have any girls by the name of Kellogg query . . .'

'Don't worry about the punctuation, sir,' Dobbs put in. 'I think I can work it out. I think I can work out the rest of the message too. Where will you be when I get the answer?' His eyebrows signalled to the house behind Batchelor.

'I'll be . . .' Batchelor looked around. 'I believe I may go and get a haircut.'

'Really, sir?' Dobbs was dubious. 'If I were you, I wouldn't. A visit to John Burkman's only a tad better than a meeting with an Oglala hostile. Either way, you'll lose your hair. Why not go and have a chat with the doc? He's a nice enough cuss and has a hard time of it with his missus. I'll find you there.' And Dobbs trotted off, 'enterprising' still ringing in his grateful ears.

Batchelor's afternoon went rather off plan after that. The doctor, the orderly told him, was at home, resting. The barber – who he decided to risk after all – was closed until further notice, on account of him being a serving soldier. Batchelor was not to know that he had come off the worst in an altercation regarding some side whiskers, inadvertently shaved off in error. W.W. Cooke, whose dundrearies were legendary, had threatened to shoot Burkman if he so much as saw a comb in his hand. The saloon was empty save for the barman and a desultory fly. So he went off to his quarters, kicked off his boots and lay down for a read. Ten minutes later, he was fast asleep.

Dobbs, to be fair, looked in all the obvious places for Batchelor to deliver his answer and then, failing that, for Grand. But his tapping at the door of the guest rooms resulted in nothing and Batchelor wasn't in any of the other obvious places. Dobbs was on his way back to the telegraph room, to swap his kepi for his campaign hat and resume his life as Bugler Dobbs and all-round dogsbody when he turned a corner and cannoned straight into Mark Kellogg, walking in the other direction with a pad of paper in his hand, a thoughtful pencil to his lip.

'Hell, Dobbs.' Kellogg grabbed his jaw dramatically. 'You could have maimed me for life.'

'Sorry, Mr Kellogg, sir.' Dobbs was mortified. 'I didn't see you there.'

Kellogg felt his lip and checked his fingers for blood. 'Well, no harm done, as it happens. In a hurry?'

'I've been sending some wires for Mr Batchelor and I need to get back to my other duties, sir,' Dobbs said.

'Of course, of course. Say, Dobbs? Can you send a wire for me? To the editor of . . . wait a minute. Do you know, I don't know the wire address for the *Tribune*? I have it written down somewhere . . .'

'Not to worry, Mr Kellogg,' Dobbs said, enterprising as ever. 'I know the address.'

'Oh, you do?'

'Yessir.' Dobbs had a sneaking suspicion that he had just spoken out of turn but wasn't sure. He glanced at Kellogg, but the man seemed unconcerned.

'I'll just jot it down for you.' Kellogg scribbled quickly on his pad and then seemed to change his mind. 'Do you know what, Dobbs, I think I'll leave it. I won't keep you.' And with a smile, the journalist carried on with his walk, but this time the pencil was stowed away and he still looked thoughtful.

Dobbs had eventually done the obvious thing and pushed the reply from a rather offended principal of the Northfield College for Young Ladies of Quality in Minnesota under Batchelor's door. It stated in no uncertain terms that she did not divulge details of her girls, but as she had no one by the name of Kellogg in her establishment, she would be very much more than grateful if Mr Batchelor took his unnatural desires else-where and she was his faithfully, Millicent Manners, prop.

Grand chuckled when he read it – he had a strong feeling that he had, over the years, met girls from that very school.

'So, James,' Grand was indulging in a final cigar before bed. Dinner had been courtesy of the bighorn buck of the hunt, with the inevitable tasteless entrées. He thought fondly of what Mrs Rackstraw could have done with a haunch of venison and, like Batchelor, his thoughts turned more than a little to home. 'Mr Kellogg has been deceiving us, then?'

'Yes.' Batchelor was feeling vindicated and yet still very unsatisfied. He knew now that Kellogg was not with the *Tribune*, but that didn't tell him much. It might simply mean that the man had lied about his paper. There were lots of rags in one-horse towns the length of the country which a man would not be proud to own as the home of his by-line. As for the girls, perhaps he had had to put them in a cheaper school or even out to service to make ends meet. He looked well-heeled enough, it was true, but that could all be a front as well. A man didn't need that many suits of clothes to give the impression of being at the top of the style. 'But I don't know how. Or why.'

Grand pushed him with an elegantly extended leg. 'Come on, let's turn in. That meat was tough enough to give anyone indigestion, let alone if you're worrying at a problem. We'll sleep on it and it'll all be fine in the morning. You know how it works – suddenly at two o'clock, there will be a bell in your head and it will all fall into place.'

'And I will have forgotten it again in the morning.' Batchelor had decided to be inconsolable.

'Write it down.' Grand stubbed out his cigar and poured some water into the bowl on the washstand. 'The problem with this case is we don't know who we're hunting for what. When we know that, we'll know it all, and then, more particularly, we can go home.'

Batchelor knew that Grand was right. It was the going round in circles that was driving him a little crazy – perhaps he had fort fever after all.

Matthew Grand had had louder bunkmates than James Batchelor and rougher berths too. The Englishman rarely

---

snored. He muttered occasionally, often around two in the morning, the time, he had told Grand years ago, that he was born. The American, in his turn, never slept all the way through the night and that night, in particular, he had lain awake for hours, listening to the far calls of the coyotes in the Black Hills and the distant thud of the guards' boots as they patrolled the ramparts.

He was just falling back to sleep again when he sat bolt upright.

'James,' he hissed.

Nothing.

There was no moon tonight, the clouds heavy over the prairie, and the room in Officers' Row was black as pitch.

'James. Wake up.'

'Hm?' Batchelor poked his head out from the coverlet. For the briefest of moments, he had no idea where he was. 'What's the matter?'

Grand was leaning to his right, fumbling for the butt of his pistol. 'Are we . . . alone?' he whispered.

'No man is an island, Captain Grand,' a quiet voice said, 'so I guess the answer is, no; you're not.'

Batchelor was sitting bolt upright now too and his hand was snaking out for the oil lamp.

'I can see better in the dark than you can in the light, Mr Batchelor,' the voice said. 'And I suggest that both of you stay perfectly still. You've seen what I can do with a gun – the one I'm pointing at you now.'

'Kellogg!' said Batchelor. 'I thought you said that was a trick coin.'

'I lied,' Kellogg said, and they could hear the smile in his voice. 'But then, so did you.'

'Did I?' Batchelor was desperately trying to make his eyes focus in the dark. Kellogg was an indistinct blur, half submerged in an armchair. The only weapon at the pair's disposal was Grand's pocket Colt and that was where it was supposed to be – in his pocket and therefore no use at all.

'You told me you were writers on vacation,' the journalist said, 'that Grand here was visiting family and you ran into Custer by chance. That wasn't quite true, was it?'

'It wasn't?' Grand was playing for time.

'No. You see, before you gentlemen left Mr Thompson's back room the other night, I took the opportunity to turn this place over. No, don't worry – you wouldn't have noticed; I'm very meticulous in these matters. I had a little rummage among your papers, Messrs Grand and Batchelor, Enquiry Agents of the Strand. You're here on an official snooping venture, aren't you, gentlemen? And, thanks to Telegrapher Dobbs, I know you're snooping into me.'

'You?' Batchelor hoped that his voice sounded more innocent than he felt. He was not a good liar, not even in the dark.

'Dobbs *can* keep his mouth shut,' Kellogg said, 'but only when Captain Keogh reminds him to. Otherwise, he could blab for America and might as well hold forth with a loudhailer after Reveille every morning. So what have you discovered about me?'

'That you don't work for the Bismarck *Tribune*,' Grand said, 'and if you have any daughters, they sure don't go to school in Northfield, Minnesota.'

'When you told me all that,' Batchelor said, 'on the train west, I thought you were just trying to make small talk. Pictures of the kids, your editor's brief – just a little *too* much information, in hindsight. But then you made a slip, didn't you?'

'Two, in fact.' Grand was a stickler for accuracy.

'Two,' Batchelor agreed. 'First, you referred to your editor as *Sam* Lounsbury, rather than Clem, on one occasion.'

'A slip of the tongue,' Kellogg said.

Batchelor chuckled, perhaps not the wisest thing to do when there's a gun pointing at you. 'If there's one thing a newspaperman *always* gets right, Mr Kellogg, it's the name of his editor, the man out of whose arse the sun always shines.'

'Secondly,' Grand said, 'another slip of yours was your reference to "old" Clem Lounsbury, who is only in his thirties and therefore, if I don't miss my guess, some years younger than you. You've never met Clem Lounsbury in your life.'

'And you aren't a journalist either,' Batchelor threw in for good measure. He may have given up his career in the papers, but he still cared for the reputation of those who hadn't.

'So,' Grand said, after a moment's pause. 'What are you really, Mr Kellogg?'

There was a silence, 'Let's just say,' he said, 'we never sleep.'

'A Pinkerton man,' Grand and Batchelor choroused.

'The same,' Kellogg nodded. 'I guess I should have got my cover story straighter, but I didn't expect you two.'

There was a click as Kellogg released the hammer of his gun and the sound of it returning to his shoulder holster. Only now did Grand roll over and light the bedside lamp. Kellogg's dark eyes and black sideburns shone in the half-light and Batchelor suddenly felt a little silly in his nightshirt.

'So,' Grand said, 'can we assume you're not here to kill Custer?'

'Kill Custer?' Kellogg laughed. 'Good God, no. Half Washington, two thirds of the Seventh Cavalry and every Indian west of the Washita wants to do that. But me? No.'

'Who are you working for?' Grand asked.

'Ah,' Kellogg shook his head. 'Now, that would be telling tales out of school, wouldn't it? You know how this works, gentlemen. Client confidentiality and all that.'

Batchelor folded his arms, leaning back against the headboard. 'I think we're way past that,' he said. 'Somebody's trying to kill Custer. And that somebody is right here, in Fort Lincoln.'

'And you thought it was me?' Kellogg asked.

'It crossed our minds,' Grand said. 'After all, you're the common denominator. You were there in Washington when Senator Maitland was killed.'

'And when those roughs had a go at Custer in the Division,' Batchelor threw in.

'And you were here at the fort when Trooper McGee was murdered,' Grand nodded.

'Not to mention the attempt that got Sergeant Reilly.'

'Let me stop you there, gentlemen,' Kellogg said. 'The first I heard about the Hal Maitland incident was literally in a morning edition of the *Washington Post*. As for McGee and Reilly, yes, you're right, I was here at the fort. And both those incidents happened out on the prairie, in the Black Hills.'

'How are Reno and Benteen involved?' Batchelor asked.

'Come again?'

'Captain Grand and I are pickers-up of unconsidered trifles, Mr Kellogg,' the Englishman said. 'In the Dew Drop the other night, Major Reno let slip that he knew that Custer had been beaten up . . .'

'Not strictly true, by the way,' Grand chimed in.

'No, indeed,' Batchelor conceded. 'The General gave more than he got. The point is, however, how did Reno know about that? Unlike Hal Maitland, it wasn't reported in the press.'

Kellogg shrugged. 'Washington scuttlebutt,' he said. He read the disbelief in both men's faces. 'Oh, all right, *I* told them. If you must know, I'm working for William Belknap.'

'The former Secretary of War?' Batchelor liked to cross his tees.

'He wasn't former then,' Kellogg told him. 'He was still very much in post. He wanted the dirt on Custer. *Anything* to bring the man down. The trouble with Washington is that there is so much dirty linen, it's hard to find dirt dirty enough to do the job.'

'So,' Batchelor was remembering another conversation with Kellogg, 'stories about Custer's squaw and Custer's black cook . . .'

'Are just stories, as far as I know.' Kellogg said, 'I doubt that the General is *quite* the saint his wife makes him out to be, but I've found nothing yet.'

'And that's where Reno and Benteen come in,' Grand observed.

'Exactly. They've got their own agenda, that's for sure, but they've also worked with Custer on a daily basis. At least, that was Belknap's reasoning.'

'So he doesn't want Custer dead?' Batchelor wanted to make sure he'd got the story straight.

'The man who kills Custer'll just make a hero out of him. "Old Iron Butt",' Kellogg, despite being only a pretend journalist, could still sketch out a banner headline, '"The Greatest Soldier in American History".' He winked. 'Something you might write, Mr Batchelor.'

'But what about Reno's comments?' Batchelor ignored the remark, 'and Benteen's? About Custer's handling of his men? His cruelty?'

'Oh, he's a martinet, for sure,' Kellogg said, 'but no worse than any other. He's shot deserters before and I daresay will again. What's unforgiveable to Reno is that the man drinks Alderney rather than liquor.'

'Alderney?' Batchelor was in a foreign country again.

'Milk,' Grand and Kellogg chorused.

'So, what happens now?' Grand asked Kellogg.

'That sort of depends on you two,' the Pinkerton man said. 'I've shown my hand, and there's not much I can do to stop you going to Custer with it. If you're right about the attempts on the man's life, my little job seems to have paled into insignificance. I'll send in my report to Belknap and make my way home. I don't guess you'd welcome a *third* nose poking about?'

'If that's an offer, Mr Kellogg, thank you,' Grand said, 'but James and I have our own way of working.'

'I understand,' the Pinkerton man said.

'As for your job,' Batchelor said, 'finish your report. We'll continue to watch the General's back.'

There was a pause. 'I'd be interested to know who your money's on,' Kellogg said.

Grand and Batchelor looked at each other. 'Everybody,' they said in unison.

THIRTEEN

Now that the idea of going home was in the wind, both Grand and Batchelor were feeling homesick. They sat at breakfast after their disturbed night and compared everything unfavourably with Mrs Rackstraw's efforts. No newspaper. That wasn't strictly true; more accurately, it was a case of no *current* newspaper and a four-day-old Bismarck *Tribune* couldn't hold a candle to a crisp, newly delivered copy of the *Telegraph*. No kidneys. No sausages, still humming softly to themselves as they arrived on a warmed plate. Nothing recognizable that morning, in fact. Batchelor advanced his nose close to the plate and looked up enquiringly at the orderly who had just brought it across from the cookhouse.

'Any idea?' Batchelor asked.

'Grits?' The man was clearly not sure.

Grand was pitching in. He could eat anything, any time. His time as a soldier had given him a cast-iron stomach, if nothing else. 'I've tasted better,' he said, his mouth full. 'But I guess "grits" covers it. Add some syrup, James – it makes the world of difference.'

When the orderly had left, Batchelor pushed the plate away. 'Is everything maize in this place?'

Grand looked down at his plate. 'More or less, I suppose. Mustn't grumble.'

Batchelor laughed. 'Sometimes, I think you are getting to be more British than the British, Matthew.'

'I'll take that as a compliment.' Grand reached for Batchelor's abandoned plate. 'Are you eating that?'

Batchelor shook his head.

Grand pulled the plate nearer and spooned on the syrup with a lavish hand. 'They do their best, bearing in mind they don't have much to work with. I've never heard of a fort starving to death, though they might get a bit bored with the cuisine.' He looked across the table at his friend. 'Don't worry, James. We'll be home soon.'

'And no further forward.'

'Well, we know that Mark Kellogg isn't a journalist. That Belknap is out to get Custer.' Grand tried to put a good face on it.

'That a double murderer – not to mention the attempt on Reilly – is roaming free.' Batchelor was in a glass-half-empty mood.

'You have to take what you can, James. Life is different out here. Cheaper. When you can die from so many things around the next corner, whether someone is out to murder you is a detail. Anyway, George will be delighted that someone thinks he is important enough to want to kill. What he fears most of all is anonymity.'

'But still . . .' Batchelor didn't like loose ends.

'Look, why don't we have a few last goes at clearing this up? Cooke will have a list of everyone on the fort who has had his collar felt. It will take time, but I'll go through it with him, see if anyone has ever behaved strangely towards Custer specifically, made Cooke suspicious. Why don't you pay a visit to Reilly while I do that?'

'We don't really get on.' Batchelor was ashamed of his antipathy to the Irish. He would like to think of himself as a man with no tendency to dislike anyone on the basis of race or creed, but he had seen too much in his home town to be completely devoid of prejudice in that quarter.

'He's Irish, James. Get over it. He's also a man you have spent a reasonable amount of time with, who is languishing in the sanatorium with a darned great hole in him. He could do with the company. Go. Find out if he knows anyone who hates Custer enough to blast away without worrying who else gets in the way.'

Batchelor didn't move.

'Go, or I'll call for more grits and make you eat it.'

With no further prompting, Batchelor was up, coated and hatted and on his way across the square to the sanatorium.

After the heat and glare outside, the sanatorium was dim and cool. The orderly showed Batchelor through into the side room.

where Reilly was propped up in the only occupied bed. The big Irishman turned when the door creaked open and his expression showed that he was disappointed to see Batchelor.

'I thought you was breakfast,' he muttered.

'Shall I go and get you some?' Batchelor said. 'It's probably just outside . . .'

The sergeant's expression may have been one of gratitude. 'That'd be grand. I . . . well, I'm still a bit wobbly on the pins. I lost a lot of blood, they say.'

Batchelor looked out into the lobby and, sure enough, a breakfast tray was waiting on the orderly's desk. 'Shall I take this through?' he asked and the orderly nodded.

'I meant to do it,' Jenkins said, 'but I'm rushed off my feet here.'

Batchelor looked around. There were no other patients. The doctor had yet to arrive. Sick parade wasn't until eleven. Quite what the rush was he couldn't say, but then, he wasn't a medical man. He picked up the tray and took it through.

Reilly pulled himself upright, slowly and clearly painfully. Batchelor stood by and watched. He didn't think that Reilly would take kindly to having his pillows plumped by an Englishman. Finally, he was comfortable, and Batchelor handed him his tray.

Reilly lifted the cover from the plate. 'Grits,' he said. And before Batchelor could apologize and remove them, going in search of something more edible, the sergeant fell to with a will.

'Shall I fetch some syrup?' Batchelor asked.

'What, and spoil good grits? No, this is fine as it is.' The plate was soon cleared, the coffee glugged down in two. Whatever else was wrong with Reilly, his appetite seemed to be intact. Batchelor removed the tray to a nearby table and pulled up a chair.

'How are you getting on, Reilly?' he asked.

The Irishman let his head loll on the pillows. 'To be honest with you, Mr Batchelor, and I don't want you repeating this, I'm as helpless as a kitten. Dr Madden, he says that I'll mend, that the wound is nothing, but I lost that much blood that I don't have enough left to feed the muscles.' He held out a forearm the size of a ham. 'He says that I'll need to stay in bed until I've made some more blood. I get double rations for me meals, as much meat as I want, and Mrs Madden, she makes me some beef tea twice a day.' He managed a weak smile at Batchelor. 'It tastes Godawful, but she means well. Mrs Custer comes to see me, brings me little cakes and things. The General, he comes by with cigars, but I've no stomach for smoking right now.' Reilly closed his eyes and Batchelor watched for a moment, then got up, ready to creep away. The visit had been easier than expected and he could report back to Grand with a clear conscience.

The chair creaked and Reilly's eyes flew open. 'No need to go, Mr Batchelor. I was just resting me eyes a minute. I get that tired . . .'

'You've been through a lot, Sergeant,' Batchelor said, soothingly. 'Not just the other day, but recently. The Division, for example . . .'

'That was me own fault. I shouldn't have gone there, but . . . well, a man doesn't go to Washington every day. A man needs a bit of company, now and then.'

Batchelor looked at the man, lying there as if boneless. He was still big, but his face was beginning to look haggard and the hands lying on the white sheets were limp. 'Of course you do,' Batchelor said. 'Looking out for the General's back must be a full-time job.'

The sergeant gave a weak smile. 'You've no idea,' he said. 'And it's not just the watching his back for knives and bullets. The man has only to open his mouth some days and he can make a dozen enemies. Me and Libbie . . . I mean, Mrs Custer . . . we're all the time having to smooth things over.'

'You should be in the diplomatic corps,' Batchelor said, then wondered if the United States even had such a thing.

Again, the big man smiled and even tried a laugh. 'I don't think the diplomatic would welcome a bog-trotter like me.'

Batchelor raised a protesting hand, but Reilly waved it down.

'I know what you think of me and my countrymen, Mr Batchelor, and I won't say you're wrong. I doubt you could name me a country in the world without some bad apples. It's just that our bad apples are a bit . . . louder than others might be.' Reilly looked over Batchelor's shoulder and his eyes became unfocused as he went back into his past. 'I'm not an educated man, Mr Batchelor, nor yet a clever one. But I might have done better for myself, I sometimes think, if I hadn't left home at a young age.'

'What happened?' Batchelor wasn't here to find out about Reilly's unhappy childhood, but one thing sometimes led to another.

The sergeant shrugged. 'I did what boys of my class and my time did. I left home to seek my fortune. I left without telling a soul where I was going; London it was, at first, of course. Then back to Liverpool, intending to cross back to Ireland and make it all up with my folks. But a packet was leaving for America and . . . well, I got on it, landed in New York and ended up in the army. Not good timing, some would say. The Civil War broke out and I was stuck by then. I served this country well, or as well as I knew how, anyway. Then I met the General. He needed a big man at his back and . . .' Reilly spread his arms, wincing as the wound pulled under its dressing, 'here I am. Not for the first time and I guess not the last.'

'Can you think of *anyone* who would want to kill Custer?'

Reilly laughed and made himself cough. Batchelor helped him lean forward and held him steady while he fought the cough which wracked him and made him twist in pain. 'Oh, Mr Batchelor,' he managed at last. 'Don't make me laugh, sir, please. I would say, in no real order, anyone who isn't me or Libbie has wished him dead at least once. Me and Libbie – perhaps not as often, but even so, we would lie if we said he had never driven us to distraction.' He settled back on his pillows and looked at Batchelor, a wicked gleam in his eye. 'List too long?'

Batchelor smiled and nodded.

'I can't make it shorter, sir, much as I'd like to.' He closed his eyes. 'And now, I really must rest. Thank you for coming to see me, but I really must . . .' And, with a mighty snore, Sergeant Reilly, Ignatius M., of the Seventh Cavalry, slept.

The man with the biggest dundrearies in the world sat in his office later that morning, surrounded by papers. He didn't like the world to know about his deteriorating eyesight, so when Matthew Grand came in, he tucked the pince-nez away under a pile of letters.

'Captain Grand,' he smiled. 'How can I help?'

'Lieutenant Cooke,' Grand smiled back. 'I was hoping for a word. About the General.'

Cooke's smile faded and he offered Grand a chair. The captain looked at the trophies on Cooke's shelves; cups for running, cups for shooting. 'Quite a collection, Lieutenant Cooke,' he said.

'Oh, just a sign of a misspent youth, I'm afraid, Captain Grand. There wasn't much else to do in the part of Canada I come from; hence my joining this man's army.'

'Misspent youth?' Grand queried. 'May I ask your age, Lieutenant?'

'I shall be thirty next month, sir,' Cooke said, as if his wheelchair and ear trumpet were beckoning.

'Who would you say is the best shot in the Seventh?' Grand asked.

'Why, the General, of course.' Cooke was surprised at the question.

'That's not what Bloody Knife says,' Grand smiled.

Cooke laughed. 'Bloody Knife's all mouth and buckskins, Captain Grand,' he said. 'He'd die rather than admit it, but he'd follow the General to hell and back.'

'And you?' Grand closed to the man. 'Are you one of the Custer gang – or do you hate the man's guts?'

Cooke was suddenly on his feet. 'I don't care for the question, Captain,' he said, sharply. 'I am adjutant of this regiment and I follow my orders. Politics don't interest me.'

Grand chuckled. 'Relax, Lieutenant,' he said. 'I don't doubt your loyalty to Custer. But that *is* why I'm here.'

'I don't follow.' Not yet convinced, Cooke sat down slowly.

'Somebody is trying to kill the General,' Grand said.

Cooke blinked. 'What?'

'You can't have missed it, surely.' Grand leaned back in his chair. 'Trooper McGee was riding Custer's horse when he died. Sergeant Reilly was feet from him when he was hit. I suppose you heard about the runaway cab in Washington, which killed the senator for Milwaukee? Well, that was aimed at the General, too.'

'My God!' Cooke sat back. 'I knew that thirty was a milestone in a man's life,' he said. 'I just didn't realize I'd lose my marbles quite so quickly.'

'Don't concern yourself, Queen's Own . . . er . . . that is what the men call you, isn't it?'

''Fraid so,' he said. 'Comes of being born north of the border, eh. I can think of worse things.'

'So can I,' laughed Grand, remembering his own troops along the Shenandoah. 'Batchelor and I have a head start on you. We were there for the Washington attempt too.'

'My God!'

'As adjutant, you'll have punishment lists – court martials, floggings, that sort of thing?'

'Of course,' Cooke said, 'although, begging your pardon, Captain, flogging's a little old hat nowadays. Branding for desertion, double pack drill for insubordination.'

'Has Custer ever shot anybody?' Grand asked.

Cooke hesitated. 'Before my time, I believe,' he said. 'And not with the Seventh.'

'I'd much appreciate a look at the punishment log, Lieutenant,' Grand said. 'See if I can find a pattern; somebody in particular who might have it in for the General.'

'Yes, yes of course.' Cooke fumbled with his keys at a filing cabinet behind him. 'Here you are. You can use my outer office. I'm drowning in this lot, I'm afraid, or I'd lend a hand.'

'What are they?' Grand nodded at the mountain of paperwork on the adjutant's desk.

'Demands for protection, mostly, from prospectors, railway workers, property developers. If the Seventh offered protection for all of them, we'd need a regiment the size of the Army of the Potomac and then some.' He passed Grand the punishment file.

'There's going to be trouble, then?' the captain asked. 'Indian-wise?'

'Count on it,' sighed Cooke. 'We're in their sacred Black Hills,' he said. 'To the Lakota and the Cheyenne, it's a little piece of Heaven here on earth, the place given to them by

Manitou, the Great Spirit. To us, it's a windy, dusty Hell-hole that just happens to be full of gold.' The adjutant pressed his palms together. 'Two immoveable forces,' he said, 'each pushing against the other. Something's got to give.'

'Something?' Grand raised an eyebrow.

'Ultimately,' Cooke sighed, 'the Indians – and with them an entire way of life. In the short term, however, I hope it's not the Seventh.'

Grand's smile was chilly. 'And on that happy note,' he said, 'I'll just try to find the man who's attempting to kill General Custer.'

All in all, it was a morning that Matthew Grand would never get back. The offences carried out by troopers of the Seventh were the same as those in any other regiment in any army in the world: drunkenness; desertion; insubordination; dirty carbines, sloppy drill. Sergeants and corporals were busted to the ranks. Men had their hips branded, their heads shaved. They marched around the parade ground in full pack under a broiling sun, jabbed up the ass by bayonets if they slowed down. Furloughs were denied, letters from home torn up. As for a pattern among the dirty laundry of the Seventh, there wasn't one. The most persistent offender, far and away, was Trooper Henry Golding, whose multiple demerits made Marcus Reno look like a choirboy. He had died of cholera, however, six months before, and there was no one to take his place. All in all, Custer emerged in the discipline records as firm but fair. Old Iron Butt was a man's man; the army could expect no less. On the other hand, as Grand was only too aware, any one of the miscreants listed in Cooke's ledger could have borne an unreasonable grudge. Mechanically, Grand added up the number of offenders still on the regiment's active list. It gave him a depressing total of eighty-six.

That afternoon, the only sound in Grand and Batchelor's room was the slow turning over of paper, the scritch of pen nibs and sighing.

'I don't think we're getting anywhere, are we?' Batchelor asked after an hour or so.

'Possibly not,' Grand agreed, 'but we certainly won't get anywhere if we give up now. What if our man is the next on the list.' He looked up. 'What are the three piles for?'

Batchelor pointed to each in turn. 'Dead or left,' he said. 'Punishment too minor to possibly cause any resentment, drill in full pack, that kind of thing. Then, possibles.'

'I haven't done it like that,' Grand said. 'I have put a marker in my possibles; that should be clear enough. How many possibles do you have?'

Batchelor lifted the file. 'One. You?'

'Same. And I only have him in that pile because otherwise I would be too depressed to go on. You?'

'Same.' Batchelor threw down his pen in a spray of ink and rubbed his eyes. 'I don't know . . .'

Grand tapped the pile of files. 'Keep going.'

There was a knock on the door and Dobbs stuck his head around it, wearing his telegrapher's kepi. 'Message for you, gentlemen. Mrs Custer sends her compliments and hopes you will dine with her and the General tonight. Sevenish.'

'She sent a wire?' Batchelor was confused. Surely, that was taking formality to insane lengths?

Dobbs was confused as well. 'No. She just stopped me on the square.' He looked at Grand as if to warn him his friend had well and truly got fort fever.

Grand tapped his head and Dobbs was puzzled for another moment, then understood.

'Oh, no, I see. I was just taking a wire to Mr Kellogg. An answer he had been waiting for – Mrs Custer caught me on my way. So must go, gents . . . oh, is there an answer? To Mrs C?'

'Be delighted stop.' Grand chuckled and Dobbs smiled – he loved a good telegraph joke.

'Well,' Batchelor said. 'That gives us a timescale, doesn't it? We need to have gone through this list before we go to dinner. Then, we can check with the General whether anyone we have on our shortlist hates him enough to kill him.' He picked up his pen again and was annoyed to find the nib was horribly crossed. He picked at it with an ink-stained thumb. 'Some days, things are just sent to try us,' he muttered and bent to his task.

Grand didn't tell him about the ink on his forehead. Later was time enough for that.

The dining room in the Custer's home looked lovely that evening, ablaze with candles and sweet with flowers. Libbie ran forward with her strange tripping gait and took Grand and Batchelor by the hand, leading them to the table.

'You'll excuse us sitting straight away,' she said. 'I'm afraid we can't manage Washington ways here – we just don't have the staff for it, nor the room, I'm afraid to say. Land, when I think of the dining room at Mama's; well, it doesn't matter, because where Georgie is, that's home to me.' She swung her gaze to the General, standing to attention behind his chair. Some men might chafe under the constant adoration, but for George Custer, it was meat and drink. He smiled at his wife and blew her a kiss which puffed out his moustache. Batchelor was struck again at how the man managed to make the most of his clear physical disadvantages – he deserved credit for that, at least.

'Not at all, Mrs Custer,' Grand said, bowing over her hand and making her giggle. 'We're honoured to be here.'

'Oh, Captain,' she twittered, 'Libbie, please. And do come and sit. A table for four is so companionable, don't you think? And lucky me, whenever I look up, I see the three handsomest men on the fort.' She smiled round at them. 'In the state, perhaps I should say, if not the country!'

Batchelor pulled out her chair and she subsided in a cloud of tulle.

'Thank you so much, James.' She looked up at Custer. 'I don't care what you say, Georgie, Englishmen have the most *exquisite* manners!'

Georgie's smile grew a little tight. 'I couldn't agree more, my dear,' he said, sitting down. 'That's why I'm proud to be descended from them.' Grand smothered a smile and sat also.

'Now, gentlemen, we have decided to have our cocktails sitting, as I said, because we don't have that many staff in the house. The men do their best but waiting at a private table isn't really to their taste, nor ours. So Georgie has mixed a peach shrub; no alcohol, but he will add to your taste. James? What would you prefer?'

Batchelor had had a shrub just once before, at his grandmother's house, and would prefer never to have another. But perhaps with a slug of something alcoholic? 'I'll have mine with brandy, General, if that is acceptable?'

'Excellent choice.' Custer walked over to the sideboard and mixed a stiff one for the Englishman and an alcohol-free one for himself. Although his many detractors mocked his teetotalism, he never strayed from the path, not for a moment. 'Matthew?'

'The same,' Grand nodded.

'Libbie?'

His wife arched her eyebrows coquettishly and said, 'I would like a spot of brandy in mine too, Georgie, if that is all right? This is *such* a special night! Land, I can hardly recall the last time we had guests, apart from your family, that is.'

It was hard to tell, but both Grand and Batchelor, practised in hearing subtleties in what people *didn't* say, felt sure they detected a hint of annoyance in Libbie's words.

'Are you sure?' Custer was on edge for some reason he couldn't quite fathom. So, someone was out to kill him – when was someone not? But there was something wrong in his fort, and it cut him to the quick. He didn't expect the men to be happy. They were far from home, hot, uncomfortable and, for a lot of the time, scared out of their wits. They would be mad not to be. But there was something else, something lurking, like a black dog panting at his heels. He needed to send it on its way before it sent him crazy. And a drunk wife – even a tipsy wife – was just something he didn't need tonight.

Libbie sulked, prettily. 'Just a small one, Georgie,' she said, in a small, light voice. Batchelor had never heard anything so quiet with so much resolve in it.

Custer brought the drinks to the table and raised his glass. 'To us,' he said, his eyes locked on Libbie's.

'To the Seventh,' said Grand and they toasted again.

Batchelor took a sip of his drink. The brandy certainly made a difference that he doubted his old granny would approve of. It underlay the sweet acidity of the drink like a stroke from a warm hand in the small of a naked back. He would have to remember this drink, for when they got home. He glanced across and noticed that Libbie seemed to be enjoying hers too – there was a sparkle in her eye and her cheek was a becoming pink.

'I don't want to sound inhospitable, Matthew,' Custer decided to take the bull by the horns, 'but I was wondering if you had any plans for going home at all.'

Batchelor and Grand began to speak at once, then stopped as Libbie laughed.

'I think we can take that as a "yes", Georgie,' she said, with a smile. She patted Batchelor's hand. 'I shall miss you, James. And you, Captain, of course,' she added, hurriedly. 'But we do understand that you have work at home.'

'And it isn't as if you have found anything out, is it?' Custer said, bluntly. 'About these murders, shootings, call them what you will.'

Grand looked at Batchelor and he waved a hand. 'Go ahead, Matthew,' he said. 'Tell them what we know.'

'Before we begin,' Libbie said, 'let's get in the appetizer.' She rang a small bell by her plate and a maid, decked out like the smartest you might see in Washington or even Chelsea, came in with a tray, with four small dishes balanced precariously on it.

Libbie waited until the girl had flounced out, her empty tray swinging in one hand. 'It's so hard to get the staff,' she muttered, then pinned on her hostess's smile. 'I don't know whether you have ever tried this, gentlemen, but it is something we have at home. It's cheese soufflé; we can only have it for small parties, because otherwise they tend to sink.' She looked down at her dish. 'But these look splendid, don't they, Georgie?'

The General was halfway through his and merely nodded. Grand and Batchelor were both thinking the same thing; if Mrs Rackstraw sent up a soufflé like this, the next news they would hear of her would be that she had thrown herself under a train.

As course succeeded course, Grand shared what he knew with the Custers. Libbie expressed no surprise at the perfidy of Mark Kellogg.

'I said it to you, Georgie, didn't I? I said, "that man has piggy eyes", I said. He was so obviously not a journalist.' She beamed at Batchelor. 'Land, we could have been murdered in our beds!' She clutched a hand to her breast.

'I don't think so, Libbie,' the General said. 'I think you can trust a Pinkerton man, even when in the pay of the other side, if I can call Belknap that.'

'A swine is what you can call him!' Libbie was getting shriller than usual and Custer regretted the brandy he had put in her cocktail.

'Well, yes,' Grand said. 'Hopefully, he will have got what's coming to him. But what we haven't found is who has been trying to kill your husband, Libbie. The other thing, of course, is that Kellogg found nothing to George's detriment.'

'Apart from nepotism of course,' Batchelor chipped in, instantly regretting it. His 'but of course, that's the American way, isn't it?' did nothing to redeem him.

Libbie clutched her breast again and this time took Batchelor's hand with hers, much to his discomfiture. Had he just been impossibly rude? He tried to wriggle his fingers free, but her grip was like iron. 'So, he didn't find out about the gold, then, Georgie? Thank the Lord and all his Saints for that!'

Grand and Batchelor's heads swivelled as though on bearings. 'Gold?' Grand asked, at last, when the silence was so profound it had begun to make his ears hum.

Custer ran a hand over his golden hair. He fluffed up his moustache and smoothed down his little goatee beard. It didn't improve his looks, but he felt better for it. 'Just a little something for my retirement, Matthew. I am afraid I don't have family money to fall back on, like you.' The General tried a merry laugh. 'There is gold in them there hills, you know. I just happened to . . . find some.'

Libbie joined in, with a little laugh. 'It's true, you know. Georgie was out riding one day and Vic took a stumble in a dry creek bed, and when he got down to check his shoe, well!' She threw up her hands and Batchelor, taking his chance with both hands, recovered his and laced his fingers together in his lap. 'Well, there it was, sparkling in the sand. So, Georgie scooped it up, didn't you, Georgie, and brought it home.' She glanced to a cupboard set back in a corner. 'It's in the safe, isn't it, Georgie?'

Custer made a note to himself to never give his wife brandy on an empty stomach again. Better yet, never to give her brandy again, *ever*. 'Yes, indeed,' he smiled, slapping the table with both palms. 'Would you like to see it, gentlemen?'

Grand and Batchelor both nodded. Other than that, they were stuck for an answer.

Custer got up and fiddled with the cupboard door. The two enquiry agents could recognize the sound of tumblers falling at a hundred paces and raised their eyebrows at each other; the safe was one of quite sophisticated design, far more so than would normally be necessary out West. Custer clearly had a good stash in there. The General turned around with a bag, gathered in one hand at the top, supported by the other from below, and he placed it on the table, moving the flower arrangement to make room. He undid the cord holding the bag closed at the top and let the wash-leather fall away.

In the candlelight, the gold gleamed dully. There was every size of nugget, from just larger than sand to one or two the size of Libbie's thumb. Neither of the visitors was adept at assessing gold, but there seemed like a king's ransom there, give or take. Custer began to gather up the leather folds again and slip the cord through the loops to hold it closed.

'Quite the retirement you have planned, there, George,' Grand said, quietly.

'My Libbie must want for nothing,' he said gruffly, bending back to the safe and clicking it shut, the gold safely in its keeping again.

'And . . . it was just *there*, was it?' Batchelor asked. 'On the ground?'

'There or thereabouts,' Custer said, airily. 'That's what happens, sometimes, with gold.'

Without specialist knowledge, it was hard to argue, but it seemed to them that if prospecting were that easy, fewer people would die and a lot more people would be rich as God. Grand and Batchelor settled for a noncommittal shrug each and both dropped their eyes to their plates and proceeded to fiddle with their nuts.

After that, the party couldn't hope to recover. The maid came in and cleared the plates and poured the coffee. The small talk got smaller until, suddenly, Custer looked at the clock on the mantel. 'Will you just look at the time?' he said. 'I promised Dubya-Dubya I would check the guard tonight.'

Libbie looked mutinous. The brandy was passing off now and she was feeling low. She always hated a dinner party to end.

'No point in looking like that, my dear,' Custer was already putting on his hat and getting ready for the night air. 'I'm sure these gentlemen have things to do. Packing, for example. Not everyone has someone to help them, like you do. Say good-night, dear,' and before anyone knew quite what was happening, Grand and Batchelor found themselves outside on Officers' Row, hatted and cloaked and on their way home. Nobody did the bum's rush quite like George Armstrong Custer.

FOURTEEN

Batchelor had taken Custer seriously and was packed, all but a collar or two. Grand had a more casual attitude to packing; like Libbie, he had usually had someone to do it for him and was still hoping that, if he left things long enough, Batchelor would step forward and be that person. It had always worked before, after all. The gold had taken them both by surprise, but it hadn't really changed the situation; someone was trying to kill Custer; it was now not so certain whether it was for revenge or gain. Though the enquiry agents were agreed – if there was anyone out there who thought that simply killing Custer would give access to his gold, they clearly didn't know Libbie very well. She might behave like a demented squirrel who had broken into the liquor store at times, but in fact they would both rather face a rabid mountain lion than Libbie Bacon Custer if anything happened to her Georgie.

'Captain Grand! Mr Batchelor!' As they walked around the perimeter of the square that morning, Bugler Dobbs ran up, waving. He was wearing his campaign hat, so he hadn't received a wire or anything important. 'Are you gentlemen coming to the Glee tonight?'

'The Glee?' To Batchelor it sounded like his worst nightmare.

'We wondered if you might want to take part. If you had a turn you could do, singing, juggling.' Dobbs began to look less enthusiastic. 'Magic . . . Out of respect for Trooper McGee, there'll be no dressing up.'

Grand smiled. He did love a good Glee – the performances were not usually theatre quality, but what they lacked in talent, they more than made up for in enthusiasm. As a period to their stay at Fort Abraham Lincoln, there was nothing he would enjoy more. He said as much to Dobbs.

'Oh, Captain Grand!' Dobbs was crestfallen. 'Are you leaving? Do you need me to do anything?'

Grand was tempted to say 'my packing' but simply shook his head. 'We may need a little help with transportation, Dobbs, but we're not leaving today. We still have a little . . . visiting to do.'

Dobbs looked knowing. Of course – Mr Batchelor would want to say a special goodbye to Mrs Custer.

'What time is the Glee, Dobbs?'

'Starts eight sharp. It'll be fun. Everyone'll be there. It's a squeeze, but we give the ladies and the officers the chairs at the front, the rest of us make benches and such at the rear. Not me, of course.' Dobbs's pleasant face flushed a little. 'I'm on the piano, so I'm at the front.'

'I didn't know you were a pianist as well, Dobbs.'

Dobbs shrugged modestly. 'I dabble,' he said. 'I'm not what you gents are probably used to in London, but I get by. As long as they don't use any of them fancy keys, I can keep up right enough.'

A distant cry of 'Dobbs!' from the direction of Myles Keogh's quarters made the man jump.

'Sorry, I was on an errand for the captain! So, we'll see you tonight? I'll save you seats at the front.'

'Oh, don't do that, Dobbs,' Grand said, hastily. 'We'll hunker in the back with the men. Best way to see a Glee.'

Dobbs smiled and trotted off on his errand. That Captain Grand, no side to him. A few others could learn from his example, in Dobbs's opinion.

'That was clever, Matthew,' Batchelor said, when Dobbs was out of earshot. 'If we're at the back, we can slip out after a few minutes and no one will notice.'

'On the contrary, James. If we're at the back, we can watch the whole fort all at once. I don't expect anyone will take a pot shot at Custer at the Glee, but we'll never have a better chance to see everyone gathered together, watch their expressions, see who sits by who – and beside, I *do* like a good Glee!'

The square that evening was just a swirling mass of people. All the ladies had dressed in their best, with flowers in their hair and just light shawls across their bare shoulders. The sun was still in the sky but low on the horizon, sending mellow beams up into the clouds which constantly lowered in the mountains. The gentlemen were dressed in their best and the smell of Macassar oil hung in the air, mixing with old lavender and violet. Batchelor stood watching for a moment from the veranda of the guest quarters; it was like a dance so complex it was impossible to see the pattern, and yet there was a pattern to it, he was sure. A stately quadrille, with hatred and death in its metre. He felt a chill run up his spine.

Grand came out, slamming the door and making Batchelor jump. 'Come on, James,' he said, poking him in the back. 'We don't want to miss the start.'

The Other Ranks' Mess Hall had been transformed with swags of paper chains and flowers. A makeshift stage had been constructed at the front with bales of hay overlaid with planks. Candles burned in sconces along the walls to illuminate the performers, but for the main part, apart from the sinking sun through the windows on one side, the audience were in shadow. Dobbs's piano was to one side of the stage, propped up at one end to keep it level. The noise was deafening. The ladies were calling to each other and kissing the air to each side of each other's cheeks with extravagant cries of delight. No one seeing the performance they gave would have dreamed that they had been gossiping about those very people not minutes before. The men were shuffling into benches so tightly packed there was scarcely room for them to sit down. As it was, each man had another man's knees in their back; no one could ever accuse a Glee of being comfortable,

Grand and Batchelor were at the back, sitting on a double pile of bales piled against the wall. It was a precarious perch but in many ways the best seats in the house. They could see above the heads of the entire company of the fort, and they could also tuck their heels into the straw for purchase. Grand pulled out his watch. Less than one minute to eight; he held up a finger to Batchelor and counted down. On the stroke of the hour, Myles Keogh stepped forward and the hall fell silent.

'Laydeeeeeeez and gentlemen!'

The men erupted in catcalls.

'Settle down, lads, settle down. Now, I know what you're thinking. If we're all in here, who's watching the Plains? Are Gall and his men climbing the walls as I speak?'

More shouts from the men and a few nervous shrieks from the ladies greeted this, but Keogh was ready for it.

'Well, it wasn't an easy decision to make. So, I auditioned every single man on the fort and the five worst singers are the ones on the ramparts tonight.' He paused for the gale of laughter. 'You all know who they are, but just so no one is in doubt, tonight we are being guarded by Baumgartner, Jenkins, Smith, O'Shaunessy and Jones. Now, I know what you're thinking; Jones is a Welshman, so he must be able to sing. But the reason he's here in the West is they threw him out of Wales, because he couldn't do the harmonies.'

The men laughed and clapped. Jones was indeed such a bad singer that he had been banned from opening his mouth, even for 'My Country, 'Tis of Thee'.

'So, that's it from me,' Keogh said. 'As it is a ladies' Glee, I won't tell any of my usual jokes tonight.'

Groans from the men.

'But we are being serenaded this evening by two of our lovely ladies. I give you, Mrs Harold Chater, with Mrs Marcus Reno at the piano.'

The men exploded with clapping. They weren't expecting much but entertainment was hard to come by in Fort Abraham Lincoln. It was a shame that Susie Chater looked about ready to pop; she was an attractive piece of skirt otherwise. Mary Reno was a dried-up old stick, but she was good on the piano, if a bit flowery.

While Susie Chater warbled something tuneless in clear disregard for Mary Reno's arpeggios, Batchelor turned to Grand and spoke in his ear.

'Isn't Custer a bit vulnerable, out there at the front?'

'I'm not expecting an attack, not here. I think he'll be safe enough. Though if I was sitting behind him, that damned hat would be annoying. He never thinks of anyone but himself, that one.'

Batchelor smiled. 'I suppose . . .' he craned his neck, 'Mrs

Madden should just be grateful that he hasn't got Reilly standing behind him, for good measure.'

'True. Poor old Reilly, he's missing all the fun.'

'When I saw him yesterday,' Batchelor said, 'he wasn't feeling up to much fun at all. He's really feeling sorry for himself. A bit homesick for Ireland, I think.'

'Oh, they all get like that.' A voice from behind Batchelor's head joined the conversation. 'Even O'Riordan gets maudlin sometimes.'

Batchelor had been wondering about the smell and now understood where it came from. Calamity Jane Cannary was sitting above them on a windowsill, perched even higher than the bales.

Grand craned round. 'Does he?' He was a little surprised to see her there, but not as surprised as he was to find that O'Riordan had poured out his heart to her.

As if she had read his mind, she said, 'Not all the time, you know. And I think he was just making me feel better. I . . . I'd had a bit of a run-in with Dobbs.'

Grand and Batchelor hadn't been in the fort long, but they knew that the men who had not had a run-in with Calam could be listed on the fingers of One-Hand Mossberger, the bouncer at My Lady's Bower. If O'Riordan was taking on the job of comforting Calam every time that happened, he would be a busy man. They nodded to the mule skinner and turned round to applaud the women, who were taking their bows and being helped down off the stage.

Dobbs took his place at the piano, to cries of 'Dobbsie!' and whistles and hoots from the men. He bowed extravagantly and tossed his imaginary tails behind him before giving a spirited, if not totally accurate, rendition of the 'William Tell Overture'.

Batchelor turned to Grand in amazement. 'Is there anything Dobbs can't do?'

'I guess we just haven't found it yet,' Grand said, with a smile. Every fort had a Dobbs, usually underestimated and not missed until suddenly they weren't there any more. But the men certainly appreciated him and stamped along with the rollicking tune, breaking into applause even before the final chords.

Batchelor found himself beginning to enjoy the Glee and had to make a special effort to remember that he was supposed to be watching the crowd. In the gloom, it was hard to see what anyone was doing, but as far as he was able, he couldn't see anyone behaving oddly. He turned to Grand and raised an eyebrow. Grand shrugged. His plan had been sound, but nothing was coming of it so far. Everyone just seemed to be there to have a good time. Which, after all, was the point of the Glee Club.

The songs followed, one after another, with a few magic tricks interspersed. There were some surprises. Marcus Reno, for example, accompanied by his wife and Dobbs in duet, turned out to have a bass baritone that rattled the windows. If the applause was muted, it was not for the performance, but because Reno was widely considered – and quite rightly in Grand and Batchelor's opinion – to be a total asshole.

Batchelor nudged Grand and nearly knocked him off his perch.

'Sorry,' he said, hauling him back by the back of his coat. 'Is that Kellogg at the front?'

Grand peered in the direction of Batchelor's subtly pointing finger. 'It is! He's got a nerve, that one. I wonder if he's still posing as a journalist?'

'Writing a review.' Batchelor chuckled. 'I have a grudging respect for the man, I have to say.'

Keogh was back on the stage, waiting for quiet. 'And now, a special treat for us all. After much negotiation, Bloody Knife has at last consented to perform in this Glee.'

The announcement was met with a moment of stunned silence, followed by mutters and then by applause. Custer looked around and was seen to mouth something at Keogh, who smiled and mouthed something back.

'This should be something,' Grand said, settling back. 'The whole Custer clan can't stand Bloody Knife – or any Indian, come to that. The General only keeps him on because he's damned good at what he does and Charley Reynolds can't do it all alone. I hope he doesn't give away too many tribe secrets, though; Gall has eyes everywhere and he won't appreciate his dances being shared at a fort Glee.'

'Don't you worry, none,' Calam breathed disconcertingly in Grand's ear. 'I heard him practising. His scalp is safe enough.'

Into the circle of candlelight stepped Bloody Knife. He didn't appear to have taken any extra trouble with his appearance. He was wearing his usual shapeless hat with a feather thrust carelessly into the band. His layers of doeskin hung unevenly over greasy trousers and his moccasins were the colour of the dust of the plain. He *might* have polished up his corporal's stripes; it was difficult to tell in the dim light. He stood foursquare in the middle of the stage and cleared his throat. He nodded to Dobbs, who struck a series of chords and Bloody Knife opened his mouth. It wasn't a war dance. It wasn't a rain dance. It was 'Largo al Factotum' from *The Marriage of Figaro*. Most of the men – and for that matter, most of the officers and their ladies – were oblivious of where it came from. All they knew was that Bloody Knife's voice filled the hall with glorious sound. 'Tra ra ra ra ra!' Bloody Knife's habitual stone expression didn't change. 'Tra ra re ra!' Even Dobbs's indifferent playing couldn't detract from the glory of the scout's voice. Grand and Batchelor could not have been more surprised if he had suddenly sprouted wings and flown around the room at ceiling height.

'How . . .? How did he ever hear that?'

'And how did he ever find he could sing it?'

'Sshh!' Calamity Jane was enjoying the music. 'I'll tell you when he's done.'

And, like the rest of the room, the enquiry agents just sat back and basked in the glory that was Rossini, Bloody Knife and Dobbs.

Finally, without putting a note wrong, Bloody Knife delivered the final 'Della Cittaaaaaaaaaaaaaaaaaaaaa,' finished by a triumphant 'da da, da daaaaaaaaaaa' from Dobbs on the rackety old piano.

The crowd erupted. The men were on their feet, packed as they were on their benches. Grand and Batchelor clapped and whistled in a way they would never dream of doing in Covent Garden – not that they had ever heard such a performance there. They turned eagerly to Calam, sitting as proudly as if she had invented Bloody Knife herself.

'Well?' Grand said. 'How did he learn that?'

The mule skinner laughed. 'A few years back, we had a parson come to Lincoln who had a bit of a thing for his music. He had this machine, we never knew how it worked, it was sheets of paper, he put them in and turned a key and music'd come out through this horn thing.' She pointed at Bloody Knife. 'One day, the old parson, he heard Bloody Knife a'hummin' along with his music and he give him some lessons. That there's his favourite. Mine too, ask me. Parson explained it was a funny song and tried to get Bloody Knife to smile a bit, but he don't do that. But he sounds good, though, don't he?'

'He certainly does,' Batchelor agreed. He had seen a lot of bad things in his time in the West, but the glory of Bloody Knife's voice would be a good memory he could treasure, to perhaps ameliorate somewhat the horrors of the little Indian boy, Trooper McGee and the prospectors.

Keogh was on stage again. 'I can't top that,' he said. 'But I wouldn't be an Irishman if I didn't try. So, if the boys of the Glee Club would like to stand. Don't come up; I know you're stuck back there.'

Benches scraped and, all over the hall, men struggled to stand between their seated comrades.

'Ladies and gentlemen, the gentlemen of the Glee Club and I will sing you out. If you could make your way out onto the square when we're done, I believe Cookie has some warm punch and some biscuits for you under the awning to the left.' He looked at Dobbs, who was, as ever, poised over the keys. 'So, Isaac, if you please . . .'

Dobbs struck up the jingling introduction to the 'Garryowen'.

Keogh took the first verse.

'Let Bacchus' sons be not dismayed
But join with me each jovial blade
Come booze and sing and lend your aid
To help me with the chorus . . .'

The scattered men of the Glee Club joined him, their voices from the dark having an added resonance.

> 'Instead of spa we'll drink down ale
> And pay the reck'ning on the nail
> No man for debt shall go to jail
> From Garryowen in glory.'

From somewhere just in front of Batchelor, a plaintive tenor rose alone. It came from a short, balding trooper whom Grand and Batchelor had often seen lounging where the work was lightest. The night was full of surprises; his voice rose pure and true to the rafters.

> 'We are the boys who take delight
> Smashing the Limerick lamps when lighting
> Through all the streets like sportsters fighting
> And tearing all before us.'

Anyone less likely to be seen fighting through the back streets of Limerick it was hard to imagine, but the chorus was already swooping across the hall. Custer was on his feet now, facing his men and conducting with a will.

'See what I mean?' Grand muttered to Batchelor. 'He couldn't carry a tune in a bucket, but that's what everyone will remember about tonight.'

The next verse began on a wave of laughter as the horse doctor got up and ground it out in an indifferent bass.

> 'We'll break the windows, we'll break the doors
> The watch knock down by threes and fours
> Then let the doctors work their cures
> And tinker up our bruises.'

The next chorus sounded just the same as always, but Grand and Batchelor couldn't help notice that the Glee Club were looking around them, man to man, some shrugging. The chorus led into the next verse, which for a line or two was just Dobbs hammering out the accompaniment. Then, with great aplomb and a look at the pianist, Keogh stepped in.

'We'll beat the bailiffs out of fun
We'll make the mayors and sheriffs run
We are the boys no man dares dun
If he regards a whole skin.'

Calam poked Batchelor between the shoulder blades. 'Where's O'Riordan?' she asked. 'This is his verse.'

Suddenly, as if a firework had gone off in his head, Matthew Grand knew what had been happening these past weeks. Custer, for all his bluster and lust for glory, was not the intended victim. Batchelor was a second behind him. They hardly heard the chorus begin, punctuated by shouts and imprecations as they jumped from their perch into the back row of the Glee Club. They missed Dobbs adding one last string to his bow as he added his very pleasant tenor to the final verse.

'Our hearts so stout have got us fame
For soon 'tis known from whence we came
Where're we go they dread the name
Of Garryowen in glory.'

The chorus and applause was the only sound beside the clatter of boots on the boardwalk as Grand and Batchelor raced each other to the sanitorium. A guard patrolling the ramparts across the parade ground paused and watched them, but nothing seemed amiss to him. They were that pair of visitors, weren't they? And wasn't one of them a Limey? No accounting for any kind of behaviour, with people like that. Cookie and his helpers stood behind their trestle away to the left. Their punch wasn't the best in the world, they knew that, but there was no need to run away quite so obviously.

The sanitorium was deserted. There was no Jenkins nor any other orderly on duty and Dr Madden's office was empty. That, however, was not why Grand and Batchelor had come. Their hearts in their mouths, they crashed into the outer office, the one that led to the ward. Grand's revolver was already in his hand and he banged aside the door with his shoulder.

Sergeant Reilly lay on his back, eyes closed, head back on the pillows.

'We're too late,' Batchelor hissed.

There was an abrupt snore, like a rifle shot, and an empty bottle of hooch clattered to the floor from Reilly's bed.

'The hell we are!' Grand muttered and put his gun away.

He grabbed Reilly by the shoulders, ignoring his bandages, and shook him. The Irishman groaned, rolled his eyes and snored some more. Grand let him fall back on the pillows and stepped back from the bed.

'All right,' Batchelor said. 'So he's all right at the moment. But we need somebody to stay with him, just in case.'

'No, we don't,' Grand said, loudly. 'We're wasting our time here, James. Let's get back to the Glee Club. You can give them your "There's no shove like the first shove".'

'Steady, Matthew,' Batchelor said. 'I mean, I know this is an army fort and all, but I'm not sure . . . Anyway, what are you talking about?'

'I'm talking about getting back.' Grand kept up the level of his voice. 'Some bastard'll have helped himself to my punch if we're not careful. My money's on Keogh,' and he hauled Batchelor out of the door. The Englishman was still protesting as they strode away across the square, the dust scuffed up by their boots.

'What . . .?' Batchelor was still asking when his companion in crime swung him round a dark corner and pinned him to the wall.

'There was somebody in the pharmacy,' Grand hissed, his hand over Batchelor's mouth.

'There was?'

Dr Madden's pharmacy was more of a shed, nailed onto the side of the sanitorium as an afterthought. It was next to the ward where Reilly lay. Grand nodded. 'I could hear him breathing; only just, over Reilly's snores, but there was someone there for sure. Whoever it was was waiting for us to leave. We'll give him a minute, then double back.'

He had relaxed his grip on Batchelor now and the two of them waited there, nerves stretched, hearts thumping.

'How long . . .?' Batchelor began, but Grand answered the question by dashing back across the open ground, the shorter man in his wake. Again they crashed through the door and this time, a figure was crouching over the drunken Irishman, a pillow in his hand.

'We've been expecting you, Corporal O'Riordan,' Grand said, his pocket Colt pointing at the man's head. The corporal straightened and looked at the pair.

'The devil you have,' he said. 'You two gentlemen couldn't find your arses with both hands. Now, be on your way – I've got a score to settle.'

'We know that,' Batchelor said, 'although what kind of score it is to suffocate a helpless man, I can't imagine.'

'It's none of your damned business,' O'Riordan said.

'Humour us,' Grand told him. 'Your number's up, O'Riordan. I must admit, you had us fooled.'

'Mr Grand here thought,' Batchelor said, 'and at the time, I had to agree with him, that it was General Custer somebody was trying to kill. That first time, when Senator Maitland was murdered.'

'Ah, that wasn't me,' O'Riordan said.

'Really?' Grand's hand was steady on his gun, the barrel outstretched to the corporal's head. 'Do tell.'

'As soon as I saw Reilly, I recognized him,' he said, his voice dripping with venom. 'You lads were there too, weren't you? At the recruitment in Washington? I'd heard a whisper that Reilly was in the Seventh, but I couldn't believe my luck when he turned up like that, all strutting bantam cock. I wanted him dead, but I didn't fancy swinging for it, so I used my day left in Washington before they sent us to Jefferson Barracks to hire a cabbie with a bit of a murderous streak. Unfortunately, he wasn't up to the job. He could drive fast, sure, but his aim wasn't true enough.'

'Killed Maitland by mistake,' Batchelor nodded.

'So you hired the thugs in the Division?' Grand checked. All this would be useful for the court martial that lay ahead.

'What thugs?' O'Riordan asked, puzzled. 'And what's the Division?'

'Um . . . six of your countrymen ganged up on us; the General, Reilly and us. We thought it was another murder attempt.'

'Jesus, that's just a few of the lads letting off some steam. What were they carrying?'

'Shillelaghs,' Grand told him. 'Maybe the odd knife.'

'Well, there you are,' O'Riordan said. 'No malice in it. If they'd have meant business, they'd have used the gelignite.'

That was comforting, thought Batchelor.

'Then you made the mistake about the General's horse, didn't you?' Grand asked.

'I kicked myself when I found out,' the corporal said. 'Everybody here told me that Reilly rode Vic for the General, so I waited for my opportunity. We all slope off from the fort now and again – you must have noticed, Captain Grand, how lax the security is. It was the General's horse, it was a man in blue uniform, but I was too far away and I was losing the light. When I went to check on the body, I realized my mistake. Not only was it not Reilly, it wasn't Custer either. Actually, I was glad about that – old Iron Butt's not a bad stick, as Yankees go.'

'Tilly McGee wasn't a bad stick, either,' Batchelor said, straight faced.

'Yes, what about that, eh? I didn't realize her little secret either until I hit upon the plan to make the whole thing look like an Indian attack. Call me a Dublin fart if I've ever seen anything like it.'

'But finally, you got your man,' Grand said, glancing at the still-sleeping Reilly. 'On the hunt above the Rosebud.'

'Tricky shot, that,' O'Riordan said. 'I had to double back behind the bluffs so's no one'd see and that made it difficult. After all,' he winked, 'I wouldn't want to kill Custer, now, would I?'

'All right, O'Riordan,' Batchelor rested his hands on his hips. 'Just tell us why. Why do you want Reilly dead?'

'Oh, I don't want Reilly dead,' the corporal said. 'I want Ignatius Murphy dead – and I've yet to achieve that.'

'Who's Ignatius Murphy?' Batchelor was on the verge of losing the drift of this conversation.

'He is.' O'Riordan jerked his thumb contemptuously at the man in the bed. 'And while we're covering all the points, my name isn't O'Riordan, either. It's Dempsey, as Offaly as you please. This son of a bitch's da hanged my sainted mother back home. And he,' and this time he prodded Reilly, who groaned, 'lied to make sure it would happen.'

'So, this is all about revenge?' Grand asked, the pistol wobbling imperceptibly in his hand.

'Of course. When I first saw Murphy posing as somebody else, I thought I'd died and gone to heaven. What were the odds, I asked myself, on finding the man I'd been looking for for ten years and more? And not in the Old Country, but this new one.' He smiled at Grand and Batchelor. 'Anyhow, it's over now, isn't it?'

A gun barked in the half-light and a bullet tore a hole in the pillow resting against Dempsey's stomach. A second shot rang out before the report of the first was over and the Irishman spun sideways, dropping his gun and the pillow. Batchelor stood staring sideways, blinded momentarily by the flash of the guns and the smoke. Matthew Grand was slumped in a corner, blood oozing from his head.

'Matthew? Matthew? Oh, for God's sake!' Batchelor was on his knees, cradling his fallen partner. He dabbed his temple, brushing away the blood and the hair. 'It's all right,' he said. 'You'll be all right. The bullet just grazed you, that's all.'

'Get after him, James,' a shocked and bewildered Grand muttered. 'Don't let him get away.'

'To hell with that,' Batchelor said, staunching the blood as best he could. Perhaps Matthew Grand wasn't indestructible after all. Batchelor looked across at Sergeant Reilly . . . Murphy . . . whatever the hell his name was. He was still snoring softly. 'It takes an Irishman,' Batchelor said softly, shaking his head, 'to sleep through something like this.'

They called out the guard as soon as the shots rang out and Dr Madden, already shaky from his punch, came to patch up Matthew Grand. The General heard Batchelor's story in astonishment and the whole fort positively rattled with rumour. The Murphy in B Company swore it had absolutely nothing to do with him. Keogh, as an Irishman himself, understood it a little. It was only a mule skinner, back in her smelly, greasy buckskins and shapeless hat, who understood it all. And she wasn't talking. Not to anybody.

Of Corporal O'Riordan Dempsey, there was no sign. The blood trail on the sanitorium floor proved that Grand's bullet had found its mark, but the man's horse and saddle had gone and he was nowhere to be seen. In the morning, General Custer and Companies C, D and I rode out in a fruitless search, coming back at sundown, tired and empty-handed. Another snowbird had flown.

Neither Grand nor Batchelor could believe it. Grand seemed to have caught some of Custer's luck. The bullet, as they said in Ned Buntline's dime novels, hadn't done much more than part his hair, although his eye was black and shiny and his ear would never be *quite* the same shape again. In three or four days, he was fit enough to travel. So was Sergeant Reilly Murphy, and Custer was still trying to decide what to do with him.

It was a little after Reveille one morning that a horseman was seen walking a tired pinto along the trails that led to Fort Abraham Lincoln. A couple of dogs barked at him, but he hushed them with a word and rode through the fort gates, acknowledged by the sergeant on duty. Grand and Batchelor were standing on the edge of the parade ground, preparing for their departure, when they saw Lonesome Charley Reynolds easing himself out of the saddle. The man was covered in Plains dust and he looked old and tired. Strapped to the back of his horse was a makeshift travois and, on it, wrapped in a blanket, was a body.

'Seen this before, Mr Batchelor?' Reynolds had pulled a Bowie knife from his belt.

'Er . . . it's a knife, Mr Reynolds.' The English greenhorn was coming on no end.

'It's *my* knife, Mr Batchelor,' Reynolds said. 'You were with me when I left it with that little Indian boy.'

'Yes.' Batchelor remembered only too well. 'Yes, I was. But, how . . .?'

Reynolds jerked his thumb behind him. 'That, on the travois, is Corporal O'Riordan or Dempsey or whatever the hell his name was. At least, what's left of him. I found him out on the Plains, in the Black Hills. He must have rode into a Lakota war party. Hunkpapa would be my guess. My knife was buried in his heart. No, I wouldn't look, Captain Grand. It's him, all right, but it's not pretty.'

'So . . .' Batchelor was trying to make sense of it all. 'The knife . . .'

'. . . was returned to its rightful owner. I guess Gall would say I meant well. Then again, I guess he didn't appreciate the gesture. You may not have got O'Riordan, Captain Grand,' Reynolds stuffed the knife away, 'but somebody sure did. I'll be sure to thank the chief when I see him next.'

FIFTEEN

G rand and Batchelor did not have Libbie Custer's problem when it came to packing. They had not bought anything since they arrived at Fort Abraham Lincoln. In fact, apart from keeping Calamity Jane happy at the Dew Drop Inn, neither man could remember having spent so little in so long a time. The food was bland and boring, but it was free. The clothes they needed for anything other than lounging on the veranda had been willingly lent by anyone who had a set to spare. In fact, with one very notable exception, they had never met a nicer bunch of men than those who made up the contingent at Fort Abraham Lincoln. Even Reno and Benteen had unbent sufficiently to say goodbye in very civil terms. The ladies had thrown them a tea party, where they were twittered over to further order. Libbie Custer had taken James out for a long walk outside the fort, with two troopers walking ahead, two behind. Just because someone wanted to be private didn't mean they had to risk kidnap and worse as well.

On the morning the stage was collecting them to take them to the station, the enquiry agents went for one last ride on the prairie. The grass waved away to the horizon, where it met the foothills, shimmering in the heat.

'If it's this hot now, what's it like in summer?' Batchelor wondered.

'Worse is the only way I can describe it,' Grand said. He loved his country, but apart from a few places where the climate was mild all year – and he had never found those places – he could do without its weather.

'Why do they do it?' Batchelor continued. 'Staying out here, with nothing to do for weeks on end, nowhere to go that doesn't look like the place you just left from?'

'They do it because they think they have to. They've got thousands of square miles, but they won't be happy until they have *every* square mile.'

Batchelor gave him a piercing look. 'You don't approve?'

'Do you?' Grand knew his man. Batchelor had never met a cause he didn't want to espouse.

'Of course not. There's plenty of room for everyone. It's just that I thought . . . well, I thought every American wanted to own the lot.'

'Not *this* American. You haven't seen my trust fund papers – I own *quite* enough for one man, thank you very much. No, to my mind, they should just leave the forts, leave the tribes to their own land. They managed very well before we got here. They'll manage just as well if we went away.'

'True words well spoken,' said a bush to Grand's left and Lonesome Charley Reynolds stepped out, silent as a grave.

'I didn't see you there,' Grand managed when his heart stopped beating in his mouth.

'Sorry, didn't mean to startle you none. It's a habit I got into. I just wanted to say goodbye to you gents on our own. You did a good job back at the fort. O'Riordan was not good people.'

'He fooled everyone, though,' Batchelor was forced to admit. 'Calam had a really soft spot for him.'

Reynolds took off his hat and scratched his head. 'She did and that's what had me fooled. Calam can usually spot a rotten egg at a hundred paces, but she fell for him hook, line and sinker.' He put his hat back on and shaded his eyes to look back at the fort. 'She even had a bath.' The incredulity in his voice made all three men laugh. 'Don't remember her doing that since . . . oh, I don't remember since. But O'Riordan was eaten up with wanting revenge. Revenge does no one any good.'

'It makes you feel better, though?' Grand didn't indulge in it himself, but without it, the firm of Grand and Batchelor, Enquiry Agents of the Strand would be the poorer.

'It does, it does,' Reynolds agreed, but shook his head. 'But it can eat you up, as well. You stop seeing right from wrong, except through the goggles you make for yourself, of hatred and regret. You blame everyone for what might be your own fault.' He stopped. Lonesome Charley Reynolds didn't share his life with anyone and he wasn't going to start now. He coughed and dragged his gaze from the far horizon, where,

whenever he looked, a beautiful Lakota woman and her two
little children gazed at him with nothing but love in their eyes.
'Anyways, I just thought I'd say thank you, boys, and good
travels.' He chuckled. 'I heard as you don't travel too well,
Mr Batchelor.'

Batchelor bridled. 'I travel as well as the next man,' he
spluttered. 'Sometimes I get a little . . . tired. That's all.'

'Well,' Reynolds rummaged in a pocket. 'Next time you're
tired, try this. My wife . . .' he looked them in the eyes and they
said nothing, 'swore by this. Just light one end and wave the
smoke around. It's just herbs and such. All natural. But you'll
feel all the better for it, guaranteed.' He thrust some grey-
looking bundles into Batchelor's hand and, wheeling his horse,
rode off across the plain.

Batchelor looked down at the bundles of what looked like
slightly mouldy grass and went as though to throw them down,
but Grand stopped him.

'Keep them, James. You never know.'

'I won't need them,' Batchelor said. 'I'm sure my travel
sickness has improved.'

'Really? Because of course you have made so many trans-
atlantic voyages in the last few weeks. Keep them, James.' He
took one and sniffed it. 'Sage. A few other bits and bobs. If
you don't need them, you can give them to Mrs Rackstraw
for her stuffing.'

As if mentioning her name had conjured her up, a waft of
cooking smells came to them on the breeze.

'Breakfast?' Grand ventured.

Batchelor wheeled his horse. 'I'll just have a little,' he said.
'As long as it isn't grits.'

If Matthew Grand had been given a choice, he would have
slipped off back to the Port of London without calling in on
his parents, but the thought of his mother's trusting face looking
up into his, eyes big with tears, made that choice impossible.
He and Batchelor had an afternoon tea party in New York,
with his parents, sister and her little one and her husband. He
had never really liked his brother-in-law, a shifty piece of work
if ever he saw one and as clearly mixed up in the Belknap

scandal as it was possible for a man to be. But he was soon to put a whole ocean between them, so he could afford to be civil. He shook hands with the men, allowed an inordinate amount of kissing and stroking from his mother, dandled Martha's child on his knee to the ruination of one of his favourite pairs of trousers and generally was the Son of the House for as long as it took. Batchelor came in for some kissing and stroking too, when Mrs Grand was at a loose end and her darling Matthew was otherwise engaged. All in all, it could have been a worse send-off and Batchelor, with four of Reynolds's bundles of sage still in his pocket, was prepared for the Atlantic Ocean to do its worst.

'James?' Grand put his head around the stateroom door. 'James? Are you awake? Mrs Vanderbilt was wondering if we could join her at her table for dinner? James?'

The voice from the bunk was so low it was almost inaudible.

'Sorry, James. I can't hear – I think the waves slapping on the side . . .'

'If dinner means food, then no. If Mrs Vanderbilt is the large woman with the two ugly daughters, then hell no. Now, go away and leave me alone.'

'Have you got any of Charley Reynolds's . . .?'

'No! Now, leave me alone!'

Mrs Rackstraw was a happy woman, happy being a relative condition with her. The house had seemed very empty without her two employers. She complained when they were there – of course she did – but when they weren't there, she all but pined away. She cooked for herself and Maisie. She still had a woman in to do the Rough. She washed down all the paintwork, she had all the carpets up to beat half to death in the back area. She swathed the furniture in cambric cloths then unswathed it all again because it reminded her of a funeral and the shrouded shapes gave Maisie the ab-dabs on her way up to the garret every night. She spent hours inventing new dishes and then invited the postman in to try them out. When the postman tried a little something over and above her kidney cobbler, she fetched him a nasty one upside the head with the dustpan and kept herself to herself after that.

But now, they were back. It was true that Mr Batchelor was not looking his best, but the poor gentleman never was a good traveller. She didn't know why he wanted to go gallivanting off to foreign parts. No good ever came of it. Mr Grand had to see his family; she had family herself, disreputable though they were. It was important to keep in touch, though. And Mr Grand's family looked very respectable, judging from the portraits on the sideboard, though they created a lot of dusting. But she promised herself she would never complain about their socks, their cigar ash, their late nights; she would never complain about *any* of it, *ever* again.

'Maisie!' Mrs Rackstraw almost sang her name and Maisie stiffened in fear. Mrs Rackstraw had as many moods as London weather, most of them just as grey. But when she was in a good mood, Maisie was on the alert; someone was overdue a smack upside the head, in her experience.

'Maisie! Have you ironed Mr Grand's paper?'

This was a new departure and it drove Maisie almost to distraction. While the gentlemen were away, Mrs Rackstraw had gone to some classes at Travers Employment Agency for Gentlewomen in How To Be the Perfect Housekeeper. Mrs Rackstraw had had to lie somewhat; the classes were only for those seeking employment, but she told Maisie that it wasn't really a lie if it was to help Mr Grand and Mr Batchelor to be more comfortable. Maisie had been doubtful, but she knew it was fruitless to argue with Mrs Rackstraw when she had made up her mind. Maisie had had to go to classes on How To Be the Perfect Maidservant, but when she told Mrs Rackstraw how little her job should entail, Mrs Rackstraw forbade her to go to any more.

The classes had taught Mrs Rackstraw a lot, mostly unhelpful, but the one thing she came away determined to do was to iron the newspaper every day. Not only – the rather condescending tutor at Travers's told her class – did it give a smoother feel for the delicate fingers of one's employer, it also killed ninety-nine per cent of all household germs. So, from that day forward, ironed the newspapers had to be.

The first week of July was hot, and Maisie could have done without the blazing fire and the row of flat-irons lined up on the hob. She had heard Mr Grand say to Mr Batchelor in no uncertain terms that he didn't like an ironed newspaper, or so she had convinced herself. But it was no good telling Mrs Rackstraw that. It was a tricky business, making sure the pages were smooth but not scorched. She expended so much spit checking on the temperature of the irons that she was as dry as dust by the time she got to the end of the *Telegraph*. And now, today, there was extra to do. Mr Grand's copy of the *Washington Post* had arrived, sent regular as clockwork by his mother. Maisie sighed and set to with her smoothing iron. She must have had a mother, but she didn't remember her. Mr Grand was so lucky.

She laid the paper out straight on the table, smoothing it out. The iron flashed back and forth as she fell into her favourite dream, the one where Mr Grand took her into his arms, let down her hair at the back and told her she was beautiful.

The smell of warm paper filled the kitchen. The smell of Matthew Grand's bay rum aftershave filled her nostrils. She passed the iron across the page and something caught her eye and she raised the iron, eyes wide. She hadn't had much education, but she could read newspaper.

'Soon, an officer came rushing into camp,' she read, 'and related that he had found Gen. Custer dead and stripped naked, and near him his brother, Capt. Tom Custer, his nephew Lt. Reed, Capt. Keogh, Lieut. Cooke, Lieut. Porter, Lieut. Chater, Dr Madden, Mr Kellogg, the Bismarck *Tribune* correspondent, and one hundred and ninety men and scouts, including the bugler, one Isaac Dobbs. Gen. Custer went into battle with Companies C, L, I, F and E, of the 7th cavalry, and the staff and non-commissioned officers of his regiment, and a number of scouts, led by one Charles Reynolds, and only one scout remained to tell the tale. All were killed.'

Maisie put the iron back on the grate. Her hand was shaking so much she didn't trust herself to hold it. She had heard the two young gentlemen talking while she waited on them at table and, anyway, they often told her of their adventures. She felt she knew these men.

Mrs Rackstraw put her head around the door. 'Not ironing, Maisie?' she said.

Maisie sniffed and picked up the iron, testing its temperature with her tears.